Acclaim for Kathryn

The Thin Place

"*The Thin Place* is that rare, brave, and original thing: an honest and energetic glimpse into an author's head. . . . Kathryn Davis has done something great here, something heathen, anarchic, democratic. She has given everyone and everything a voice: animals, plants, children, coma patients, even the earth itself. . . . Generously, Davis never underestimates her readers and assumes that we value the natural world and mourn our eventual removal from it."
— Lucy Ellmann, *New York Times Book Review*

"Davis has let her seemingly boundless imagination loose and provoked us into following. She is one of the most inventive novelists at work today. . . . I'm in awe of her achievement with this book, of her utterly fantastic and unfettered mind."
— Beth Kephart, *Chicago Tribune*

"No amount of character sketching or plot summary can begin to convey the experience of reading this strange and delightful novel. . . . Davis is sly, and playful, but also serious about exposing the spiritual lining of everyday phenomena."
— Julia Livshin, *Washington Post Book World*

"*The Thin Place* is full of subtly funny moments. . . . It is difficult not to be exhilarated by Davis's soaring ambitions, her hallucinatory use of language, her fearlessness. Her voice is utterly original, crucial even, a breath of fresh air at a time when so much contemporary fiction seems reluctant to experiment with style and form. With *The Thin Place,* Davis is at the height of her powers."
— Irina Reyn, *San Francisco Chronicle*

"*The Thin Place* features a Jane Austen–like country setting and a Virginia Woolf–like sensibility. . . . Davis takes the events and characters of a recent small-town spring and uses them for an extended meditation on time and mortality and the mysterious web of connections among all things." — *Library Journal*

"Kathryn Davis is a writer who appears to be able to do, well, almost anything. Cosmic without being florid, funny without being flip, terrifying without being trite, in her new novel, *The Thin Place,* Davis gives us a world animated by spirit. . . . The wonder of the book is the way she weaves pure beauty and prickly humor into her doomsaying."
— Claire Dederer, *Seattle Times*

"A kind of wry humor is the one constant in *The Thin Place,* but with exquisite skill Davis tailors every observation to the character making it. . . . Mees's miraculous gift is less the center of the novel than a gleaming speck in its lustrous fabric, a single sequin sewn onto a bolt of satin. . . . Davis shows how even events that her human characters barely notice are like keyholes through which eternity can be glimpsed." — Laura Miller, *Salon*

"Both telescopic and microscopic, Kathryn Davis's sixth novel is a rare fusion of grand sweep and fine detail. . . . *The Thin Place* asks, in its quiet, poetic fashion, that we learn to let the world in." — Lydia Millet, *Raleigh News-Observer*

"Brilliant. . . . Davis writes hallucinatory, literate prose, and adopts a cosmic perspective." — *The New Yorker*

"This is a deeply religious book in its way. The natural world is full of wonder and terror. Human beings squander the abundant resources at their disposal."
— Barbara Fisher, *Boston Globe*

"Exquisitely mysterious, sinewy yet soaring. . . . *The Thin Place* moves from minor crisis to minor crisis, and from minor joy to minor joy, while slowly, almost imperceptibly, tightening the spring on a clockwork that will eventually blow apart in a climactic epiphany that is as tragic and as comic as life itself."
— Harper Barnes, *St. Louis Post-Dispatch*

"Nothing is predictable in Kathryn Davis's thrillingly strange new novel. . . . As this original tale gradually reveals its deeper, spiritual concerns, you may feel as if you've been watching Thornton Wilder's *Our Town* while under the influence of some benevolent consciousness-altering substance."
— Francine Prose, *People*

"Daring and original, Kathryn Davis constructs each of her fictional worlds with a precision and an earnestness that come from her fascination with ideas. Her sixth novel, *The Thin Place,* continues this bizarre and delightful trajectory."
— Fiona Foster, *Toronto Globe and Mail*

"Amazing and idiosyncratic. . . . Using a point of view that tacks restlessly from mind to mind, and zooms in and out, as in a novel by Virginia Woolf, *The Thin Place* studies the reality of Varennes from all angles. . . . Davis's mobile perspective also gives *The Thin Place* an impressive vitality."
— Celia Wren, *Newsday*

"It's tricky to find an authentic voice for an adolescent girl, but Davis finds the bridge between sugar-and-spice innocence and the darker side of being twelve. . . . While the girls are the entry into the story, *The Thin Place* encompasses the entire life cycle of a town. . . . Never has Davis's prose seemed more effortless. . . . *The Thin Place* is a bright, shimmering book."
— Jessa Crispin, *Chicago Sun-Times*

"There's excitement in hanging on to Davis's newest novel for dear life, exulting in the quiet glow of her virtuosity — and sometimes even laughing out loud at the precision of her descriptions. . . . Davis writes from a generous vantage point where a fervent appreciation of the world's physical and spiritual glories — the Gerard Manley Hopkins in her, a graceful observer of nature's opulent fragility — collides happily with a down-to-earth understanding of teenage preening, of lust, of pettiness and meanness and human ridiculousness. . . . Although this startling book is not at all like Marilynne Robinson's *Gilead,* it is touched by the same love of life and gift of grace."   — Lisa Schwarzbaum, *Entertainment Weekly*

"The quirky, immensely gifted Davis has been compared to Kafka, Dinesen, and Hans Christian Andersen. One might also say she is to contemporary fiction what Emily Dickinson was to nineteenth-century poetry. A delightful, surprise-filled narrative: Davis's best yet."
          — *Kirkus Reviews* (starred review)

"A riveting read, the kind of novel that flows through your mind like clear, fresh water after a long thirst. . . . If Davis's new novel signals the kind of year we're going to see in American fiction, we can settle in for a very good year indeed."
          — Charity Vogel, *Buffalo News*

"Cosmic in her vision, provocative and comic in her storytelling, Kathryn Davis draws on sources as diverse as quantum physics and tales of saints and miracles and makes place a key element in her exploratory fiction. . . . As strange and deadly events unfold, Davis works out a calculus of the accidental and the inevitable and maps the interface of the natural and the supernatural, the human and the divine."
          — Donna Seaman, *Booklist* (starred review)

"Kathryn Davis's sentences have the bite of Jane Austen's and the scope of Gabriel García Márquez's. I hope that the gods who preside over such matters know enough to confer the next big literary award on this wondrously human and magical novel." — Howard Frank Mosher, *Burlington Free Press*

"The imaginary worlds of Kathryn Davis are as mysterious and enthralling as any vanished Celtic kingdom . . . . Henry James and Virginia Woolf are usually mentioned by critics reading Davis. *The Thin Place* is likely to suggest Thoreau and D. H. Lawrence, too, with some of García Márquez's Macondo thrown in, or else Bruno Schulz rewriting *Winesburg, Ohio*."
— John Leonard, *Harper's*

"Davis's writing doesn't boil down neatly into punchy catch-phrases. Plot synopses don't do her justice, and adjectives don't really help much, either. . . . *The Thin Place* left me scraping the plate and looking around for stray crumbs. . . . I wasn't ready to vacate the town of Varennes."
— Yvonne Zipp, *Christian Science-Monitor*

"When was the last time you read something truly lovely? And not only lovely, by which I mean pleasing to the imagination and the mind's eye, but funny, too? Think about it — funny and exquisitely lovely. Now hold on to those two qualities and add these to the mix: fiercely intelligent, spiritual, and thought-provoking. . . . Davis's most amazing feat may be that she has managed to make something this dense and jam-packed also accessible and entertaining. Reading this book is a little like looking at a huge painting, the canvas covered with details, too many to take in at one time, and being mesmerized by a piece of art filled with a passion that is violent and beautiful. . . . *The Thin Place* is a love story, or perhaps more accurately, a love letter to life."
— Mary Guterson, *Believer*

The Thin Place

A NOVEL

Kathryn Davis

BACK BAY BOOKS
LITTLE, BROWN AND COMPANY
NEW YORK   BOSTON   LONDON

Back Bay Books / Little, Brown and Company
Hachette Book Group USA
1271 Avenue of the Americas, New York, NY 10020
Visit our Web site at www.HachetteBookGroupUSA.com

Originally published in hardcover by Little, Brown and Company, January 2006
First Back Bay paperback edition, February 2007

The characters and events in this book are fictitious. Any similarity to real
persons, living or dead, is coincidental and not intended by the author.

The author would like to thank the Bogliasco Foundation for its
generous support, Phyllis Roth for offering an ideal work space, and
Louise Glück and Elaine Segal for providing irreplaceable help
with this book, as they have with all of my other books, with
superhuman generosity and intelligence.

Library of Congress Cataloging-in-Publication Data

Davis, Kathryn.
     The thin place : a novel / Kathryn Davis. — 1st ed.
         p.   cm.
     HC ISBN 0-316-73504-3
     PB ISBN 0-316-01424-9 / 978-0-316-01424-3
     1. Girls — Fiction.   2. Near-death experiences — Fiction.   I. Title.

PS3554.A934923T48   2006
813'.54 — dc22   2005007981

10 9 8 7 6 5 4 3 2 1

Q-FF

Book designed by Brooke Koven

Printed in the United States of America

*For Jan Armstrong &
for David Hall*

Beloved, I am so glad that you are happy to see me.
Beloved, I am so glad, so very glad, that you have come.

— Hāfiz

The Thin Place

There were three girlfriends and they were walking down a trail that led to a lake. One small and plump, one pretty and medium-sized, one not so pretty and tall. This was in the early years of the twenty-first century, the unspeakable having happened so many times everyone was still in shock, still reeling from what they'd seen, what they'd done or failed to do. The dead souls no longer wore gowns. They'd gotten loose, broadcasting their immense soundless chord through the precincts of the living.

At the lake the trail branched right and left. Right to the town beach, a grassy plot with six picnic tables, two stone grills, a pit toilet, a trash can, and a narrow strip of lumpy gray sand. Left to the Knoll, where the overlarge houses of the rich nestled among shade trees and tasteful redwood play structures — and then back to town. Straight ahead was the boat ramp and the Crocketts' chocolate Lab, Buddy, going down shoulder-first on a dead fish. Beyond the ramp was the water.

The sky was the palest blue and fluttered over the girls' heads like a circus tent at the apex of which the sun was pinned. It was a Saturday in mid-May, the sun only just starting to heat up, it being the northern latitudes, but even so Mrs. Kipp had made sure they all wore sunblock. You couldn't be too careful. Like many objects of worship, the sun had grown impatient with its worshipers, causing some of them to sicken and die. As she larded on the sunblock, Mrs. Kipp informed them that these days only stupid people had tans.

When they got to the beach, the three girls came to a halt. A very large man, dressed in a pair of khaki shorts and not much else, was lying on his stomach in the sand with his head facing the lake. From where the girls stood, they could see the bottoms of the man's feet, which looked smooth and white. Almost as if he were a baby, observed Lorna Fine, not only the tallest and least attractive but also the most fanciful of the three. The older Lorna got, the prettier she would become, but for now she was like a bespectacled monkey wearing red-and-yellow plaid seer-sucker pants and the vintage Ramones T-shirt she'd found in the back of her brother's closet under a stack of dirty maga-zines, so she was sure he wouldn't ask for it back.

Sunny Crockett let out a loud sigh Lorna knew was meant to be overheard by anyone inconsiderate enough to be hogging the entire strip of sand when obviously there were other people who wanted to use it.

"It's Mr. Banner," said Mees Kipp.

"Who?" Lorna asked.

"Mr. Banner," said Mees, "from Sunny's church." She walked around to the man's right where she planted herself, a small round thing in a pink tracksuit, in the sand next to his face. Mr. Banner's eyes were loosely shut, and his black eyeglasses were shoved up so the left lens was wedged over the bridge of his nose, which was bruised and bleeding. His mouth was partly open, and a little foamy drool was coming out of it; there were several blackfly bites, the first of the season, on his bald head, and four long fine hairs were growing out of the middle of his nose halfway between the bridge and the nostrils.

Noon. The sun shone down; Mees leaned closer. Mr. Banner smelled like perspiration but also sweet like cotton candy, and there was something about him, about the way he lay there so perfectly still yet with a sense of something enormously alive inside him, something almost insanely teeming with slumberous hidden vitality deep inside, that made her feel like she was looking at a cave full of sleeping bats.

"Don't," said Lorna, when Mees reached out a finger. "Don't touch him."

"Germs?" guessed Sunny, but Lorna, a great fan of Agatha Christie, shook her head.

"I don't think he's breathing," she said. "Look at his chest." Tentatively she held her hand near the man's nose. "I think he's dead." The sand was coarse and gritty, the entire beach hard as a rock. If there were any footprints, Lorna couldn't make them out, though despite the trash can, there was a lot of trash on the ground, including cigarette butts and a beer bottle. Molson. Canadian.

"We should do something," said Sunny. "We should get help."

"You get help," said Mees. "I'm staying here."

"It's not like he's going anywhere," Lorna pointed out, but once Mees had made her mind up, forget it. "Just try not to touch anything," Lorna added sternly. "Okay?"

Of course Lorna knew perfectly well that the minute she and Sunny were out of sight Mees would do just that — it had been so obvious, her hand visibly itching to touch the man's cheek.

"Sure," Mees said. She nodded her small round face, a face that, no doubt due to its exceptionally round dark eyes and full bow lips, its fringe of dark hair and pronounced widow's peak, tended to remind people of a pansy. Such a sweet little flower, with such a fierce expression!

Mr. Banner, Mees was thinking. Mr. Banner Mr. Banner Mr. Banner Mr. Banner.

Think of me. That was what Pansy said in The Language of Flowers.

Mon Jan 1, 1872 — Taught school. Bertie in eve played dominoes.

Tues Jan 2 — Taught school went home at night quilted on my skirt in eve.

Wed Jan 3 — Taught school. Came home at night hooked Bertie a mitten.

Thurs Jan 4 — Taught school.

Fri Jan 5 — Taught school.

Sat Jan 6 — At home done house work. Aunt Tiny here all day.

Sun Jan 7 — At home all day read some. George Wheeler and Hinkson here.

Mon Jan 8 — Taught school. Went to singing class in eve with Bertie. I hope it is not so.

Out the window the sun was shining on the lake, the whole surface a radiant copper-blue pricked with dazzling specks of white. Out the window, sunshine and fresh breezes, a family of ducks riding the little swells near shore. Mallards. The dull brown mother and her cute yellow babies — *I hope it is not so.* Andrea Murdock stiffened with the usual mix of impatience and affection as for the third time that morning she listened to her husband take the stairs from the second floor two at a time, like a man half his age, prior to yanking open the cellar door and sharpening his pencil in the sharpener he'd insisted on attaching to the wall just below the light switch. Sharpening and whistling the same five-note phrase that came from nowhere and went nowhere, over and over, like birdsong. Murdocks since the dawn of time had kept their pencil sharpeners at the head of the cellar steps.

Taught school. Taught school. Chick a dee dee dee.

What else was there for an unmarried woman to do? thought Andrea. At least Miss Fair had been lucky enough to have a profession. At least she wasn't stuck washing and churning and baking and cleaning and churning and chatting and washing and baking, day in day out, like the author of that last diary Andrea had restored, though this one's pages were in worse condition, ready to flake away at the lightest touch. Lucky Miss Inez Fair, Andrea thought grimly, peeling endpaper from cover board. Young and unmarried and teaching school.

Andrea Murdock's bindery extended from the southeastern wall of the house and had windows on all three sides, providing an unobstructed view of Black Lake and a maple- and beech- and cedar-obstructed view of the bike trail and the Upper Varennes Road. Midges, mayflies, blackflies, bees. Atmospheric vapors. A little higher than everything around it, the bindery perched at the lower tip of a five-mile-long esker, wide-eyed and hopeful, in the spirit of a space capsule finally ready to break from the mother ship.

Back in the days of Inez Fair none of it had been here — house, bindery, nothing. Nothing, that is, except the esker, which had been here forever, or at least since the Pleistocene, when long cracks appeared along the surface of the ice sheet. The lake also had been here for a very long time, though possibly not as long as the esker. If Andrea paid closer attention when her husband was talking, maybe she'd remember better.

Esker. Ice sheet. She tugged at the last section of endpaper, which had decided to hang on for dear life.

Tenacious, just like Inez. Tenacious, doomed Inez Fair, Varennes village schoolmarm. *Thurs Jan 12 — Taught school. Mr. Bacon asked me to go with him to the donation Tues eve. (Thinking of thee. Art thou of me?)* Though who exactly was this "thee"? It didn't seem like she meant Mr. Bacon, since Tuesday eve she went to the donation — whatever that was — with someone named Mart. In 1872, the year Inez Fair began the diary, the tip of the esker would have been a popular location for picnics, given its fine view of Black Lake, which had once been full to the brim with glacial melt. Picnics, parties, maybe even donations, though certainly not in the dead of winter. It was also from here, a year later, that a band of mothers and fathers would watch Miss Inez Fair set forth in a leaky boat with the eight victims of the Sunday School Outing Disaster.

Nowadays water levels everywhere were way down — the beach on the east side of the lake was twice as big as it had been thirty years ago when Andrea first moved to Varennes. She'd been Andy Aikman then, and lived in a geodesic dome on French Hill with four Toggenburg goats. And while life had certainly been simpler, could you also say it had been happier? Once Andrea managed to grow a blue Hubbard squash the size of a manatee, but did that constitute happiness?

The doorbell rang. No one who knew the Murdocks ever rang the doorbell, most of their friends and acquaintances tending to walk straight in without knocking. "Could you get that, Danny?" Andrea yelled, and then the bell rang again, and she realized her husband must be back in his study with his box of bones and the radio tuned as usual to the country music station's drawn-out stories of heartbreak and betrayal. The news turned a person's heart to stone, he said.

Wed Jan 16 — Taught school. Went to oyster supper with Eve. Came home late. Mother gave me a scolding that I guess I shall remember . . .

A scolding. Those were the days. Andrea opened the front door and found two girls standing on the porch. Two girls, the usual combination, one pretty, one plain, and both vaguely familiar. Girl Scouts? Though when they went around selling cookies, weren't they supposed to wear their uniforms?

"Sorry to barge in like this, Mrs. Murdock," said the pretty one. "We'd like to use your phone, if that would be all right." Her blond hair was coiled over her ears, Princess Leia style, and her perfectly regular features were perfectly distributed on a perfectly oval face that Andrea knew wouldn't hold up over time.

She told them to come in and noticed that the blonde made a great show of wiping her feet on the welcome mat, whereas the brunette stumbled across the threshold and looked around wildly the way a horse would if it thought it was going into a barn and suddenly found itself in a flagstone entry hall instead.

"Sorry to disturb," said the blonde. "My name is Sunny. Sunny Crockett. We live just up the road? And this is my friend Lorna."

"Of course," said Andrea, recognition striking at last. "Kathy Crockett's your mother." She handed her the phone, since Sunny so obviously appeared to be the one in charge, and then watched, interested, as Lorna calmly but firmly took the phone away from her and punched in 911.

A man, Lorna reported, presumed dead, on the Varennes town beach. When Andrea gasped, Lorna held a surprisingly well-manicured finger to her lips. Balding and heavyset, she said, probably about 220 pounds or so, the skin pink but not bright red, meaning he couldn't have been there for more than an hour. No obvious signs of foul play, unless you counted the head wound. No one else's footprints visible. She and her friends had been careful not to disturb the scene. And while she herself hadn't recognized the man, one of her friends said his name was Banner.

Lorna listened intently to the dispatcher for several seconds, then shook her head. "Not T," she said. "B. B as in *baby*." She sounded exasperated, going on to explain that naturally she couldn't swear the man wasn't breathing, since as she thought she'd mentioned, they'd been careful not to disturb the scene.

Andrea felt her face turn red. Menopause, she realized, not embarrassment, though the girls couldn't be expected to know the difference.

"Carl Banner?" Andrea asked. She tensed, hearing the sound of feet on the stairs. Wasn't Carl Banner *ever* going to leave her alone? Already she could imagine the change coming over her husband's calm blue eyes and smiling mouth, like a front moving in from the Great Lakes. It was hard being married to a man who treated the least impropriety like the end of the world, like freezing rain and a tractor trailer jackknifing right in front of him and everything going so fast it might as well not be moving, the immense tire and the windshield racing toward each other yet frozen in time. It was hard being married to a romantic.

The world was already acting strange millions of years ago.

Water had its way with rock. Liquid beat solid. Ice is supposed to be obdurate, unyielding, but back then it rippled and flowed. The glacier rode the world, and the world let it change it, like a girl riding her lover and turning his prick to foam. Exactly the way it is today.

The world was strange from day one. Let there be light, God said, and there was light. There is probably nothing more beautiful and implausible than the world, nothing that makes less sense, the gray bud of the willow, silky and soft, the silk-white throat of the cobra, the wish of nature or humans to subsume all living matter in fire and flood. I will hurt you, hurt you, hurt you, says the world, and then a meadow arches its back and golden pollen sprays forth.

Everyone prefers to stick with the subject of people, but how shortsighted to leave out the question of how we got here and where we're going.

At least four glaciers covered Varennes over the past three million years.

And even then, how beautiful! Rock cased in ice, the sun extracting greens and blues. Though to say everything was more beautiful without people, before people — even to go so far as to imagine *after* people — is obscene.

Banner, Mees was thinking. Think.

But what is this stuff? What is it? Where do we go and how? We are just human beings.

Pink. Blink. Stink.

The inside walls so unexpectedly thick, yellowish, and made of small pieces piled in alternating rows similar to bricks. Curving, beehive shape, toward the top. The bread oven they visited on the class trip, and *zees ees where zee smuck goes out,* said the handsome French baker, and Sunny blushed, the fool.

Hurry! It's not like you've got all day.

Mr. Banner Mr. Banner Mr. Banner.

Like reaching your arm into a box you can't see inside of except — guess what? — you're already there. Like the man who put his arm in a jar full of mosquitoes in the filmstrip about yellow fever to test his hypothesis, even though he knew he would die. So easy to die here, squashed under a landslide of fat and blood. Quick. Quick. Ship in a bottle. Harp strings.

Move your fingers around. Snag the thing and give a little tug.

Four-masted schooner. Pure white note. Eye sliding open. Daystar. Walnut. Daisy.

On the second floor of the Crockett Home for the Aged, in the most coveted of the second-floor bedrooms, its windows facing the backyard gardens and the verandah of the Locust Inn next door, sat Helen Zeebrugge, ninety-two years old. She was a large-boned and handsome woman whose great head of wild white hair had been momentarily tamed by a set of earphones. "'So extraordinary, my dear — so odd!'" said the voice in Helen's ears, and Helen laughed, just as she had the first time she read *The Forsyte Saga* over sixty years ago, at the thought of Aunt Hester trying to "shoo" Bosinney's hat off the hall chair because she thought it was a cat. Poor Bosinney. Not dead yet and still full of that boundless erotic energy that made men so attractive to women, even old ones like herself who would no more dream of succumbing to it than going over Niagara Falls in a barrel. It certainly formed the explanation behind her son Piet's many marriages, though he was nowhere near as rash as Bosinney. How many was it now? Four? Helen had lost count after Amy, the massage therapist. Of course Piet was a banker, and Bosinney was an artist.

"'Like an artist,'" concurred the voice in Helen's ears, "'forever seeking to discover the significant trifle which embodies the whole character of a scene, or place, or person, so these unconscious artists — the Forsytes — had fastened by intuition on this hat...'"

"Helen?"

Tentative and bold and, as usual, without knocking, Marjory Mason had once again managed to slip into Helen's room like she was made of ectoplasm. You could pretend you hadn't noticed Marjory for only so long before she stood right in front of you — visibly sensitive to the fact that you were visually impaired. Even if you were blind as a bat, you'd know she was there, because she stood way too close and spit on you when she talked.

Helen shook her head and pointed to her earphones, all to no avail. Marjory seemed to be crying. Rummaging in the sleeve of her apricot-colored cardigan for one of those unsanitary floral hankies she kept hidden away up there — rummaging and sniffing, sniffing and rummaging. Helen wanted to take her by the shoulders and shake her until every single distasteful thing she'd hidden on her person throughout the course of a long deceitful life came fluttering to the floor, but instead she removed the earphones and tossed them on her bed, only remembering to switch off the tape when she heard the reader's fruity British baritone continue to buzz away like a bee on the white candlewick bedspread.

"Don't be mad," Marjory said, literally wringing her hands.

"What makes you think I'm mad?" Helen replied. "Don't you mean 'angry'?"

"Mrs. Crockett," Marjory whispered. She looked at the door.

It was late Saturday afternoon, almost suppertime. Beauty Parlor Day, which would explain why Marjory's hair seemed to have turned the same shade of apricot as her sweater. A nice enough color for a sweater, but on an old woman's head? Sometimes Helen thought she'd rather be moldering in the grave than having to witness these final pitiful gasps of female vanity. Lipstick. Jewelry. The way the French Canadian woman's eyelashes were glued on crooked. Not to mention Boo Makepeace's false teeth.

"What about Crockett?" asked Helen.

"She said George isn't allowed to come here anymore."

George was Marjory's son, a hapless but amiable fellow who taught sixth grade at Varennes Elementary. A confirmed bachelor, as Marjory would explain whenever one of the other Crockett ladies dredged up a potential girlfriend for him from out of her vast pool of unmarried relatives, though any fool could see George was gay as a box of birds.

"George?" Helen said. It was hard enough to imagine George doing *anything,* let alone something so bad Crockett wouldn't let him through the door.

Marjory mimed turning a key between her lips before girlishly tossing it over her shoulder. Too many people in the hall, Marjory explained. Too many *ears.* The smell of something roasted to within an inch of its life drifted up the elevator shaft, along with the smell of a boiled member of the crucifer family.

"Hold it, hold it!" yelled the new woman, the one who could never bear to wait for anything because she was originally from New Jersey. The hallway filled with the sound of shuffling feet, of the rubber tips of walkers, three-pronged canes — you couldn't stay at the Crockett Home if you weren't able to ambulate or if you were incontinent, though if, like the woman from New Jersey, you couldn't bear to stop for anything, Death included, you could be sure Death would kindly stop for you, as he had only last week for poor Anita Sommers, screaming her head off up there on the third floor before the horses arrived with their heads toward Eternity.

Helen, on the other hand, was in no hurry to get to the dining room.

She leaned forward and retrieved the earphones, switching the machine back on. "'Come now,'" the fruity baritone was inquiring, "'should *I* have paid that visit in that hat? No! It would never have come into my head...'" So comfortable, Helen's English lounge chair; so beautiful, the pink light of the setting sun. "'What indeed was this young man, who, in becoming engaged to June, old Jolyon's acknowledged heiress, had done so well for himself?'"

Meanwhile downstairs the ladies were settling into their assigned seats. They'd get their new seat assignments Monday, but until then Helen was stuck at a table with Crooked Eyelashes, who had once known how to speak English but refused to speak anything these days but French, and Jane Shippee, who ate like a pig, and Selena Blum, who felt compelled to relate the story of her husband's suicide at every meal. Gun, mouth, brand-new Oldsmobile.

"'Never had there been so full an assembly, for, mysteriously united in spite of all their differences, they had taken arms against a common peril. Like cattle when a dog comes into the field, they stood head to head and shoulder to shoulder, prepared to run upon and trample the invader to death.'"

Group mentality! You might as well head straight to the slaughterhouse as to the dining room. At least mad cow disease had provided a little change of pace. No more shepherd's pie, no more American chop suey. Helen hated groups as much as she hated meat. She had been a vegetarian ever since the day she watched her amah's handsome slant-eyed son kill a chicken by cracking its neck between his teeth. This was the sort of thing that happened if you had missionaries for parents and spent your formative years in Japan. Though maybe it wasn't vegetables she longed for so much as some fascinating tidbit, the sort of thing the world would drop in your lap from time to time if you were lucky, which is to say not stuck sitting at a table with Gargantua and the Ancient Mariner. Maybe when you were ninety-two years old what you really wanted was what Helen's young friend Billie referred to as a scoop — what the little girl with the bad eyesight, who sometimes came to read to her, called "dish."

Police Log — Saturday May 17

1:59 a.m. Noise disturbance on Bank Street.

2:45 a.m. Trash dumped in Dumpster.

4:06 a.m. Domestic complaint at French Hill residence.

8:55 a.m. Wandering dog brought to Humane Society.

9:15 a.m. Drug activity on Route 3.

10:30 a.m. Threatening phone call reported at Terrace Street residence.

12:40 p.m. Subject sold car without brother's consent.

2:10 p.m. Vandalism complaint on Perry Street. Vehicles egged.

3:06 p.m. Juveniles riding wheelchairs in roadway on Bank Street.

3:10 p.m. Protesters blocking traffic at Summer Street rotary.

4:03 p.m. Subject unconscious on town beach.

4:12 p.m. Dog loose on Summer Street.

6:20 p.m. Double-headed meter stolen on River Street.

8:58 p.m. Bear reported in Terrace Street yard.

It was still there early the next morning or had returned after being scared off by the trooper who responded to George Mason's call, and it reappeared several times the following week. A medium-sized black she-bear, dull-eyed and mangy from her recent hibernation and obviously ravenous — it was unclear what had drawn her to that particular yard, though the Mason house was at the end of Terrace, a dead-end street on the northeastern edge of town, beyond which there was nothing but several hundred acres of forest and beyond that the boggy remains of Goneaway Lake. Acres and acres of nothing, which is to say everything a black bear might find desirable. Acres and acres of tamarack and black spruce, balsam fir and white cedar. Silvery hemlock in the cool shady ravines, sphagnum moss and cinnamon fern. Jewelweed and nettles, witherod and nannyberry. Fish. Lots of fish. A beautiful black salamander with yellow spots hiding in the leaf mold under a fallen cottonwood.

Monday night was a half-moon. Wednesday, waxing gibbous. The bear removed the lids from all of George Mason's recycling bins and licked out the insides of the spaghetti-sauce jars George hadn't washed thoroughly enough, also the mushroom and chicken-noodle soup cans. She made a mess of the newspaper, some of which ended up Thursday morning plastered against the front of the Canfields' house across the street, a cold front from the Canadian Maritimes having arrived around midnight, bringing with it wind and rain. Thursday night was clear and bright. The bear sat on her haunches in the middle of George Mason's yard. She looked like an old man in a sweater, George thought, peering at her through the curtains over the kitchen sink. Like his father, which is to say *not* cute, *not* adorable, but full of pent-up anger that could be released at the drop of a hat.

Where did the bear come from? What was she doing there?

Of course, beyond the acres and acres of forest there was the world. The world with its houses and cities, its people, machinery, weapons, germs, and noise — something always encroaching from somewhere. Encroaching and pushing until something else had to give. Until it had to shoot loose like a storm of invective from a father's mouth or a weapon from an underground silo. There was only so much room.

Eventually George began putting honey out for the bear. He would pour it into a cereal bowl that he would set inside the otherwise empty newspaper recycling bin and then tightly replace the lid. He loved to watch the whole operation, but in particular the deft way the bear opened the lid and then paused for a fraction of an instant before looking inside the bin, as if to dwell for a moment in that happy place where almost anything is possible.

The universe a doughnut. A teacup. A scroll. Like a garment turned inside out. The outside of a bag without anything in it. No throat. No tongue. No mind. Also, no ventriloquist.

Let there be light, God said. But what was God that God could say that? Where did His mouth come from?

Piet Zeebrugge was running through the woods above Black Lake, having the usual argument with himself in his head. An astonishing view across the lake to French Hill, where he could just see the roof of his house, and eastward all the way to Mount Washington, home of the strongest recorded winds in the world — but only because they had a weather station there, superlatives being relative.

The trail had been a streambed before it was a logging road; every year the spring runoff washed away the dirt and left behind rocks, making it difficult to run. You had to concentrate. You couldn't let your mind wander — which was the main reason for running in the first place, Piet knew, along with warding off depression — or you'd twist your ankle, a depressing thought. Wakerobin was in bloom along the banks. Red trillium, also called stink flower. He'd have to tell his mother, who experienced nature vicariously these days. The only flowers it was okay to pick were black-eyed Susans.

Piet Zeebrugge: a tall man in his sixties with a little pot-belly, wearing unfashionably scant black jogging shorts and an unfashionably big black T-shirt with a picture of a dog on the front. All four of his wives had found him irresistible due to his boyish charm, which turned out each time not to be charm after all but a kind of mania resulting from his unceasing communion with the material universe. Just because he couldn't stop talking about it didn't mean he was a real conversationalist, that he loved the ebb and flow and give-and-take of real conversation. What Piet needed to do was plant the seed of his thought in his wives' minds and hearts and watch it take root there. Things would sprout, and he could monitor their growth, strange things that had nothing whatsoever to do with his wives, but which they were permitted to keep warm for him, since the place where an investment banker lives his life is full of money and excitement, but cold and lonely.

Piet had been wifeless for over two years. It was time for a new wife, ideally one to accompany him to the grave. For the past year he'd been dating Chloe Brock, who taught French at Varennes High, though lately he'd found his eye wandering, since Chloe seemed uninterested, and in any event was too athletic for his taste. His type was more along the lines of the brunette shooting past the intersection going a hundred miles an hour while simultaneously applying lipstick in the rearview mirror.

He might have computed the odds: how many times could a distracted woman drive her car way too fast around a certain blind curve before she hit another vehicle?

Every single thing that happens in a life is like Chekhov's Gun, trustfully casting before it the shadow of its own final shape, if only we knew how to see it clearly.

Fourth Sunday after Easter: the Baptism of Emma Starr Brackney. Processional hymn 182. "Christ is Alive! Let Christians sing." Billie Carpenter had run out of service leaflets, the congregation being larger than usual, due to all of the baby's fans.

"The Lord be with you," said the Reverend Richard Jenkins.

"And also with you," replied the congregation.

"Let us pray," said Reverend Jenkins.

Everyone was on their feet, praying, as a woman in the last pew on the left took Billie's jacket by the scruff of the neck and shook it.

"This is *my* pew," the woman said. "Quentin and I always sit here."

Sometimes it seemed to Billie that everyone in the church was very old. "I'm sorry," she said.

"It's okay, Mrs. Quill. Billie's an usher," said James Trumbell, Billie's ushering partner. He leaned over and gave the woman a brisk pat on the back as if to dislodge a sourball. Mrs. Quill still wore a mink stole, despite the lateness of the season and the fact that she'd been spat at more than once, the town being full of political activists of every stripe.

"Quentin's dead," whispered James. He was standing next to Billie and staring toward the front of the church, where Chloe Brock had taken the lectern, a wild look in her eye.

"A reading from the Book of Ezekiel," Chloe was saying.

She tossed back her long blond hair, tilted her chin defiantly, all but shook her fist. "'Woe be to the shepherds of Israel that do feed themselves! Should not the shepherds feed the flocks?'" Ever since the previous summer, when her ne'er-do-well husband dumped her, Chloe's style at the lectern had become increasingly dramatic. "'Ye eat the fat, and ye clothe you with the wool, ye kill them that are fed: but ye feed not the flock!'"

"He died four years ago," James added. "Left her a bundle."

Billie was looking straight ahead, but she could tell James was drawing closer, the sleeve of his houndstooth sports jacket brushing against her arm, catching on her arm hairs. His breath smelled minty, and his slightly too long dun-colored hair like the dandruff shampoo her father used to use. James was lanky, though out of shape. A runner? No, that was Helen Zeebrugge's son, Piet, whose long leg Billie could just barely see, sticking out into the aisle way up front, a running shoe on his foot. Piet Zeebrugge wore bifocals and was balding but not trying to hide the fact like James Trumbell. Piet was cute. He had a nice mouth and no wedding ring, though maybe that just meant he was difficult to live with.

"'The Lord is my shepherd, I shall not want,'" sang the choir member with the gray braids and the overheated, operatic voice, adding a touch of misguided vibrato on *herd* and *want*.

There seemed to be some sort of sheep and shepherd theme going on today. Of all the psalms, this was the best — what could be better than to be led beside still waters? Billie found herself picturing the formal pool in the little park near where she grew up, marble terraced, rectangular, its water a glaucous motionless green, though the stream that fed into it was as dark and ungoverned as the behavior of the bad teenagers who came there in the dead of night to do things Billie would never dare to do. Good Billie. What was she afraid would happen?

Get over it, girl, she told herself, though she was almost fifty years old. A current ran through the church, the tremulous dark current of excitement that she thought of as God's nerve.

Now there was a pasty-faced young man at the lectern, and someone's dog barking just outside the big double doors, setting off all the babies. "'The wind bloweth where it listeth and thou hearest the sound thereof . . .'" The young man's *t*'s emerged as glottal stops. Outside the big double doors the spring sun was shining, the spring wind blowing. Blowing where it listeth — why on earth had Billie invited her neighbors for dinner when she could be paddling her canoe across Black Lake instead? The moon was going to be full. Hare Moon, Cassiopeia ascendant. The lake water still cold. Tadpoles, little fish.

Billie looked at Piet, who was looking at Chloe Brock as she turned to follow the reverend's progress up the aisle, the gold-plated Gospel held aloft, gleaming. "The Holy Gospel of Our Lord Jesus Christ according to John," said Richard Jenkins. "'I am the good shepherd: the good shepherd giveth his life for the sheep.'"

Sheep again, Billie thought. Piet leaned forward to scratch his ankle.

Cute, she thought. Cute, but not for me. James Trumbell is more my speed.

Mees folded her hands. She bowed her head and seemed to close her eyes but left slits to look through. Mr. Banner was looking back at her, his heavy black-rimmed glasses and the brilliant orb of his hairless head catching the last sunlight that came through the window over the sideboard. Looking back at her with a puzzled and cagey expression on his face — a very strange disposition, Mr. Banner's. What was he thinking? *You didn't imagine it,* Mees told him with her brain. *But it's a secret. Shhh. Shhh.* Spring breezes and the whooshing sounds of skateboards on the sidewalk — the Banners lived in town, two blocks up Main Street from the Crockett Home for the Aged. Car stereos, *boom boom boom,* bells ringing, *bong bong bong,* the Devil, God, the Devil, God. Nothing fancy.

"For what we are about to receive," Mrs. Banner said, "may the Lord make us truly grateful."

She was a religious person of sixty or so, with long gray hair that she wore in pigtails and a relentlessly pleasant expression that made you think eternity would be exhausting. At least they hadn't had to join hands, like at Ginny Makepeace's house.

"Sunny, would you kindly pass the gravy?" asked Mr. Banner. "Lorna, may I help you to some roast beef?"

He was a man plucked from the jaws of death. A man given a second chance. A man who couldn't stop talking about the kind of man he now was.

"It's going to be different around here," Mr. Banner was exulting. "Didn't I say, Glenda? Help yourself to some of Mrs. Banner's mashed potatoes, girls. No one makes mashed potatoes like Glenda."

On the school bus the next day, when Sunny repeated this last sentence in a sonorous voice, opening her small blue eyes as wide as possible and ducking her chin into her neck, Mees pretended to gag, and Lorna — tenderhearted Lorna, who sometimes cried over the faces of the men in the Wanted posters in the post office — twisted across the back of the seat in front of them to object. "Just because we saved his life doesn't mean we have to like him," Mees pointed out.

For the moment, though, Mees was behaving herself, having been instructed to do so by her mother, who also happened to be the person who'd made her accept Mr. Banner's invitation in the first place. It had been such a nice day, a day when you could pack a lunch and head into Fair's Woods and no one would ask any questions and you and Margaret could stay as long as you wanted. Assuming, that is, you didn't have to be packed off to town in a dress, of all things, to eat dinner with people you barely knew at a ridiculously early hour. A perfect day, Mees thought. The trail sun-splotched and shadowy and down you'd go past the Five Erratics and the next thing you knew there'd be that first little invisible hand slipping shyly into yours, but so shyly to begin with it wasn't so much like *slipping into* as *slipping through*.

"Your gravy is very good, Mrs. Banner," Sunny said.

"The hallmark of a great chef," said Lorna, adding that that was what her dad always said, though Mr. Fine never took his head out of the newspaper long enough to see what he was eating, and Mees figured that, as usual, Lorna had gotten the line from a book.

"A great chef," repeated Mr. Banner. "I like that. Are you going to let the girls in on your secret, Glenda?" he asked.

"I thought you said it was going to be different around here," Mrs. Banner replied, cutting her roast beef into tiny pieces as if there were an infant hidden away waiting to be fed. She had a very high-pitched voice, the exact opposite of Mr. Banner's. Mrs. Banner's voice was like the hot evening breeze coming through the window over the sideboard, parting to make its way around the roast. A hot breeze, with a lot of floral aromas in it, whereas Mr. Banner's voice was like the roast, overdone and hard to chew and clogged with blood and fat. When you did a Saturday night sleepover at Sunny Crockett's, everyone went to church the next morning, and so Mees also knew what Mrs. Banner's voice sounded like, singing. The only one in the choir who could, according to Sunny's dad, though he usually slept through the entire service.

Speckled brown-and-gold wallpaper, a mahogany sideboard, a mahogany breakfront filled with many different kinds of dishes and ceramic figurines, including several Indian maidens, and on either side of the arched doorway into the living room a very tall snake plant in a brass pot. A spinet piano, with *The Fireside Book of Folk Songs* open to "The Foggy Foggy Dew." The room smelled like potatoes and varnish and baby powder, though they weren't having potatoes but Le Sueur canned peas, which Mees recognized because that was the only thing her sister, Mersey, would eat after one of her migraines. Unheated, straight from the can. Over the piano there was a large oil painting of a naked woman with a sort of blurry face and very large boobs, reclining on a sofa. "You didn't know I was a painter, did you?" Mr. Banner challenged when he saw Mees looking at it, adding that there was nothing more beautiful on God's earth than the female form. Then he excused himself and went into the kitchen to refill the yellow aluminum water pitcher.

"The gravy's from a package," Mrs. Banner said, the minute he was gone. She looked around the table without making eye contact. "But don't tell that I told," she added, blushing.

And then Mr. Banner was back with the yellow pitcher and Mees was whispering, "I don't get it," and Lorna was whispering, "Shhh," and Mrs. Banner was saying, "So are any of you girls natives, originally?"

"My mom's from here," said Sunny. "She met my dad on spring break in Fort Lauderdale. He's from Massachusetts."

"Fort Lauderdale," Mr. Banner mused. "I was there once. Excellent sand beaches."

"I was born here," said Lorna, "but my parents are both from New York."

"And what about you, young lady?" Mr. Banner asked Mees, leaning across the table to pour tepid water into her glass.

"I just live with my mother and sister," she answered. "My mother's from England *originally*."

"Ah," said Mrs. Banner.

"She doesn't have an accent," Lorna added, to change the subject.

Mees could see the wheels turning inside both Banners' heads — big slow wheels, generating a look of concern on both their big slow faces. What business was any of this of theirs? Lorna was patting Mees's arm, trying to get her attention, trying to soothe her. Mees could feel her own anger like a many-headed snake darting its tongues and hissing and striking its many poisonous blows again and again and again into all her extremities. "My father made a rubber mallet for me," she said. "To hit the bottoms of my feet."

A series of jolts, really, like when you accidentally bumped against a strand of electric fence, or in the winter when the house was so dry that everything you touched including your dog's nose gave you a shock. Even Margaret's nose. That was why the mallet was so great: you didn't have to jump off the top of the piano anymore to punch the anger back.

"My father's dead," Mees said.

"I'm sorry," said Mrs. Banner.

"Why are you apologizing?" Mees asked.

She was thinking *Margaret Margaret Margaret,* because her mother had taught her to think of her dog when she got angry like this. "It's not like it's your *fault.*" Margaret's smell, Mees thought, and she could feel herself calming down, thinking of the way the top of Margaret's head smelled like popcorn and the way Margaret would settle her black moist nose between her two white front paws and then stare up at Mees. A crescent of white under each dark brown eye. Those long black whiskers.

"That's not what she meant," Lorna whispered, giving Mees a look. "You know that."

There is nothing more wonderful than a dog's nose, Mees was thinking. "No, you're right," she said, but she was still thinking of Margaret's nose. Why couldn't people's noses be like dogs'?

"Save room for dessert," said Mr. Banner.

And all of a sudden Mees found herself remembering what it had been like in there that day on the beach, hardly enough room to do what she had to do and get out and certainly not enough room for that *and* a bowl of butterscotch pudding with nondairy whipped topping, which seemed to be what Mrs. Banner was this very minute bringing to the table.

It started just the two of them, Margaret and Cam, but at the pit toilet Buddy joined up, slowing things down as usual because he got carried away by stuff that wasn't worth it like leaves or wadded-up tissues, and even though Cam was a little too careful, a little too afraid he might get himself into trouble, a little too *good dog Cammy,* he could always tell the difference between worth it and not. Also Cam smelled divine and Buddy didn't. He couldn't help it. His person sprayed him with something.

Where to? Where to?

The moon was round, divine for singing. Sometimes Margaret could get Cam to sing with her, but never Buddy.

Buddy wouldn't sing. He was like, *Quick before that dachshund finds us.* That was Buddy for you — always trying to sound tough.

Except guess what, Buddy? Margaret loved the dachshund. So bold, so dashing, so fast to catch a mole! Also the divine way he ran right under her, sniffing. Doozie. Quite a stinking name but no worse than Margaret. Margaret the Malamute. Not their real names anyway.

So, okay, four of them.

Little pack tonight. The tall one had let Margaret out by accident. The tall one never shut the back door right. Margaret always got in trouble when she ran away like this. Her girl was angry and Margaret loved her girl more than anything but sniffing air divine from deer and also porcupines.

Buddy smelling a Popsicle stick.

The tall one never shut the back door so it stayed shut. Push it with your nose! Margaret always got in trouble when she ran away like this but it was golden.

A little pack tonight, running up the long grass hill, Margaret in the lead and Cam right behind. Many deer beds and some human pee in a bush and also birds in trees and lots of squirrels too high to eat and then a house. Never a good idea to go too near a house unless you knew the person put out suet.

The rule was: bad dog! Bad Margaret! Bad to run off like that! Bad dog! Bad!

The rule was: ignore some things, some things you howl and Cam barks and Doozie barks.

But wow it was getting good now! Stupendous!

Chickens.

All together in one place like kibble and way too fat to fly!

It seems solid enough, the world. Drop a thing to the world's surface from a great height and the thing breaks, painfully if it's alive. Alpinists strung together like charms on a bracelet, spurned lovers, cats on their tenth life. An airplane crashes, foundation stones quake, the elevator cable snaps in two. Total strangers hold hands and jump from a burning building.

The tempter took Jesus to the pinnacle of the Temple. This was on top of Mount Sion, at the corner where Solomon's porch and the royal porch met, and there was a sheer drop of 450 feet into the valley of the Kedron below. "Jump," said the tempter. The River Kedron looked no bigger than a golden thread, the noon sun winking off it.

Of course Jesus was afraid, but that isn't why He didn't jump. We are always tempted through our gifts. Simon Magus promised to fly through the air and perished in the attempt.

The world seems solid enough. The valley of the Kedron is an area of yellow sand and scattered shingle, glowing and shimmering with heat. And under the sand and shingle? Under the streets of a big city? Under the new spring grass of Bliss Hill? Aside from the obvious holes and tunnels made by animals and people, rabbit warrens, subway systems, missile silos, rumpus rooms, it seems solid enough, though in fact it's a set of interlocking pieces, sometimes bound tightly together and sometimes drifting far apart, its composition various, but in the case of Varennes, say, a blend of igneous rock, schist, and granite batholith, of dark slate and lignites containing a fossil flora of tropical nuts and fruits, the whole plate pressing down into the viscous mantle below — descending a few inches every thousand years like the Garden of Paradise in the fairy tale, only in the wrong direction. Nothing's really pinned in place. Everything's moving, up and down and back and forth. Moving pieces around a ball of fire.

If you jumped at just the right moment, you'd fall through all the gaps and out the other side.

Except isn't that like thinking that if you start jumping when the elevator cable breaks you have a fifty-fifty chance of being in the air when the car hits bottom?

There are natural laws, but they're pretty strange, too.

Billie Carpenter's camp was almost exactly opposite the Varennes town beach, tucked among fir trees in a small cove where the same family of mallard ducks Andrea Murdock often watched from her bindery had taken up residence. It was about seven o'clock — a half hour before the Murdocks were due to arrive for dinner — and the sun hadn't quite set, though because the house was hemmed in on three sides by fir trees, you couldn't really tell, despite a few pinkish-red wrinkles in the surface of the water. Above the beach the sky was already darkening to a violet-gray-blue, yet it hadn't lost its daytime opacity, the full moon on it like a vaccination mark. It used to be you could tell how old someone was by whether they had that mark, Billie thought, but like lots of other things, that was about to change, too.

Several people, teenagers probably, remained smoking on the beach, the orange tips of their cigarettes moving around in the dark as if they were trying to send messages. Far away, beyond the beach, she could hear the sound of barking, echoing off the long ridge that followed Lake Road from Canton to Varennes and all the way to Canada. Adder Ridge, named for the harmless little snakes that lived in its forests; the old-timers called them milk snakes because of how they'd sneak into barns and milk cows with their mouths. The ducks were getting ready to sleep now. They slept swimming, Billie guessed, and she felt herself yearning for her own bed in her own bedroom that continued to smell reassuringly damp and provisional even after she'd been there for a year.

Like a camp, not a home. Like a place you might visit from time to time to get away from home, and if you actually lived there it meant you didn't *have* a home, which also meant you didn't have a life, a condition which until recently Billie had found desirable.

Most of her furniture came with the camp. Her bed, for instance, as well as the matching maple dresser and the mint-green chenille bedspread. All of the living-room furniture, including a sofa and two chairs with big wooden armrests and lumpy cushions printed with pictures like the ones you used to find on the linings of Boy Scout sleeping bags. A wooden pump-handle table lamp some previous owner had made in junior-high wood shop, its shade held in place with clothespins, also a "modern" floor-to-ceiling lamp from the fifties, with three adjustable fixtures shaped like the domes of professional hair dryers. Two elegant end tables made of mahogany and in tiers; a faux rough-hewn coffee table more or less shaped like the state of Vermont; and a large salmon-pink ashtray shaped like a hand, palm up. A framed picture cut from a magazine of an English cottage surrounded by hollyhocks. A Reliant wood stove.

The only things of Billie's in the living room were her sandals, a notepad, and a pile of newspaper.

Whereas the kitchen smelled overwhelmingly of curry powder, and aside from the white tea towels with red rooster borders that Billie was using as napkins, the three place settings on the gray Formica tabletop were clearly not indigenous, the cutlery being sterling, the plates bone china, and the wine goblets crystal. The silver candelabrum wasn't indigenous either, though unlike the other items, it hadn't been a wedding present from her ever-hopeful in-laws, who'd never given up on trying to turn her into a homemaker, but something Billie had bought by accident at an auction.

The phone rang. Seven-fifteen. Thank goodness, she thought. They're calling to say they can't make it. But why invite people if you don't want them to come?

Only it wasn't the Murdocks, it was Piet Zeebrugge. Seven-fifteen on a Sunday night — where was his girlfriend, Chloe? Billie felt as if she were a teenager again, hiding on the floor of her mother's closet amid a sea of high-heel shoes, talking to Kenny Kottler. Above her head, size nothing dresses on padded pink hangers, and everywhere the smell of Chanel No. 5. Of course Kenny only called for help with his English homework and to pump her for information about Sara Dinardo.

"Billie Carpenter?" Piet said. "Sorry to bother you at home."

"Don't worry about it," Billie said. "I'm not busy" — though as the words were leaving her mouth she remembered that was the last thing in the world you were supposed to say to a boy. She could see headlights advancing toward her from the south, dramatically lighting the trees along the road from beneath, an effect enhanced by the fact that the Murdocks, or whoever it was, had their car windows down and were listening to the country station full blast.

"We need to talk," Piet continued. "Sorry. I don't mean to sound melodramatic." Billie heard a cork pop, the *glug-glug-glug* of liquid pouring from a bottle. A woman spoke, and Piet put his hand over the receiver. "Walkie-talkies," she heard him say, and the woman laughed.

Billie Carpenter was a strange creature. She'd chosen a profession in which it was essential to get to the bottom of things, and yet she believed in her heart of hearts that no such place existed. She was a regular churchgoer, and yet in her heart of hearts she found it almost impossible to believe in God. Of course she would never come right out and say any of this, so most people took her for a woman of strong convictions. She had the kind of face — borderline homely, with a long narrow nose, thin lips, and deep-set brown eyes — that bore out this impression, despite the fact that she wore her brown hair girlishly long, and her whole body was covered with freckles. Her ex-husband was one of the very few people who'd known this about Billie Carpenter, but — as very few people also knew — her ex-husband was dead. He'd been murdered. Murdered! Who knew anyone who'd been murdered?

A car pulled into the driveway, funneling light across the lake. A betrayed woman was pouring her heart out at the top of her lungs, the oven timer was going off, and Piet was explaining how the vestry had decided ushers should carry walkie-talkies, in case of trouble, and had enlisted his help.

Walkie-talkies? Billie pictured orange-juice cans. "What kind of trouble?"

Suddenly the woman stopped midnote. A car door slammed. Another. *Bang* from across the lake, *bang bang,* though surely it was too late for target practice. Billie could once again hear the sound of barking. Voices, loud knocking on the porch door, the door opening, and Andrea Murdock saying, "Knock knock?"

"Never mind," Piet said. "I'll tell you later. It sounds like you're busy."

"I'll call," Billie promised.

Of course if you called people you might end up inviting them to dinner, and then you'd have to cook it, and then there they would be, standing in your kitchen, staring at you, disappointed, holding out a bottle of wine.

Andrea was heavier than Billie remembered, also prettier.

She had short curly hair without a trace of gray and extremely shiny eyes and what you'd have to call a luscious set of lips. Her husband, Daniel, reeked of cigarette smoke and looked a little freakish, like an albino, but sexy. He was also, it turned out, deaf in one ear.

"I haven't been in this place since the Lesters owned it," Daniel said. Maybe he wasn't sneering but just had to twist his face like that in order to hear better. "Used it mostly as a hunting camp," he added. "Gutted deer right on this table."

"I'm sure it's not the same table," Andrea added, though she looked doubtful.

Billie lit the candles; they all sat down. The wine turned out to be surprisingly good and went a long way toward improving her mood. Andrea, who claimed she never drank, got tipsy immediately. "This casserole is delicious," she said, her mouth full, chewing. "You've got to give me the recipe. Isn't this delicious, Danny?"

Daniel shook his head and pointed to his own mouth. But did the head shake refer to his inability to talk or to the quality of the casserole, which Billie thought wasn't all that bad really, though maybe a little heavy on the curry powder?

"Danny's the cook in our family," Andrea explained. "He's a genius in the kitchen. I starve when he's gone."

"No she doesn't," Daniel retorted, emptying the bottle into his glass. "Look at her."

"That's right," Andrea said. "Look at me." She had a smug, cat-that-ate-the-canary expression on her face. "When you're gone I pine away to nothing."

"Face it, Andy. You married me for the food."

"I'm a supertramp," Andrea explained cheerfully, helping herself to more casserole. "That's another word for 'opportunistic,' among scientists."

"Come on, sweetheart. We're boring our hostess."

If you are a single woman and you invite a couple to dinner, you may be asking for trouble. If only for the duration of that dinner, you may be required to lend your presence to the formation of a three-sided, three-dimensional object, a drama with three starring roles — Adam, Eve, Snake.

Billie opened another bottle of wine, not so expensive as the Murdocks' bottle, but serviceable. Meanwhile, in response to her question, Daniel launched into a description of the island where he'd be heading mid-June. It was called Pitsulak, which was Inuit for "sea duck," because it was small and made of smooth gold rock and shaped like a duck riding the waves. Archaeologists who worked in the Arctic had it easy, since permafrost made it impossible to bury anything and consequently you never had to dig.

"Wouldn't that take all the fun out of it?" Billie asked, but it was clear that Daniel wouldn't hear of any attempt to turn monologue to conversation. Or maybe he couldn't.

If you didn't count the underdone chickpeas, there was nothing on the table left to eat. The candles burned unevenly, subject to a draft whose source Billie had never been able to locate. Hare Moon. The lake was quivering all over and had turned the color of mercury; a loon cried, another loon answered.

"Do you mind?" Daniel asked, slipping a yellow pack of American Spirits from his breast pocket, and just as Andrea was giving him a look and saying, "Of course she does," Billie was returning from the living room with the salmon-colored hand.

The north was dangerous. A plume of smoke drifted to the ceiling and began to loop downward. Everything beautiful was dangerous. The Arctic Sea made that famous Caribbean turquoise appear tawdry and meretricious by comparison. Cold heaven, Daniel said. The Arctic Sea was the color of cold heaven. Yeats. Clearly he was showing off, but the activity seemed to agree with him. Billie could feel Andrea watching her, measuring her response, which had the effect of making her get up to get the salad. The more Daniel talked, the less like a shoe-bomber he looked, the more like a wild animal. His eyes were an interesting shade of pale blue, translucent like a husky's.

"No one up north knows how to swim," he said. "If you fall in, you've got thirty seconds before you're a goner."

Hare Moon, danger of frost. Some mornings there'd be the thinnest layer of ice on the birdbath.

Billie tossed the salad with her fingertips. "Speaking of goners," she said, "whatever became of that man those girls found on the beach?"

"Who?" Andrea asked, pouring the last of the second bottle of wine into her glass and then staring at it with apparent deep interest.

"Carl someone," Billie said. "His wife goes to my church," she added, waiting for the usual response, but neither Murdock seemed especially surprised to hear that Billie was a churchgoer. "She's in the choir. My friend Helen heard that he almost died. Carl Banner. That if those girls hadn't come along when they did, he would have been dead."

"He sold you that car, didn't he, Andy?" Daniel lit another cigarette. "Banner," he repeated in a tone that Billie thought was meant to sound speculative, but didn't. It was more like someone pounding a nail in place with a single blow of the hammer.

Police Log — Sunday May 25

12:01 a.m. Loud music at Msgr. O'Rourke Avenue residence.

12:16 a.m. Kids drinking and smashing beer bottles in Pioneer Street driveway.

2:45 a.m. Bear reported in Terrace Street yard.

3:18 a.m. Hit-and-run accident on Tucker's Gore Road.

7:30 a.m. Caucasian male looking out of place in Credit Union parking lot.

9:10 a.m. Skateboarders blocking sidewalk on Summer Street.

11:13 a.m. Raccoon acting suspiciously outside Brooks Drug.

2:06 p.m. Accident on Dump Road.

4:28 p.m. Subject sleeping on mausoleum in Canton Cemetery.

10:25 p.m. Dogs chasing chickens at Bliss Hill residence.

10:32 p.m. Drug activity behind St. Luke's Church.

11:56 p.m. Single-vehicle accident on Main Street.

Late Sunday night clouds moved in from the Canadian plains, covering the moon. A heavy wind began to blow; all the trees began to toss their branches like lunatics and torrential rain to pour from the sky. From time to time the whole world lit up, not bright as day but like fluorescence, a flicker to start and then bluish-white and chill, followed by muffled grumbles of thunder. The storm itself was still miles to the west, busy driving lightning bolts into the central mountain peaks, pounding the already-stunted tundra vegetation into mush.

On Bliss Hill the rain was hitting the roof of Sula Bliss's trailer and scattering like BB shot. She'd only meant to scare the dogs off, not hurt them. Thanks to the storm, her TV reception was lousy, too staticky to block out that other sound, that whining noise coming from below the coop. Five chickens! The fucking dogs had killed five chickens and injured at least two others. It wasn't that Sula didn't love animals, just that she didn't love them the way people from down country did, treating them like their own flesh and blood.

The storm moved closer. A fork of lightning struck a butternut tree that had been standing on Adder Ridge for over two hundred years, splitting it neatly down the middle and setting loose a family of milk snakes. From the kitchen table, where she sat sipping tea spiked with whiskey, Sophy Kipp saw the lightning hit and had just started counting — *oneone-*

thousand, twoonethousand — when she heard the sound of paws on the back porch, followed by a peremptory bark and a crash of thunder.

"Darling, she's back," Sophy called, but her younger daughter was already downstairs and at the door, her coarse black hair sticking out all over her head and her plump little body shivering in the pink shorty pj's with black paw prints she insisted on wearing all year long.

Margaret got home before the other dogs because she had the least distance to go, straight down Bliss Hill and across the Dump Road, but also because she was the fastest. She had eaten two chickens and killed two more. Despite the driving rain, her beautiful muzzle was still streaked with blood and had a few soggy white feathers clinging to it. "Margaret," Mees said. "Oh, Margaret, where have you been?"

Margaret lay on her side in her favorite corner, with her head on the wood floor and her body on the rag rug. A little like a wolf except not quite so rangy, she appeared blissfully happy. But she couldn't stop panting, her dark almond eyes staring oblivious out of her sleek white mask, and her elegant plumed tail streaming behind her across the rug like a boa. The trip down the hill had been difficult for her. A northern dog's eyes are angled skyward in the brow, inviting rain in instead of keeping it out. Mees wrapped Margaret in a yellow beach towel and began to rub her dry. She smelled terrible and her stomach was rumbling loudly.

"Margaret," Mees whispered adoringly. "Bad Margaret."

"You should try to go to sleep now," Sophy said.

"Just a minute longer," Mees said.

The phone rang, one anxious little ring, but if you tried to answer, lightning would shoot through the receiver and zap you in the ear.

Over the mountains to the west the rain was letting up, the wind dying down. The storm was racing toward the far-off coast, where it would move out to sea and vanish.

In the restored farmhouse at the head of the Canton Road that she shared with her husband and dachshund, Mrs. Roy Diamond was sleeping like a drugged baby in her pencil-post bed when Doozie finally showed up, so wet he looked almost black, and after scaling the front steps in seven dolphinlike leaps, activating the porch light and alarm system. It wasn't that Mrs. Diamond didn't think the world of Doozie, but an elementary-school principal needed her sleep, and Mr. Diamond had generously offered to wait up for the dog, though in fact the alarm had been going off for several seconds before it finally managed to rouse him from his own deep slumber. Doozie climbed the stairs and jumped into bed with his mistress, snuggling up against her and staining her nightgown and sheets with mud and silt and blood and bringing with him the same bad vacuum-cleaner-bag smell Mees had noticed on Margaret, though Mrs. Diamond didn't bat an eye.

The sky began to clear. As the scalloped edges of the thunderheads slipped apart like stage scenery, the moon once again shone through, perfectly round and small, shining into Lorna Fine's bedroom window. Lorna was wide awake and had been for hours, unable to put down *A Pocket Full of Rye,* which she'd started reading to Mrs. Zeebrugge right after leaving the Banners and had picked up the minute she got home. Agatha Christie was so clever — no matter how hard Lorna tried, she could never figure out who the culprit was, though with Agatha Christie it always made sense, unlike those other mystery writers who'd suddenly introduce a guilty party two pages from the end. The poisonous yew trees had been there all along. Did yew trees grow in America? It was surprising how many ordinary things ended up being deadly.

Lorna switched off her light and looked out the window. The German shepherd that lived in one of the hippie houses on French Hill had just crossed Canton Brook and was trotting along the far side of the millrace, the moonlight reflecting off its eyeballs. Demon dog, Lorna thought. "The Mystery of the Demon Dog." Something about a dead man on a beach? A dead man with a *secret!*

Meanwhile on the northernmost edge of the Knoll, the phone was ringing in the Crockett house. Real ringing, not the storm. Shit, thought Kathy Crockett. She'd given strict orders at the Home that unless it was a major emergency she wasn't to be disturbed, but the night staff lacked all judgment. The last time it had been a mishap with a smoke alarm. "Let the machine get it," said her husband, and Kathy sighed and rolled back onto her side, pulling the sheet over her head. First she could hear the Crockett family message — Sunny brightly explaining that no one was available at the moment to take the call — then some breathing. Then an unfamiliar voice. "I'm calling about your dog," it said.

The storm was gone. It had stormed off, you might say, sweeping its dark velvet skirts and fox-fur tippets behind. The storm was confident it had made an impression, confident that while the town of Varennes would go back to what it considered normal, it would never be precisely the same as it had been before the storm.

Everything in the world was still wet, dripping. Pendent from the tip of every single thing in the world, a diamond.

In her desirable second-floor bedroom at the Crockett Home for the Aged, Helen Zeebrugge was once again having a hard time tempting Morpheus to join her. The driveway between the Home and the Locust Inn next door was blacker than black, glistening, and she could hear a ripped sound like a Band-Aid being pulled up every time a car drove past on Main Street. Not much traffic though, at this hour. Witching hour. Someone moaning on the third floor, and the quick movement of rubber-soled feet along the corridor.

A premonition of death had come to Helen through her headphones just before supper, and she was still feeling sad, thinking of the sunlight creeping up old Jolyon Forsyte's toes, and of his soft, slow, imperceptible decline — impatient Nature clutching his windpipe one early morning before the world was aired. "Help me, Lessie, help me, Lessie," a person on the third floor was moaning. It was a terrible thing to be ninety-two years old, Helen thought, and all of a sudden she was filled with so much anger that when she heard the crash outside, she thought it was the sound of her anger breaking out of her, something big and out of control, like a two-tone Chevy Impala with Quebec plates hitting something big and hard and immovable, like the concrete abutment of the bridge over the railroad tracks.

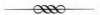

Nature, on the other hand, adores breaking things, and despite the patience she's been known to display when grinding mountain ranges to dust, she can also work with lightning speed, turning meticulously nurtured perennial borders to wasteland overnight, uprooting trees that took centuries to grow, and flooding rabbit holes. The day after the storm she reclaimed a number of her trails, in particular the steep ones draining into the Canton valley, filling them with muddy runoff and flattening the newly sprouted spring flowers, the wood anemones and violets and bellflowers.

The closer Andrea Murdock got to the crest of Adder Ridge, the more uncertain her footing became. Early that morning she'd been summoned on the telephone by Ellen Fair, the diarist's great-grandniece, who wanted to lodge a complaint with the town select board. Andrea had been elected to the board the previous spring; this would never have happened if there weren't a large population of urban dropouts in Varennes, people who voted for Andrea because she was one of their own and not because they'd paid the least attention to what she'd said about the town's need to move forward while looking back, a statement that, given their equation of progress with blight, might very well have turned them against her. As for the old-timers — the ones who voted for her were mostly men.

The stone outcroppings were slippery and the blackflies were terrible, thriving as they did on moisture, but when Andrea swatted at them she lost her balance. Still, it was a beautiful morning, the sun shining through the branches of the trees on either side of the trail, burning away the night's mist. Hemlock and white pine mostly, a few sugar maples. According to Danny, the forest used to be so immense and thick and uninterrupted that a squirrel could travel from the East Coast to the Mississippi River without ever touching ground. Then along came the sheep and ate everything up. Danny was always telling Andrea things like that; for all she knew, they were absolutely true.

Of course *there* was the problem. She believed every last word Danny told her, and he never believed a word she said. Carl Banner, case in point. It had been horrible, the way his hand slid in under her shirt. The way he'd feigned innocence, as if it were an accident. As if he'd never meant to touch her breast at all.

Adder Ridge was about two miles across. The dirt road transecting it was one of the oldest in the county and had provided the main carriage route to Canada before the arrival of the automobile and the construction of Highway 10. The Fair homestead was situated facing this road, with its back to the valley, about halfway between Canton and Varennes. It consisted of a large brick farmhouse with an enormous hay barn, a smaller cow barn and milk house, as well as numerous outbuildings. The southern edge of the property was marked by the butternut tree that had been struck by lightning the night before, the northern edge by the road to Hebron. To Andrea's left, the family of displaced snakes slithered through the stalks and stems of a hayfield long gone to vetch and milkweed. All of the air was alive with flies.

The foundation of the one-room schoolhouse where Inez Fair had taught so many years ago was no longer visible. It burned down decades earlier, the year after Andrea moved into the geodesic dome. The lake was frozen solid, so the volunteer firefighters arrived too late. Had Inez Fair been a good teacher? She gave a person so little to go on. *Taught school* every day, and each weekend *done housework,* with here and there the occasional *Bertie.* No doubt about it, Inez Fair liked men. Flakes of candent ash had drifted past the goat pens; it was a big blaze, but no one was hurt.

Huge sugar maples lined the road, banks of daffodils at their feet. A herd of cows with numbers stapled to their ears gravely watched Andrea pass. FAIR 1808 it said over the open door into the hayloft, where a little calico cat sat switching her tail.

Sun Feb 18 — At home. Dreadful windy. When eyes are beaming what never tongue can tell when tears are streaming from their cruel crystal cell . . .

Andrea and Daniel Murdock had been married for about thirty years; they no longer turned to each other like starving people for love, and when they fought (as they had this morning), they tended to fight in the manner of declawed cats hissing on a fence. Nor would they dream of staying awake till all hours talking about the existence of God or the meaning of life. It was as if the big questions no longer mattered to them, the more money they were forced to make in order to keep living the life they thought they wanted to live together in the beginning.

In the beginning the Murdocks weren't so much hungry for love as murderous for it, the one partner's wish to devour the other a wish to turn the infuriating recalcitrant other into food and, hence, into the self, going on the assumption so popular back at the time when Andrea and Daniel fell in love that we are what we eat.

Certain issues remained sticky between them: their mutual reluctance to be pinned down about anything, which created in turn a need to pin blame somewhere (i.e., on the recalcitrant other) for so many colossal failures to act. There was a period when Danny wanted children and Andrea refused, though she never told him that her reproductive system had been messed up by a teenage abortion, just as she managed to withhold her true nature from him until her dying day. But you could tell everything about them you needed to know just by looking at them — Andrea so opaque and fleshy, Daniel so translucent, with his alabaster skin and pale eyes, like a raw shrimp.

Andrea walked up the front steps onto the disintegrating mat that said ELCO and tapped on the door.

Ellen Fair turned out to be a perfectly pleasant old woman, about eighty years old and probably always quite small, with hands like a little girl's and a little girl's quiet confiding ways, but without a trace of girlish innocence. She was dressed in overalls and wore a bandanna tied at the nape of her neck; as she led Andrea into the kitchen, she removed the head scarf, revealing a head of very sparse, pure white hair. To keep the damn bugs out of her ears, she explained. They got inside and you could hear them buzzing in your brain. The cows had broke loose where a tree fell on the electric fence; the couple who usually helped out were visiting kin in Magog.

From Ellen's kitchen table it was possible to see that Black Lake was indeed black and an almost perfect oval, if it weren't for the esker. Just a small section of roof and a little plume of smoke rising from the chimney — that was as much as Andrea could see of her house. Danny didn't have an ounce of fat on him, which he said meant that up north there was less to tempt the mosquitoes and the polar bears but which also meant he kept a fire going in the wood stove all summer long.

No house in 1873, just the empty tip of the esker, nor had the bay window where they were now sitting been there in 1873 either, Ellen said, when Andrea asked. There had only been a couple of windows on the east-facing side of the house, to protect from the wind. So no, Ellen said, Inez Fair wouldn't have had to look at the esker and be reminded of her tragic mistake every day for the rest of her life. She had plenty of other reminders.

It was obvious that Ellen didn't want to talk about Inez. The past was the past, she reported grimly. She found it surprising that a relatively young woman like Andrea would want to spend any time in it at all. Let the dead bury the dead, Ellen suggested. She didn't know who Bertie was or why Inez would have knit him a mitten. Aunt Tiny was her own great-great-grandmother. She'd been christened Bettina, but Fair women had always been small boned, until you got to the present generation — big tall women like Chloe Brock, that is. Had Andrea by any chance run across Chloe, who lived in town and worked at the high school? Modern women were too damn big, if you asked her. You couldn't live in the past, but the present was even worse, inhospitable, toxic, even . . .

"Which brings me to my point," Ellen said, interrupting herself and directing Andrea's attention across the lake to the opposing ridge, where billows of thick black smoke were pouring into the pale blue sky. "Sula Bliss," she said. "It's a crime. Just look at it." Ellen explained that Sula Bliss persisted in incinerating her trash in the open air in violation of the town ordinance. Poisoning the air for everyone — she'd been warned, but she didn't care. She also jacked deer, though that was another matter. Perhaps you couldn't blame her — she was simple, or at least that was what she wanted you to think.

"I'll talk to her," Andrea said. "I'll see what I can do."

"Good luck," Ellen replied. She seemed suddenly discouraged, looking down at her hands and sighing, as if the conversation had taken every last ounce of her energy.

The refrigerator rattled to a halt; the little yellow birds in the apple tree outside the kitchen window stopped singing. Andrea became aware of what sounded like a million clocks ticking in a far-off room.

"What happened to her?" Andrea asked.

"Happened?" Ellen looked up, and her eyes were cold as ice. "Nothing. Nothing ever happens to a Bliss. She's still there, burning her trash."

"I didn't —"

"I know what you meant. And I meant what I said. There will always be Blisses, burning their trash." Ellen got up wearily and walked to the screen door, to let Andrea know it was time to leave. "I appreciate your help," she said. "It's going to be a hot summer. Listen to the frogs." She stared out across the road at the thick green meadow. "We got here first," she said.

"I'll let you know what happens," Andrea replied, but Ellen was already far away, inside her mind in the deep purse of the thick green valley where we go when we want to get away from other people.

Had she been beautiful, Inez Fair? Andrea pictured her that way, small like Ellen, with pale skin and eyes so brown they looked black. The same little hands. The same wry smile. Or maybe it was just that Inez loved men more than anything, the smell of them and the dark pit their voices traveled up from. Ellen Fair had never married. Maybe that was why she regarded the past with such hostility.

Inez would have walked down this road every day on her

way to the school, Andrea thought. Her small nose sniffing the fresh spring air. Her small ears hearing the little yellow birds.

Happy enough to be alive. And then, after?

The most Ellen could say was that Inez never had any children, as if that explained everything.

Very few of the children at Varennes Elementary ever actually found themselves inside the principal's office, since Dorothy Diamond only called a child into her office as a last resort. The office was a dark little room at the back of the school, its one small window blocked by a blue spruce that had started life as a potted Christmas tree but that now towered moodily over the entire building, contributing either to feelings of impending doom or helpless gratitude or utter indifference in the building's inhabitants, depending on their relationship to the natural world.

The tree had been a gift from a guilt-ridden parent; Dorothy had planted it, watered it, fed it. She wasn't so much a gardener as a druid, though she would never have described herself in such terms: a strapping middle-aged woman who invested trees and stones and animals and — most significantly — children with a kind of magical power. And while she didn't exactly subscribe to the cult of the child, she tended to shy away from situations equating maturity and constraint. Her wide-set hazel eyes would roll to one side, and her upper lip would roll back, showing not only a row of big white teeth but also bright pink gums; you could almost see the bridle.

"So, what's the problem?" Dorothy asked the two girls sitting opposite her on the orange-and-green-plaid sofa. The room had no decoration aside from a framed photograph of Dorothy's husband gripping their dachshund under the dog's front legs and holding him aloft for the camera like bagged game. Doozie had an aggrieved expression on his intelligent russet face; seconds after his mistress snapped the picture, he'd snapped at his master's nose, missing by inches. "Girls?" Dorothy prompted. She hated fluorescence, and the little brass desk lamp barely illuminated its own feet. The blue spruce pawed ceaselessly at the window. They might have been in a cave, the brilliant midmorning May sun a dream of long ago.

One girl was crying, one was breathing hard, and they were both drenched in mud. George Mason had hauled them in off the playground where a fight had broken out at recess. Lorna Fine, the out-of-breath girl, whose behavior was usually exemplary, seemed to have started it. She had accused the Bliss twins' mother of murdering her friend's dog, and Brittany Bliss, the smaller of the twins and a known troublemaker, had called Lorna Fine a fucking liar and punched her in the chest, and the next thing everyone knew they were rolling around on the playground, which because it was overshadowed by the blue spruce, hadn't had a chance to dry out yet from the storm.

"Well?" said Dorothy Diamond.

"It's not my fault, Mrs. Dee," Brittany said.

As if that were the point. As if Diamond were hard to remember or pronounce. Whose idea had that idiotic nickname been? Certainly not Dorothy's. Brittany Bliss sat primly, every inch the little lady, though she was dressed like one of Carmen's coworkers in the cigarette factory, which is to say in the whorish style currently popular among sixth-grade girls. She looked stupid but cunning, primly dabbing at her face with a tissue she'd extracted from the box on the desk.

"I never said it was your fault," Lorna replied. In the struggle her glasses had gotten broken, leaving one of the lenses cracked and a stem missing, and making them sit crookedly on her long sallow face. Lorna wasn't dressed like a whore, nor was she dressed, as Dorothy had been when she was Lorna's age, like a baby. Lorna's T-shirt was much too big, and whatever it said on it was obliterated by mud. The name of some band, no doubt — Lorna's brother, who had been a world-class troublemaker in his own time, was now a successful musician with a band of his own. Sump Monkey, or some equally pointless name. "I said it was your *mother's* fault," Lorna corrected. "Your *mother* shot Sunny's dog. Your *mother* shot Buddy, not you."

Lorna kept her eyes on Brittany; Brittany kept her eyes on Dorothy.

"They killed five chickens. It's against the law for dogs to run loose. We're not made of money, you know."

In fact, Dorothy had arrived at school knowing that her own dog had been involved in some questionable activity the night before. The sheets were ruined — her treasured Irish linen sheets from Portugal. You could pretend not to notice; it was in a dog's nature to hunt and kill. Even a little dog like a dachshund.

"She could've fired into the air," Lorna said. "She didn't have to kill him."

It might have been Doozie, Dorothy thought. The stupid dog would get away no matter how hard she tried to keep him in, digging a hole under the fence or once even jumping out the window. It was all because of that malamute. Mees Kipp's dog — it was like the Pied Piper. That malamute was a bad influence. But then Mees Kipp was a little like the Pied Piper herself. She even played recorder in the school band, aggressively tooting and tooting a single note . . .

"Lorna, look at me," Dorothy said. "Murder is a strong word. Brittany's mother was only protecting her property. I think you owe Brittany an apology."

The minds of twelve-year-old girls are wound round and round with golden chains, padlocked shut, and the key tossed out the car window on the way to the fast-food restaurant. This is probably a good thing, since what they keep in there isn't always very nice. Human sacrifices, cockeyed sexual adventures both sadistic and masochistic, also kitties with balls of yarn and puppies chewing on slippers and soft pink babies and disembowelings.

"I guess that's like 'getting away with murder,'" Lorna said. She was picking a scab on her ankle. "But okay. I'm sorry."

Brittany Bliss smiled at Dorothy, a version of the smug disdainful smile Dorothy remembered seeing on Sula Bliss's face at parent-teacher conference night. A painfully thin woman in acid-washed jeans — but you couldn't blame the mother on the daughter, just as you couldn't blame the daughter for being named Brittany.

"You have to apologize, too," Dorothy said. "Lorna's not a liar. She wasn't lying when she said your mother killed the dog. It was just a difference of opinion about what happened."

Brittany smiled even more disdainfully, and Dorothy thought she was going to have to murder her, when there came a tapping at the office door. Mr. Mason — couldn't he keep order in his classroom for one lousy minute? His face was splotchy and beet-red and his orange-red hair was plastered to his skull unattractively. There was a little white circle in the middle of his lips where he'd been sucking on the chalk, and he was clad in the usual plaid cowboy shirt with mother-of-pearl buttons and the infuriating leather vest and boots.

"Excuse me," he said, looking at Lorna. "Do you have any idea where Mees Kipp has disappeared to?"

I might as well be invisible, Dorothy thought, and the thought made her happy.

"I don't know," Lorna said. Mees had been there for attendance, and Lorna had seen her in the playground just before the fight broke out. It had been her turn to present her report on gladiators, but Mees wasn't the kind of girl to skip out because she was unprepared. Besides, Mees loved gladiators.

Harder this time. Much. Last time there'd been room and light and Mr. Banner still there, the body still warm and the sun shining on it on the beach, but this time it was rigid and cold and wrapped in an old pink baby blanket of Sunny's on the Ping-Pong table in the cellar.

A gladiator never knew what to expect, whether another gladiator or a lion.

Hey boy. Hey Buddy. Mees patted his neck. It was stiff as a board, while the life in the cellar went on and on, clicking and ticking around him. Luckily the Crocketts were off to work or at school. Also lucky, the pink blanket. A lucky color, pink. The coming-to-life color. Thank you, Jesus, Mees said.

What was inside Buddy was like stars connected by strings of light, a chain of stars, strings linking star to star to star, and not just in *there* but the strings were everywhere, in her arms, for example, and a whole lot of them strung to the star at the back of Buddy's nose. The closer she got, the more densely knitted it all was and also clumped with debris, dark clots of stinking matter, buzzing like bees and restless, fidgeting around, bumping themselves into place and taking up all the room. A smell like what came from the sanitary-napkin disposal boxes in the school bathroom and also, weirdly, banana skins.

Buddy, Mees wanted to say. But you couldn't talk. You couldn't be in the world and in there at the same time. You couldn't scratch the blackfly bites behind your ears no matter how much they itched, no matter how crazy they were driving you. Otherwise, you might never get back.

The gladiator came out of the dark tunnel and into the bright arena — that was where the danger was. In the bright arena, surrounded by people eager to be entertained.

But if blood and pieces of bone were where they weren't supposed to be, it made the clumping worse. Mixed with those buzzing stinking clots, and the stars going out like matches. There were only so many of them — if you didn't get in soon enough they'd all have gone out and then there wouldn't be a thing you could do. Nothing.

As if a man fled from a lion and a bear met him, or went into the house and leaned with his hand against the wall and a serpent bit him.

The net dragging like strings of shadow across the sandy floor of the arena.

A little thump, a million miles away. *Thump thump.*

The smell of the cellar returning, damp concrete and fabric softener and mothballs. A square of sunlight coming through the window set high in the front wall, lighting the jars of apple butter and dilly beans Mrs. Crockett had spent hours and hours putting up thousands of years ago and would no more dream of opening than flying to the moon. There was a Ping-Pong ball in the corner under the sink, lodged like an egg in a nest of lint. A spider dangled from the ceiling.

Buddy was wagging his tail.

"This is a test," whispered Piet Zeebrugge into his walkie-talkie. "Testing. Testing." He was standing at the very back of the church next to the table where every Sunday the Elements waited to be carried up for Communion, when they would turn from ordinary water and wine and bread into the body and blood of Jesus Christ. But today was Thursday, the table was empty, as was the church, except for Piet and James Trumbell, the sexton, who was in the chapel atop a wobbly ladder, reaching like Adam with trembling fingers for a dead bulb, and Billie Carpenter, who was standing in the pulpit with her own walkie-talkie.

"Do you copy?" Piet said into Billie's ear, and Billie made a face intended to be charming before she remembered that the whole point of the experiment was whether they could *hear* each other. In any case, Piet was standing with his back to the church, looking out the open front doors at River Street. "Ten four, good buddy. One Adam twelve. One Adam twelve." A panel of brilliant yellow sunshine had been erected behind him, and every now and then a passing car with its radio turned all the way up drove straight into Billie's brain.

"See the man," Billie replied.

Piet Zeebrugge had dark presbyopic eyes, a wicked smile, and a long dent in his left cheek that looked like a dueling scar but was a dimple — he ought to have been a pamphleteer in eighteenth-century Paris not an investment banker in twenty-first-century Varennes. He had studied English literature at McGill and economics at the Wharton School. He could recite Eliot's *Four Quartets* from memory, and like the eighteenth-century technocrats, he believed pictures of fire and air and water should be printed on our currency instead of the faces of dead presidents, to remind us of what was actually being spent.

Piet wasn't a religious man, but he was a devoted son. After his father died he moved his mother from the city to Varennes, and while there'd never been any question of the two of them sharing a house — especially two people as strong willed as they were and in a house as isolated and Spartan as Piet's — they genuinely enjoyed each other's company. If it weren't for Helen, Piet would never have set foot inside a church, preferring to spend his free time gardening and running and lamenting the sorry state of the world. He'd been born in Sault Ste. Marie, and the sound of foghorns or train whistles filled him with the profound melancholy of the adolescent, which is without peer.

"Don't switch it off," Piet said. "I'm not done yet."

He had turned around and was once more looking down the long central aisle toward Billie, when Kathy Crockett emerged through the chancel door. She bowed with military precision before the altar and was in the process of removing the silver candlesticks and dumping them into a large canvas tote bag when Billie's walkie-talkie made a noise like a parrot.

"Billie?" Kathy said with a start. "I didn't see you there." Kathy was her usual self, a public conveyance, a bus maybe, doors opening, doors closing, moving briskly from stop to stop. Her sleek brown hair had just been cut in a chin-length bob, clearly expensive and definitely not local.

"A bold move!" Piet said into Billie's ear as Kathy dropped the last of the candlesticks into her bag.

"Shh!" Billie replied, then turned to Kathy and held up the walkie-talkie. "We're testing the system," she said.

"We?"

Billie pointed, and Kathy whirled around, suspicious, but Piet was nowhere to be seen. He had in fact left the church and crossed to the café on the other side of the street, where he was sitting in the sun at one of the outdoor tables facing the river. On the opposite bank below a row of gray tenements, a shopping cart lay in the mud, waterlogged soft drink cups and paper bags and even two unmatching dress shoes trapped inside it. A large glistening creature — a weasel or an otter or a beaver or a rat — was swimming along the deep central channel with something in its mouth. The river had settled down following the storm, but it was still the color of Coca-Cola.

"Piet?" Billie said into the receiver.

"You're breaking up," Piet replied.

"I'm just taking these to the vestry to polish them," Kathy said.

"Is she still there?" Piet asked. "Tell her we've got her red-handed."

"I'm hanging up now," Billie said.

"I can't hear a word you're saying," Piet replied. "Plant the bomb and make a run for it. I've ordered you a mocha latte."

Midmorning, late May. A cloud of midges hung above the church's granite entry porch, and a Popsicle stick lay in a raspberry-colored puddle halfway down the flagstone path to the sidewalk, on the verge of which sumptuous Mimi Jenkins, the rector's "bad" daughter, dozed in a lawn chair, soaking up the sun. The yard between the church and the rectory had been recently mowed, and for once there was a message on the message board: "Behold, the eye of the Lord is upon those who fear Him. Everyone Welcome!"

"Hey there," Mimi said as Billie's shadow passed across her. On the nod? There were rumors, but more likely it was too much trouble to fully open her eyes, given the quantity of eye shadow she was wearing.

Billie crossed the street and joined Piet at his table. He was sitting in the shade of a red-and-white-striped umbrella, sipping from a blindingly white cup and reading the latest issue of the *Varennes Voice,* which had started life as an advertising paper but which now included movie reviews, advice to the lovelorn, horoscopes, the police log, local gossip, and an assortment of cracked editorial opinion, much of it the handiwork of one small, overachieving woman who also bred German shepherds and repaired chain saws and lived not far from Piet in one of the hippie houses atop French Hill.

"It seems to work," Billie said, and Piet nodded without looking up from the paper. He was so much friendlier through the walkie-talkie.

She sat back and sipped her latte, her eyes on the river. Two could play this game. Jigsaw-shaped pieces of sky swept past on the current like items on an assembly line, and across the water the tenement porches were festooned with laundry, mostly undergarments. It was getting warm; the new leaves of the maples were already less yellow, less babyish. Unlike you, Billie said to herself. *Baby.* She'd been married, after all. Her husband had also been a banker. Well, a teller. It wasn't like she couldn't deal with a man.

She made a noise with her spoon in her cup, and Piet looked up over his glasses. "Nice message," she said, and when he blinked at her, she added, "I mean, does anyone really think someone's going to plant a *bomb* in the church?"

"My guess is they're more worried about the collection plate." Piet swung around in his chair, looking for the waitress, when his eye lit on Mimi Jenkins, who Billie saw was in the process of taking off her shirt. "Ever since that old babe in the mink started dropping hundred-dollar bills."

"Mrs. Quill?" Billie asked, but Piet was busy watching Mimi Jenkins apply suntan lotion from a tube, squirting it lavishly across her wide creamy thighs. "I suppose she knows she's a thorn in her father's side," she reflected.

"Speak of the devil," Piet said.

Richard Jenkins was headed toward them across River Street. He wore a black windbreaker over his clerical shirt and collar and a pair of black wind pants over what everyone in Varennes knew were white tennis shorts. A kind of centaur, Richard, a house divided against itself — he'd been rector of St. Luke's for well over twenty years, such a long time that almost no one in the congregation could remember why his appointment had set off such a firestorm of controversy. Was it because the church had been Low and — without going so far as to introduce incense and bells into the service — he'd made it High? Tom Templeton, the former rector, had wanted no part of transubstantiation of matter, and Richard Jenkins claimed the Eucharist was meaningless without it. His sermons had taken some getting used to, as well. He jumped around, as old Mrs. Makepeace said, like a flea. He quoted from the strangest sources, Sheridan Le Fanu and Julia Child. Also, he was very smart, so that if you conflated creator and rector, as many people tend to do, you wouldn't always end up feeling all that comforted. Mary Holst-Jenkins, his wife, who worked for Legal Aid, was very smart, too. She refused to run the Christmas bazaar, or to teach Sunday school, or to lead a Lenten discussion group, or to bake a single cupcake, whereas the previous rector's wife, Ronda, had been a world-class baker.

But Richard Jenkins was a great man in times of personal and spiritual crisis, and Mary had opened the rectory on more than one occasion to the homeless.

And unlike Tom and Ronda Templeton, Richard and Mary Holst-Jenkins were well married. They excelled at mixed doubles.

"Can you join us?" Piet asked, and the rector took a quick look at his watch.

"For a sec," he said, sitting. "We've got a court reserved for eleven, and Mary goes ballistic when I'm late."

He was a very big man, with a big head of graying auburn hair and a big chest and big long arms and legs. "What a day!" he said, lavishly stretching and kicking Billie in the ankle without so much as batting an eye. Could it be that she *felt* like a table leg? Then he leaned into the shade under the umbrella, and she could see his pupils expand. "How well do you know Kathy Crockett?" he asked.

"Hardly at all," Billie said.

"She was just telling me the strangest thing," Richard went on. "About her dog."

According to Richard Jenkins, Kathy Crockett told him she'd gotten a phone call from Sula Bliss in the middle of Sunday night, informing her that Kathy's dog, Buddy, a chocolate Lab, the nicest and sweetest of dogs, a dog who wouldn't harm a fly, had been shot while killing chickens, and if she didn't come get him right away he'd probably be dead. Which he was. Dead, that is — or so Kathy claimed. She said she wrapped him in an old baby blanket of Sunny's and drove him home and put him on the Ping-Pong table in the cellar. Why they kept it, she told Richard, she couldn't say — no one in the family had played for years. This would have been around one o'clock in the morning: at one o'clock Monday morning Buddy definitely wasn't breathing. They were going to bury him late the next afternoon, but when the kids got home from school, he was alive.

"She must have been mistaken," Piet said.

"A Crockett's never mistaken," Billie said, and Richard laughed.

"Kathy said she checked Buddy before leaving for work in the morning. He was cold and hard and his wound had stopped bleeding. But when Sunny and the boys got home, he was warm and soft and blood was running from the wound. He was looking around the cellar, and when he saw Sunny, he whimpered. Sunny called Kathy, and they took him to the vet, who cleaned the wound and sewed it up and gave him an antibiotic shot. The vet said it was a miracle, but I think she meant medically."

"I know that dog," Billie said.

She pictured Buddy, his wide panting mouth, his bright shoe-button eyes, his round wet nose. On the porch, happy as all get out, having just knocked over her garbage. Maybe it was because dogs have an abundance of life in them. Maybe after what seemed like all of the life got taken away, there was still life left over. Math, Billie thought, sighing. Some things are impossible to compute. Piet and Richard were now deep in discussion of the prime lending rate. Though maybe we all died ages and ages ago. We all died and continue dying, this being the hell we're all too stupid to recognize we've fallen into or too filled with wishful thinking to acknowledge.

Such a sweet-smelling hell, though! Coffee and cut grass and the sumpy aroma of the river. Sweat and soap. Ivory. The sweet-smelling sweat that forms just below the hairline. The dead come back sometimes this way, in the smells of the living.

Billie let out another little sigh and watched as Piet carefully replaced his coffee cup in its saucer. Richard said it was time he was going. Was he sensitive to some signal that had passed between Billie and Piet, or was he merely dying to hit the courts?

"By the way," Richard said to Piet. "When you see Chloe, could you tell her I'm looking for her?"

"Sure thing," Piet said, folding the paper and putting it in his Danish school bag.

"Vestry business," Richard added. "Chloe will know."

As if your dance card said you were pledged to Mr. Darcy for the mazurka, Billie thought, and then you watched him sail off in the arms of two-faced Miss Bingley.

"Buddy's a nice dog," Billie said, after Richard had gone. "I should get a dog."

Who cares, she thought. Besides that school bag is pretentious.

"They're a lot of work," Piet reminded her. "Especially puppies."

Only a ball, a big round ball, the materials it's made of end-lessly changing place, changing shape, changing essential form, moving round and round and round, mountains bowing their heads and oceans swinging open like doors, fists of rock un-clenching, all that dark matter geologists call scum in endless tireless motion on an otherwise featureless ball.

Forty-six hundred million years old.

One billion six hundred and seventy-nine hundred million days, one billion six hundred and seventy-nine hundred mil-lion nights, the sun and the moon having always been with us, even before there was an *us* to be there with. Also, the Word. Let there be light. The greater light to rule the day, and the lesser light to rule the night.

He made the stars also.

In the Pleistocene, hands of ice gripped the ball top and bot-tom, the fingers moving around for purchase, a thumb on Varennes. This was not long after Noah's flood. The sun shone on the waters; the moon came out. Underneath, of course, every living substance was destroyed which was upon the face of the ground, man and cattle, and the creeping things, and the fowl of the heaven . . .

All the paired creatures on the ark drifted oblivious above the dark restless scum of utter annihilation, regarding the moon in all her phases: new moon, waxing, waxing gibbous.

Full moon. The best time to gather herbs and fruit — best, that is, if the planet isn't covered in water. You may notice a heightened awareness of personal relationships. The body is at its peak for absorbing substances. Waning gibbous. Waning crescent. You may feel drawn toward introspection.

You may wonder, for instance, why, despite its obvious imperfections, God decided to flood the world. Was He planning to make another one?

The moon, as usual, above it all.

Showing only her one face, as usual. Though not the best but the pockmarked side.

Then the fountains of the deep and the windows of heaven were stopped, leaving behind oysters and clams and whales and so forth and so on in the mountains.

Eons passed, or no time at all. Time is the first requirement of evolution.

If the earth is just a ball, no one place on it is any more important than another. Human time is much too thin to be discerned. The slow steady march of geologic time is punctuated with catastrophes.

Before the Flood the air was soft and warm and still as death. The moon was full. All the animals were nervous.

Sunday, June 1

Aries (March 21–April 19) — You might feel as if a rocket ship is being launched right under you. Take advantage of your energy to do those jobs around the house you've been putting off for way too long. Clean out those cupboards! And while you're at it, throw away those clothes that haven't fit you for years.

Taurus (April 20–May 20) — Reach out to people at work. Your coworkers have a lot to tell you, probably more than you're willing to admit. Also, you should have that mole looked at. Tonight: live it up!

Gemini (May 21–June 21) — Just because there are two of you doesn't mean it's OK to be two-faced. Tell it like it is, Gemini, and maybe one of these days you'll get to play double solitaire with somebody besides yourself. Lucky numbers: 5 and 6.

Cancer (June 22–July 22) — That standoffish member of the opposite sex is ready to give you a tumble at long last, so don't blow it like the last time by playing it cool. You're at your best in the wee hours of the morning. A nap might be in order.

Leo (July 23–August 22) — While you're shaking your head at what others say and do, take a look in the mirror. Maybe, just maybe, someone's got a mote in their own eye, Leo, if you know what I mean. Lucky numbers: 2 and 8. Stay away from foods containing dairy products, cream cheese, in particular.

Virgo (August 23–September 22) — No one likes a busybody, Virgo, especially a busybody who doesn't know what they're talking about. Keep an eye on your wallet and avoid dangerous intersections. Tonight: early to bed and no television, not even Andy Griffith reruns.

Libra (September 23–October 23) — You might not be feeling comfortable with what is happening, but then you never do. A shopping spree will be just the thing to lift your spirits, but don't go overboard or you'll feel even worse. There's nothing wrong with you, by the way, that a little Prozac won't help. Aries figures prominently.

Scorpio (October 24–November 21) — When they say there are no bad signs in the zodiac, they haven't had their eye on you, Scorpio. Who do you think you are? Shame on you!

Sagittarius (November 22–December 21) — You have more vision than most people, especially when dealing with affairs of the heart, as long as they're not your own. Wise up! That attractive coworker wants to share more than your morning latte!

Capricorn (December 22–January 19) — Your unpredictability is driving everyone crazy. Consider sticking with your most recent employer for at least another month. Red is your lucky color. Watch out for falling objects.

Aquarius (January 20–February 18) — One-on-one relating brings surprise after surprise. Someone new on the scene turns out to be a hotbed of energy and enthusiasm. Don't move too fast or you're sure to get burnt. Tonight: remain goal-oriented.

Pisces (February 19–March 20) — What do you think you're doing with that hairdo? It isn't fooling anyone, least of all a certain someone who shall remain nameless. Otherwise, you've never looked so good. Go for it!

If your birthday is today: *You're full of fun and life, though you might want to find sturdier ground to stand on. Consider striking out on your own. If you are single, you may meet Mr. or Ms. Right, easily disarming them but shocking them as well! If you are attached, your relationship will blossom if you let your sweetie be a little bit more of a wild one. That cloud on the horizon is getting closer every day. Don't underestimate its potential to do harm. Wishful thinking is your middle name.*

Leg of lamb. Baby peas. Roast new potatoes.

Of course it was too much to hope that just this once Kathy Crockett wouldn't have gone overboard, ornamenting the light fixtures with pink crepe-paper ribbons, stringing gold letters spelling HAPPY BIRTHDAY across the French doors, and putting pastel nut cups at each place setting, as well as party favors, this year charms — ballet shoes, kittens, jingle bells, roses, etc. etc. — as if to reinforce the notion that in our old age we revert to sugar and spice and everything nice and not a sorry bundle of rotting bones and decomposing tissue and tumors hidden in all the darkest corners.

Helen Zeebrugge sat in the place of honor, which is to say at the head of the long central table. The white napery was out in honor of the occasion, as well as the "good" china, whatever that meant. Ninety-three years old, going on a thousand, and full of fun and life. The year Helen was born Teddy Roosevelt had been President, though not a single woman had voted him into office. Deadly diseases roamed the earth — Helen's own sister had died of diphtheria, named for the leathery gray membrane that clogged her breathing passages, choking her to death. Pandora let the diseases out of the box, and then they got coaxed back in. And now they were going to be let out again, not by accident but as weapons. No good could come of this.

Helen thought she'd like to see how Crockett would handle

turning ninety-three. She'd obviously had an eye-lift at the very least and hogged the exercise bike in the so-called gym that was supposed to be for the exclusive use of the home's residents, not its owner.

"Move your arm," said Lois, the newest member of the wait staff, a sullen teenage girl with terrible skin and hair the color of oxblood shoe polish.

"Please," said Marjory Mason, on Helen's right. "You should say please, dear," but Lois just kept moving, dealing out food-filled plates as if for blackjack. She didn't even have the energy or imagination to roll her eyes.

"Please dear," said the woman from New Jersey. "Please dear. Please dear." She picked her slice of lamb up in both hands and began tearing into it like a wild animal. Nor was the meat pink, as the birthday girl had requested, but dark gray, nor were the peas baby, but big and wrinkled, nor the potatoes new, but scooped from old Idahos with a melon baller.

It wasn't all that long ago that Helen Zeebrugge had been a cook, and a very good one. She supposed she still was, in the same spirit that she was still a woman, even though she'd more or less ceased to behave like one. When she used to fix roast lamb for her family, she wouldn't have dreamed of serving it with mint jelly from a jar but would prepare a sauce of finely chopped fresh mint and champagne vinegar. No one in her right mind would put something the color of mint jelly in her mouth or, for that matter, on her body, except in the form of jewelry, though Helen preferred her gemstones less flashy, garnets and pearls.

At least, she thought, Crockett had seated Janet Peake, her best and only friend at the home, to her left. Janet was a youngster — she hadn't turned eighty yet — and due to the drop of Cherokee blood she'd received from her renegade mother's side of the family tree, she possessed that truly excellent bone structure without which the aging facial skin falls into folds like a deflated parachute. Straight backed and without a hint of dowager's hump, her eyes wide set and refined to a blue verging on silver, her abundant white tresses twisted into a Psyche knot at the back of her head — so splendid a physical specimen did Janet Peake present that you might be justified in wondering what on earth she was doing in the Crockett Home for the Aged until you noticed the way the hand holding the spoon trembled on its way to her lips or the way her lips trembled as they opened to receive the spoon or the way the hand holding the napkin trembled in her lap or the way her whole body couldn't stop vibrating, every inch of it, lightly and without cease, like a struck tuning fork — an appropriate simile given the fact that before her exhausted and impatient family packed her off to Varennes, Janet used to teach piano to the children of the well-to-do in New Haven, where her father had headed the Classics Department at Yale and her mother had made brief appearances between jaunts to the peanut- and cassava-rich fields of West Senegal, where she refused to stop trying to convert the natives despite their lack of interest verging on hostility.

Janet Peake had Parkinson's disease, and her two sons and ex-husband had convinced themselves that she was better off in the hands of Kathy Crockett, which may in fact have been a sound assumption, given how infernally busy they all were, day and night, night and day, not unlike the beavers Billie Carpenter had been describing to Helen only last week. The beavers were damming the southern outlet of Black Lake with whatever they could lay their cute little hands on, which in many cases turned out to be jagged pieces of rusty metal, as if they'd somehow stumbled on a punitive connection between all human attempts to dismantle their work and lockjaw.

"Okay, ladies, eat up!" Kathy Crockett appeared in the doorway to the dining hall, a cardboard carton in her arms. Never a welcome sight, one of Crockett's cartons — this one turned out to be full of hats to be worn while eating cake. A beanie with a pinwheel. A pink flannel hood with ears. A sombrero with tassels hanging from its brim.

"*Je refuse,*" Janet said.

"Come on," Crockett urged. "Don't be a party pooper."

"I don't see you wearing a hat," Janet said.

Crockett took a black cowgirl hat from the box and set it on her head at a rakish angle.

"Cheater," Helen said. "You've got to look like a fool, or it doesn't count."

"You wear it, then," Crockett said. Of course she knew perfectly well that Helen's head was twice the size of her own.

Helen and Janet exchanged a glance. They'd discussed this at length — there was no denying the fact that no matter how fundamentally stupid the woman was, she certainly thought on her feet.

Meanwhile Crockett rummaged around in the box, eventually unearthing a ruffled white mobcap. "Satisfied?" she asked, ramming it into place atop her chic hairdo, where if anything, it made her look better than ever, more delicate, vulnerable even, almost like a flower, though with a sour expression.

At a signal from the kitchen, the dining-hall lights were extinguished. Of course because it was the custom in this rustic place to eat dinner at midday and because the June sun was shining brightly, furiously you might say, it made no difference. You couldn't have seen the candles even if there'd been ninety-three of them, which there weren't. No, there were ten candles — one for each decade, and one for luck or to grow on, assuming you equated longevity with luck. The cake was a yellow sheet cake with white frosting. As if "yellow" and "white" were flavors. 93 YEARS YOUNG, it said in pink frosting across the middle, its perimeter bordered in pink roses with green leaves.

Lois deposited the cake in front of Helen and then backed off quickly, like a terrorist leaving a bomb. There was some singing going on, also some other noises that might have been singing though it was hard to say, moanings and yappings and loud snorelike barks.

"Make a wish," Crockett suggested, leaning across the table to stop the New Jersey woman from dragging her fingertip through the frosting. "Patience, Selena," she said. "You'll have your very own piece soon enough."

"I know what *I'd* wish for," Janet whispered to Helen, making a neck-slicing gesture.

And then, for just a fraction of a second, the room grew silent.

It was like the moment when you slid the silver blade of the letter opener into the envelope: a small, self-contained gesture, measured yet violent.

The light shifted. The boring red geraniums in the two wrought-iron étagères fronting the garden windows all at once changed color, becoming so mysterious, so impossible to recognize or call by name that you might think you'd left this world. A smell like humus, wet stone.

To be poured out like water. The seven secret folds deep within the heart preparing to unfold. To be poured out like water. For your hand was heavy upon me day and night.

You almost died and you didn't.

These things happened when you were ninety-three.

The sun returned from behind a cloud.

A beeping sound.

The moment was over, as suddenly as it had begun. Something very big and not too far away was beeping as it backed up.

"Look who's here," Crockett said.

"Hello, Mother," said Piet Zeebrugge, bending his tall body practically in two to give her a kiss on the cheek. He was her *son,* her only living son, and he was sixty-three years old! At least he'd shaved. At least he was still vigorous and good-looking, though it wouldn't kill him to give a little more thought to what he wore.

"I'd have been here sooner," Piet said, "but the traffic's a mess." He handed Helen a package and a bouquet of yellow roses.

"Thank you, darling," she said. "They're beautiful."

"I know you prefer wildflowers."

Helen shushed him, eagerly tearing the wrapping paper from her present. Even when Piet was a little boy and she was a new and doting mother, she'd always been scornful of that sentiment about the thought being what counts. If you were going to give someone a gift, you should make every effort to figure out what would please the recipient the most. Helen's own gifts were famously inspired, though that meant that her husband wore the same necktie to work for years. It also meant that she was impossible to shop for.

"I'll just get these into some water," Crockett said, relieving Helen of the flowers. As usual, when there was a man in the room, she couldn't take her eyes off him. "Did you get stuck in that traffic jam on Main Street? They're fixing the bridge," she explained. "Some drunk ran into it last Sunday."

"Nice hat," Piet said. He patted Janet on the shoulder. "How have you been, gorgeous?"

"My son told me whoever it was hit the bridge just high-tailed it out of there and left their car behind," put in Marjory Mason.

"I suspect I might have done the same," Piet said.

Crockett picked up a knife and began slicing.

"Nice hat!" yelled Selena. "Nice hat!"

"Here," Crockett sighed. "Have a rose."

Then she glanced across the room and saw Lorna Fine hovering in the doorway, package in hand.

"Lorna," she said. "What on earth are you doing here?"

"I don't think the driver was drunk," Lorna said, approaching the table. She blushed, her cheeks bright red in her pale yellow face, an unusual color combination. "I came to wish Mrs. Zeebrugge a happy birthday."

"He was running from the law," Marjory added. "George told me." She lowered her voice. "Stolen car."

"Hello, Piet," said Janet.

She was happy to see him — women were always happy to see Piet, including his ex-wives. It was hard to stay angry with a man so obviously delighted to find himself tied to a woman's heartstrings.

"How about a slice of cake?" asked Crockett.

So *that's* what I heard the other night, Helen was thinking. That crash. A piece of machinery slamming into concrete. Sometimes she thought all the horrors of modern civilization might have been avoided if we'd remained content to get around on our own two feet, but then she'd remember how easy it had been for Cain to slay his brother, sneaking up on him from behind and hitting him with a rock. Or was she making that part up? The image was so vivid in her mind, she must have seen it somewhere. In any case, it was a different order of magnitude.

Lorna's present was an actual book, *Murder with Mirrors,* while Piet's turned out to be an audio book. *In Chancery* — volume two of *The Forsyte Saga* and not a moment too soon, since she'd just finished *The Man of Property* that morning. Though Helen couldn't decide which was the greater pleasure — hearing the baritone voice leak confidingly into her ears through the earphones or Lorna's clear sweet voice enunciating words like "corpse" or "autopsy."

"It's a good thing no one was killed," Helen said, thinking sadly of poor Bosinney, so desperately in love with Irene and crushed under the wheels of a carriage. All he wanted was to be with her. His art was nothing to him, in comparison. Love was like that. An image of her husband's face — his red cheeks and delicate red-tipped nose and wild head of hair — came skating toward her on a frozen pond in upstate New York. Just a boy when she met him, no older than that ill-bred child who waited on their table. "Thank you, darling," she said to her son. "Thank you, Lorna dear."

How quickly everything changed! One minute you were a young woman with your whole life ahead of you, and the next minute all you really wanted was to be left alone to get some sleep. On the verge of the vast muffled blackness, as Galsworthy put it, where sudden shapes came rolling slow upon you, and now and then a light showed like a dim island in an infinite dark sea.

The baby beaver was wide awake and in her element, swimming through the ink-black lake water with an alder branch in her mouth. Her brother was swimming beside her with a piece of styrofoam, as meanwhile her parents gnawed at saplings in the boggy place where the two roads met, and her older brothers and sisters continued working on the dam, which was coming along nicely. Every day the humans took it apart; every night the beavers put it back together again, better than before.

A mild evening, milder than customary for this time of year, the water at the surface warm, though once you dove down to visit the lodge you could tell the entire lake had been covered with ice not all that long ago. To swim at the surface! Your belly in water, air on your nose! The moon was out of alignment, losing light from her right side. Big fish eating little fish and all of them eating bugs. This was the time of year for tender new water-lily shoots and delicious new duck potato. Plenty to go around.

The moon shone down on the water from above, sending a white trail from the lodge to the dam. And there was a smaller yellower light coming down along the shore past the place where the mallards lived.

A human female carrying a flashlight, swooping its beam carelessly up through the delicate pointy leaves of the treetops, then over across the lake and back to her own feet. A human female, out for a walk. A human female, talking to herself in the desperate yet companionable way of a person who lives alone. If I were you. If you were *who? Oh give me a break, Billie* . . .

SMACK! went the mother beaver's tail. *SMACK!* went the father's. Time to dive below and hide. The mother beaver knew the human posed no real threat; it was an instinctual response, the way beavers in zoos keep building dams even though they're totally useless.

For a moment Billie could see a beaver swimming right at her, and then it disappeared. There was almost nothing more touching, she thought, than the sight of an animal with something in its mouth. The bright eyes, the wet nose, the implicit sense of a project under way that far surpassed human understanding. How long could they stay down there? She realized she had no idea — that it had never occurred to her before that a creature that wasn't a fish could remain below the surface of the water for any substantial length of time. Did beavers have gills? No, of course not. So how did they do it?

Billie took a deep breath. Such a beautiful night. She and Glenda Banner had taken Communion to Helen Zeebrugge earlier that day, and she was still rattled by what Glenda had told her. Glenda didn't have the imagination to make something like that up. On the far side of the lake, the beavers resurfaced and got back to work, felling saplings and fortifying their dam . . .

But like what? Like *what?*

How little patience we have for the impossibly slow unfolding of stories about the lives of anything that isn't human! Of course it makes sense: stories about humans are more interesting to humans than stories about animals. Who's interested in the beaver family story, except, possibly, beavers? God? Jesus said, "Ye are of more value than many sparrows," but the

Word made flesh would necessarily take an anthropocentric stance, whereas God's love extends to every aspect of His creation. The mother beaver, for instance, who was already harboring the bacillus that would kill her before summer's end. God loved her, and He loved the bacillus, too, a tiny rod-shaped thing with its own will to live and reproduce, capable of existing almost anywhere, in the bodies of other living things and in every place on earth, in the Arctic ice and in the depths of the oceans, even in the stratosphere. Trees and hills. Clouds and lightning bolts. Valleys. Rain.

But what about the beaver traps, Billie wondered. What about the traps handsome young Beau O'Brien had been hired to set around the lake's southern perimeter? What did God think of *them?* A group of neighbors, led by Henry Fine, had met over coffee with Beau only that afternoon to discuss their problem. The beavers refused to take a hint, rebuilding their infernal dam by night, despite the neighbors' best efforts to dismantle it by day. The dam blocked the outflow from the lake, turning the lower stretch of Canton Brook to a trickle and the Fines' sparkling millpond to a cauldron of mud.

Metal forged in fire — clearly the raw materials used to make the traps posed no theological problem. Only, what about the traps themselves, objects of human manufacture?

Billie had missed the meeting because she'd been with Helen, but when she got home there was a message from Henry Fine explaining that if she wanted to kick in twenty bucks, there'd be a trap with her name on it. I know how you feel about this, Henry said. But think of it like rats. An infestation. The beavers have no natural predators, he reminded her, especially since the fisher-cats were virtually hunted out of existence.

Would it be different if you *ate* the beavers? Billie wondered. But she felt physically sick every time some wildlife biologist referred to the autumn "deer harvest." Meanwhile she was planning to buy herself a Havahart trap.

The next time she visited Helen, Billie decided, she'd bring the subject up, though Helen's position on almost everything (with the exception of the Crockett Home) appeared remarkably open-minded. She tolerated the appearance in her room of a pair of wafer and wine-bearing women solely out of friendship. Not to mention the fact that the entire event — if you could refer to the Eucharist that way — hadn't exactly gone smoothly. It would have been awkward enough dealing with Glenda Banner's piety — her insistence on doing everything without Billie's help, for instance, while at the same time crossing herself and dropping the wafers onto the rug and into Helen's lap — without also having Helen's son as audience.

Billie knew Piet wasn't the devout atheist he gave every appearance of being, nor did he watch the proceedings with ironic detachment or scorn or impatience but with a kind of deep interest that made her aware of how heavy-footed she was, of how (as her husband had so memorably put it) from below-stairs she sounded like someone stamping out fires.

Where are you now? she thought. Where did you go, Dougie? If you really loved me the way you said, the least you could have done was come back to haunt me. Everyone knew an unquiet grave was a breeding ground for ghosts.

On the far side of the lake, she saw a sleek little head pop up, bearing behind it a long cape of ripples. A loon cried; Cassiopeia settled more deeply into her chair.

I understand nothing, Billie thought. Nothing.

It had only been later, when she and Glenda were walking back to St. Luke's with the Communion kit and when she, Billie, was speculating about the relationship between Helen's age — so close, no matter how you might want to deny the fact, to death — and her waning interest in whatever it was the church had to offer, that Glenda let drop her remark about her husband.

"Carl had a near-death experience, you know," Glenda had said. "It changed him forever."

"I guess I didn't know," Billie had replied.

Glenda stopped walking and grabbed Billie's arm. They were in front of the jambalaya vendor's cart, where the sound of zydeco music conspired with a sudden gust of wind, sending his pile of paper napkins flying and Glenda's long gray braids aloft like streamers. "He used to hate that I went to church," Glenda said. "He hated that I gave the church money. Not a lot, and never out of his paycheck. I'm a home knitter, you know. But then he went swimming and had that attack. He says he doesn't remember any of it except right before he opened his eyes. He was dead, and a little girl was calling him back."

"Which little girl?" Billie had asked, shaking loose from Glenda's grip. She'd been mildly interested, thinking of what Richard Jenkins had told her about the Crocketts' resurrected dog. Glenda couldn't possibly mean Sunny Crockett, to whom Billie had taken an instant dislike when she sang "O Holy Night" during last year's Christmas pageant. The Annunciating Angel should have a voice pure as driven snow, not throbbing with unmet desires.

Though maybe I was just feeling jealous of the girl, Billie thought, rounding the bend in Fair Road. To her right, through the shifting branches of the trees, she could make out the porch light of the big farmhouse at the head of Canton Road and farther ahead a light in a first-floor window of the millhouse, where Henry Fine no doubt sat brooding about the beavers. Maybe I'm still bitter about being stuck with my bad voice in the back row of the Heavenly Host, Billie thought. Always a bridesmaid.

Then the jambalaya vendor had asked them if they'd mind moving on. They'd been blocking the access of customers to his cart, in this case a pair of tourists in matching blue jackets and comically large sunglasses, who'd seemed undeterred by the idea of buying food on a warm spring afternoon from someone who kept his mountain of hair hidden under a big wool hat.

Billie had apologized and had begun to move away down the sidewalk, when Glenda Banner once again grabbed her arm. "Mees Kipp," she'd whispered, and when Billie looked confused, she'd added, "the little girl. She lives out near you."

"The bookish one?" Billie had asked, thinking of Lorna Fine, whom she'd seen walk into a tree once, reading.

"No," Glenda had said, irritated, as if Billie were being purposely obtuse. "The *little* one."

By now Billie was approaching the place where Fair Road met the Dump Road. *Avoid dangerous intersections* — wasn't that what her *Varennes Voice* horoscope had said just this morning? The lake was behind her, also the beaver dam and the beavers, though if she stopped walking and listened closely, she could hear the sounds of their industry. Rustling and dragging. Gnawing. It was quite late — well past midnight, the moon dropping below the trees at the crown of Bliss Hill, casting long shadows across her path like something that could trip you. Ahead and to her right, the house where Mees Kipp lived with her sister and their mother, which Billie only just now realized had been her destination all along. The house was small but charming, with two bow windows facing the road and two eyebrow windows above. Long ago it had been a hat shop, back in the days when there'd been a hotel where the Knoll development was now. The house was also dark as pitch — though what had Billie been expecting? Tomorrow was a school day, after all.

She turned off her flashlight and walked right up onto the front lawn and stared at the house, and the house stared back. *No one likes a busybody, Virgo.* But it was Monday — the horoscope was no longer valid.

Sophy Kipp lay in her bed in the middle of a long, pointless dream about trying to find her good shoes, which always got lost while she was asleep. The two girls were also asleep and dreaming, Mersey about kissing a boy at school, and Mees about a large frightening box at the end of the town dock, though she was about to be awakened by Margaret, who had been dozing at the foot of her bed, but now jumped down and padded over to the eyebrow window, where she looked out, whining a little, excited.

"What is it, girl?" Mees asked. "Come on. Come back to bed." She patted the mattress, but Margaret ignored her.

Mees sighed and joined Margaret at the window. The freckle-faced woman who lived in the old camp near Sunny was standing in the front yard, her expression identical to the other kids' expressions in the slow readers' group when they tried puzzling out a word. Sunny thought the woman was ugly, a category Mees didn't pay much attention to, though she had to admit the woman wasn't what you'd call beautiful, just as she, Mees, wasn't a slow reader, only a reader who didn't like being *stared at.*

"Shhh!" Mees told Margaret. "You'll wake Mom and Mersey."

But Margaret didn't care, and before Mees could stop her, she'd taken off down the stairs, nosing her way for the millionth time through the imperfectly latched kitchen door, across the back porch, and around the side of the house. The moon! Margaret raised her head and let out a little howl of pleasure. The stranger on the front lawn held her interest for less than a second — a quick sniff of some smell that was not so very great, and then Margaret was *gone!*

Gone! Gone! Gone! Gone to find Doozie, whose person, for the millionth time, had locked her up like a precious jewel.

The beavers also momentarily captured her attention, but then *SMACK! SMACK!* they were gone too, under the lake, taking the divine smell of their scent glands with them. At least the ducks just ducked their heads.

It's hard for a dog to catch a beaver, even an excellent hunter like Margaret. The only animals that have ever had much success catching beavers are fisher-cats, due to their remarkable speed and viciousness. Fisher-cats and wolverines. And, of course, humans.

By 1850, when the Kipps' house was still a hat shop, and when hats and coats made from beaver pelts had become the height of practical fashion, the beavers of the New World had been trapped to near extinction.

Poor beavers. So shiny and sleek — no wonder women wanted to put that fur on their bodies. Of course they didn't love the fur the way they loved the beloved — they didn't want to slip into the beaver's fur the way they wanted to slip into the beloved's coat or vest. They didn't want to be thought of as beavers. They just wanted to be admired. Also they wanted to stay warm.

In 1873, the year of the Sunday School Outing Disaster, the appearance of a beaver in Black Lake would have been a very rare sight indeed. It would have been like seeing a freak at the county fair. A woman with a beard. A sword-swallower. It would have been like waking some morning to see the dark moon swallow the sun. It would have been enough to make Inez Fair suddenly stand up in the boat and point.

"Poor wandering one," Sunny was singing. "Though thou hast sure-ure-ly stray-ayed . . . Take heart of grace, thy steps retrace . . ."

Lorna lifted her eyes briefly from her notebook. Where had Sunny come up with that look? Surely it hadn't been summoned by the proximity of Justin Byrd, who was no more a dashing young pirate than Sunny was a tender Victorian maiden, especially in that halter top and those cutoffs. Lorna could barely believe the brightness and busyness of the classroom — plus the smell in it of chalk dust and uneaten, rotting lunches and the foul disinfectant favored by school janitors everywhere — in comparison with the gray Hebridean island where she'd been walking along the sands only moments earlier with taciturn Beau O'Brien.

"Give Frederick your hand, Mabel," suggested Mr. Mason. "Like this," he added, delicately uncrossing his legs and leaping from his chair.

"Watch yourself, Byrd," someone snickered.

"That'll be quite enough of that, William Ainsworth," someone snickered back in the patrician tones of Mr. Mason.

Mees twisted around in her seat and glared at Lorna. "When do we get to go *home*?" she asked. "School was supposed to be over *one minute ago*."

"Dunno." Lorna shrugged, returning to her notebook. She could feel Mees start to kick her desk, over and over again, and with increasing intensity — never a good sign. Mees hated injustice almost as much as she hated Gilbert and Sullivan.

They were all there, Lorna wrote. *The clues were all there, and it was only a matter of time before Beau O'Brien would stumble on the truth. The paw prints. The cigarette butt. The crumpled something or other . . .*

Beau O'Brien. Lorna couldn't get over the sight of him sitting on a stool in her parents' kitchen, his long legs looped around the legs of the stool, drinking coffee like a normal human being, even adding a little milk and sugar. "Beaver," he'd said, matter-of-factly correcting Mr. Diamond. "Looks like we're dealing with six *beaver.*" Lorna knew Beau O'Brien would stumble on nothing, being the soul of grace and elegance, not to mention the fact that "stumble on the truth" was a terrible cliché, as well as "matter of time." How hard it was to write a book! Lorna had decided not to change Beau's name, at least not until she was ready to publish, in order to experience the shudder of pleasure it gave her whenever she let it out of her pen, letter by letter, B-E-A-U, almost as if she were making up Beau, himself, his thick black hair, his hazel eyes, his long black eyelashes! Until yesterday, Lorna's hero had been named Alan Stewart, stolen from Robert Louis Stevenson.

Beau O'Brien's problem, Lorna wrote, *wasn't seeing the clues. No, O'Brien's problem was seeing Mary MacDonald for what she truly was, a child of a Black House, whose mother was a human and whose father was a seal.*

"Pirates, simmer down," said Mr. Mason. He reminded them that the show was in two weeks. The posters were up, the publicity was out: *Pirates of Penzance* at Varennes Elementary School! He reminded them they were the ones who would be embarrassed if they didn't know their lines. "Kevin Comeau, this means you."

Soon he would lose his temper, and then all would be lost. His face would get blotchy and — everyone's favorite moment — his nostrils would enlarge. Once he had made the exhilarating mistake of telling them how sick and tired he was of banging his tits on the fable.

"Ta-ake har-ar-ar-har-ar-ar-har-ararararar, har-ar-ar-har-ar-ar-har-ararararar-heart!"

Sunny was really going to town with this. Lorna could hear Mees beginning to make a familiar growling sound in the back of her throat, and when she leaned forward to touch her shoulder and reassure her that everything was okay, Mees whirled around and for a second — for just a fraction of an instant — Lorna thought she was going to bite her. But Mees burst out laughing instead.

"She looks like My Little Pony," Mees observed, and once again Lorna was filled with envy at the way these things came out of someone who had no interest whatsoever in being a writer. It was Sunny's tannish face, together with the blond hair and the wide-set eyes. The stunned expression. My Little Pony to a T.

"Shhh," Lorna said, "she can hear you," and Mees laughed even louder.

"You're so *good,* Lorna," she said. "In a past life you were a nun, and I was a soldier."

Mr. Mason clapped his hands, signifying the end of rehearsal. "Soloists, plan to stay late tomorrow," he said. "Pirate King, work on those high notes. Mabel, glorious, absolutely glorious. I couldn't ask for more. Frederick, still a trifle flat in the duet. And class, don't forget your reports on the respiratory system are due Friday."

Everyone began stuffing their books in their backpacks, stopping their ears with their earphones, beating a hasty retreat. The room, which had been so full of noise and energy seconds earlier, was suddenly completely and dramatically empty, like the body of a man dispossessed of demons.

Outside it was hot and still, the hot still air stirred by the departing bodies of all the little demons. Where were they going? Where did they go?

Sunny informed the bus driver that she and Lorna and Mees would be walking home. They had letters from their parents to this effect, she said.

"This *effect?*" Mees said, and Sunny told her maybe she could try to be a little nicer, if she even knew the meaning of the word.

"I heard you laughing," Sunny said.

Varennes Elementary was on the County Road about two miles north of where all three girls lived. For most of their walk home the town forest was to their right, the river to their left, the road gently rising and falling with only one steep hill that crested where the Hebron Road cut across it and where, on a clear day, they could see all the way down the valley, past Black Lake to the Canton hills. The sun was tipping to the west, a forest of shade falling across their sweaty bodies, cooling things down a bit, though it was still hot, the air hazy and full of the smell of coming rain, of the loggers' two-stroke oil, of wood chips, pine resin, dust, and frog spawn.

"That's what my horoscope said," Lorna was explaining. "Someone new turns out to be too hot to handle. I can't remember exactly. But it had to be *him*. Who else could it mean?"

"Horoscopes are so stupid." Sunny was walking with her face tilted skyward, working on her tan. "You know who writes those horoscopes? That weirdo with the German shepherd dog. Think about it."

A log truck made its laborious way up the hill behind them, immediately followed by a rust-colored Dodge Dart with no suspension left to speak of. The girls were forced to walk single file for a few minutes, putting a halt to all conversation, until the truck turned to the left for Hebron, and the girls and the Dart to the right, over the bridge across Canton Gorge. Far below, the river surged around a thicket of sharp black boulders. Still swollen from the spring runoff and the recent storms, it was poised to flood. The National Weather Service had issued an advisory for the following weekend, predicting more heavy rain.

"What's he doing?" Lorna asked Sunny, who'd fallen into step ahead of her, swatting at flies. Mees was in the lead, the Dart creeping slowly along just a little in front of them, the driver's eyes, attentive to their progress, visible in the rearview mirror, as well as the long ponytail on the very round back of his head, also visible through the dirt-spattered rear window.

"Just keep walking," Sunny ordered over her shoulder.

Once they were across the bridge, they could slip into the woods past Lover's Leap, angle their way along the side of the ravine, and pick up Fair Road at the bottom. Even if the driver took off after them, they'd be okay. Lorna felt her knees shaking; the Dart was going slower and slower, bumping over the metal expansion joints, the driver's round head bobbing up and down, his eyes fixed on *her,* following *her,* though maybe it was just an optical illusion like the Mona Lisa. Was he jerking off? Maybe he was having trouble with his car. The license plate, she told herself; memorize the license plate. But the thing was caked with mud and was a color she'd never seen before. J? JL something? There was an American flag decal on the bumper that looked relatively new, beside a very old sticker for Six Flags.

At the end of the bridge the Dart came to a complete stop.

"Sunny," Lorna hissed. "What should we do?"

And then to her astonishment she saw Mees run up to the car and yank open the passenger door.

"That is *disgusting!*" Mees yelled into the car. "We're *children.* What's wrong with you, mister? Don't you even care?" She started kicking the rocker panel, over and over, the way she'd kicked her desk, only harder, fiercer.

"Mees," Lorna said. "Measle. Stop." She and Sunny hung back near the rail of the bridge, horrified.

"Do you think it doesn't matter what you do? Because it does. What's wrong with you?" Mees gave the car one more good kick and then slammed the door. "God damn you," she said.

The Dart took off. Shot off, in fact, then made a K turn into Fair Road and drove back the way it had come, the driver gunning the engine and steering as close to the three girls as he possibly could without running them into the rail.

"You could have gotten us all killed," Sunny said.

"Go fuck yourself," Mees said. "That's what he said to me. He had a knife." She was staring at Lorna. "There's no reason to feel sorry for him," she said. "It's like we weren't even there."

"What makes you think I feel sorry for him?" Lorna asked, but she knew Mees had seen right through her.

The three girls continued walking, letting the chatter of the brook stand in for speech, their thoughts running around and around the dark corridors of their brains like mice, hearts ticking a mile a minute, unable to see a thing and endlessly squeaking, trapped in a maze the point of which remained beyond comprehension.

The ancient world believed unquestioningly in evil spirits; it was said there were seven and a half million of them. They lived in unclean places, places where no cleansing water was to be found. They were especially dangerous to women in childbirth, to the newly married bride and bridegroom, to children out on the road alone. They were especially dangerous between sunset and sunrise, also in the midday heat. The long-haired demons were especially dangerous to children.

"You know, you're wrong about Lorna's horoscope being stupid," Mees said to Sunny, once they'd gotten to the bottom of the hill. The brook withheld comment, disappearing off to the right behind the Knoll. The lake was on their left, fundamentally mute, blue pieces of sky and white pieces of cloud floating on its surface. "Except it was talking about that man in the car, not the one who's coming for the beavers."

Pure of heart, Lorna was thinking. Beau O'Brien was too pure of heart to see Mary MacDonald for what she truly was, a child of a Black House, whose mother was a human and whose father was a fallen angel. . . .

Meanwhile Sunny stared into space with the abstracted and vaguely sad expression she always wore when she was trying to figure out how to turn dross to gold, which is to say, to reestablish herself as the group's unwavering center. "Whatever," Sunny said. Her house was coming up just around the bend, so large and new and replete with all the Palladian details beloved of postmodern builders. Any minute now she would vanish through the door, and then it would be too late. "Did I tell you what my mother told me?" she asked, a last-ditch attempt. "About George Mason?"

"What about him?" Lorna asked. She knew she had to take the initiative, since Mees had run on ahead and had planted herself on the road in front of the Crocketts' house, small and pink and as intractable as ever.

"He stole money," Sunny said. "Over a hundred dollars."

"You're kidding. Mr. Mason?"

"From one of the old ladies."

"I don't believe it."

"Ask my mother." Of course Kathy Crockett wasn't home — she never was. No one was ever home at the Crockett house. Lorna's mother said the Crocketts made the beavers look like slackers. "She caught him in the act."

Lorna pictured Mr. Mason tiptoeing into one of the bedrooms at the Crockett Home for the Aged in the dead of night, dipping his long pink fingers into a large black pocketbook hanging from the arm of a recliner, extracting a wallet.

"Buddy," she could hear Mees calling. "Buddy, come *here!*"

The dog had appeared from behind the house. He'd come running right up to the edge of the lawn and not a step farther, then begun barking like a lunatic and running back and forth, his chocolatey ears flapping and his silver tags jingling in the sun.

"What's wrong, Buddy?" Mees asked. She turned to Sunny, and Lorna could see that Mees was crying. "What's wrong?" Mees asked Sunny, and now it was Sunny's turn to burst out laughing.

"Oh, Mees, you're such a dope," she said. "It's the invisible fence." She pointed to a small white flag attached to the top of a metal post and then to another one about three yards off. Another, another. A row of posts topped with small white flags, extending around the perimeter of the lawn. "What did you think? We had it put in after Buddy, he, well. You know."

"I thought he didn't know who I was," Mees said.

Sunny walked up to the dog, and he rolled over on his back in the new spring grass, wagging his tail and revealing his smooth pinkish-brown belly, his little penis in its sock of fur. You could still see the shaved place on his throat and two rows of black stitches where the bullets had entered.

"I thought he was afraid of me," Mees said.

In the beginning it was beautiful. Beautiful Nothing — it could have stayed that way, but.

As if motive could be ascribed before wish or need. As if out of Nothing a *moment* arose, a snag, the very beginning of what cosmologists call a singularity, the place where space and time begin and end. In my end is my beginning, sang the medieval choristers, and they believed it, lucky ducks.

It was beautiful and it could have stayed that way, but Nothing reached its beautiful endless hand-that-is-not-a-hand into the infinite Nothing of itself and turned itself inside out, giving itself form. The hand of God, which has no shape, no up or down, no end or beginning, drew the world from itself like a rabbit from a hat.

It was small, according to Julian of Norwich, no bigger than a hazelnut and round as a ball. This was in the fen country, in the fourteenth century. Despite her misleading name, Julian was a woman, thirty and a half years old, an anchoress living in a cell that adjoined the parish church. *Lewd,* she called herself, meaning ignorant. She looked at the small nut-sized thing lying in the palm of her hand and thought, What can this be? Everything which is made, came the answer, and Julian was amazed that it could last, because of its littleness. But it would last, little created thing that it was, she was told, and always would, because God loved it, even though there was no peace in it.

Whereas beautiful Nothing would never take up the sword against its neighbor, nor would it poison the wells, nor salt the fields. It would not sicken and die. A man walks upright, said Julian of Norwich, and the food in his body is shut in as if in a well-made purse. And when the time of his necessity comes, the purse is opened and then shut again, in most seemly fashion.

Who hath ears to hear, let him hear.

Make a thing and invite corruption.

A man possessed of demons was living in the country of the Gadarenes, hiding among the tombs and terrorizing anyone who came near him. In those days it was common knowledge that the human body had thirty-six different parts, each one of which could be occupied by a demon. Their favorite way to gain entry was to lurk beside a man while he ate and settle on his food. Once swallowed, the demon would endow his host with an overwhelming desire to do ill and the prodigious strength needed to satisfy that urge.

By the time Jesus came upon him, not only was the man possessed of demons so strong that he couldn't be restrained by fetters and chains, but he was also stark naked and howling. When he saw Jesus, did he run up to Him and worship Him? Did he tell Him to go away and leave him alone? The Gospel writers don't agree on this point, except to say that Jesus drove the demons out of the man and into a nearby herd of pigs. Two thousand of them, in fact, which seems like an impossibly gigantic herd — two thousand pigs ran violently down a steep hill and into the sea, where they "choked." Shortly thereafter the people of Gadara asked Jesus to go away. They were frightened by the wild man's rapid transformation into a man not unlike themselves. And they were furious about what He'd done to their pigs.

This story is one instance, Julian said, of why no soul has rest until it has despised as Nothing all which is created, so as to be able to love uncreated God.

Saturday night, the anticipated rain not yet falling. Sunday morning, actually, the half-moon submerged in a pot of murk, and Chloe's hair spilling across her antique pillow slip, dark-blond, thick. Her strong back, the faint lumps of the vertebrae visible in a row, the razor-sharp shoulder blades: Chloe Brock had crewed for Dartmouth ten years earlier. She had blackfly bites at the base of her skull, behind her ears, but was there anyone in Varennes who didn't? Now she was sound asleep, had dropped off immediately after sex the way the man was supposed to, unlike Piet, the man.

He rolled over, looked out the window. A large shade tree of some sort, then his car, and beyond it the street and the porch of the house opposite with those infernal wind chimes. Everything plainly visible despite the murkiness of the sky and the lateness (or earliness) of the hour, because of the streetlamp two doors down in front of the Summer Street Deli, where in less than four hours he'd be buying the Sunday papers and smoked salmon and cream cheese and bagels. Coffee, too, since Chloe didn't keep it in the house, being a confirmed homeo-path. The first time they had slept together she'd described the precise headache targeted by the pills she took, like her brain was loose and rolling around inside her cranium. She shook the pills, which were about the size of fleas, into a folded piece of paper and tipped them into her mouth. You weren't supposed to touch them.

Piet had been having sex with Chloe ever since Ash Wednesday, when the sight of the black smudge on her forehead had rendered her vulnerable and, hence, desirable. Otherwise her nails were long and obsessively manicured and painted a shade of red verging on black, and her eyes were a terrifying shade of aquamarine that turned out to be contact lenses. She was a gymnastic partner in bed, not Cirque du Soleil, but close. The pleasure was undeniable, and she was also interesting to talk to, even on the subject of her ex-husband, a category of subject (former sexual partners) that Piet, like most men, generally found inhospitable. Of course, it helped that the guy sounded like a loser.

Outside the window the wind was kicking up, the leaves of the shade tree showing their silver backs. A far-off rumble of thunder, abrupt flashes of heat lightning. Piet was overwhelmed with the desire for a cigarette, though he hadn't smoked since college. Probably because Chloe was so much younger — there was a sort of provisional and illegal feel to their affair, as if it were being conducted in a late-fifties dorm, where discovery would lead to expulsion. As if a housemother or hall monitor might burst in at any minute. But that was merely a bad memory: Sandra, whom he'd barely known. She'd never smoked marijuana before and had just told him she felt like a pinecone when the door flew open and in came Mrs. Murray.

"Wait up!" Chloe said. "Hey. Wait up!" Her eyes were wide open, but by now Piet knew how to recognize the signs. Not only did Chloe talk in her sleep, but she also often walked, out of the bedroom and down the stairs and, on one memorable occasion, right onto the front porch. He found her standing there without a stitch on, curtained by her golden hair.

Like a spring willow, its branches sweeping the ground, ready to bud.

More thunder, louder now, and more percussive — the day the invasion started, Piet had been in New York City on business, heading down Fifth Avenue past the Guggenheim when it suddenly began to rain. Gently at first, and then harder, and then it was pouring, and no sooner had he decided to take refuge inside the museum than there came a huge thunderclap, sending a surprising number of art lovers in flight from the upper levels, several of them weeping, not just women. "Holy Mary pray for us," a museum guard was whispering. Someone flicked open a cell phone, tapped in a number, and Piet found himself remembering what it had been like when he was first married and the sirens would begin to wail in the middle of the night and he'd hear his new wife, Ruth, turn on the immense console radio that she inherited from her grandfather and kept in the corner of their bedroom. WOWO, Fort Wayne, Indiana, broadcasting all through the night, long after the other stations had signed off. A million miles away in the dark Midwest, the tower rising out of a flat dark plain, a red light at its tip. If the world were ending that would be the end of Fort Wayne. Also the Everly Brothers. Ipana toothpaste. Ruth had called it "checking."

After a while, everyone got used to it. And then the United States made friends with Russia or at least pretended to. For a brief period everything seemed to go back to normal, meaning the idea that people might destroy an entire planet faded from the foreground. Now it turned out that countries weren't the problem, but people. Guns don't kill people, Piet was annoyed to hear himself think. People kill people. But guns certainly came in handy, also bombs, smart and otherwise, stealth missiles, tanks, planes, etc.

A flash of light, white verging on blue. An explosion. Why not assume the worst?

For a moment he found himself missing Ruth. The problem with Chloe was that she never exactly seemed to be *there,* though perhaps that was his problem, not hers. You got to be sixty-three years old and you had to face the fact that no one was going to come along and watch out for your welfare. Ruth was living on the other side of the country, in California, married to the same man now for over forty years, with three children and enough grandchildren that Piet had long ago lost count. Sondra was dead of breast cancer; Irmgard had gone home to Berlin. Amy lived in the southern part of the state, and they sometimes met for lunch. Wonderful women, all of them!

Piet slid lightly from the bed, stepped into his jeans. It was just starting to rain, a delicate tapping on the dormer roof, but if the wind chimes were any indication, the storm was gaining strength. He could go around closing windows, though that would suggest a misleading sense of proprietorship on his part. Still, if he left them open, the floors would get ruined, and Chloe, who barely eked out a living at Varennes High, teaching French and coaching women's hockey, had just spent a fortune she didn't own having them refinished.

The bedroom windows seemed all right, the wind coming from the west, driving the rain against the back of the house. Piet felt his way carefully down the hall and into Chloe's study — somewhere in the place there were two cats, and he knew what it was like to step on one of them in the dark. She kept a map of the Loire Valley pinned above her desk and beside it a signed photo of Pavel Bure, number 10, the Russian Rocket, with his petulant girlish lips.

Piet shut the window and put a sheet of paper that had blown to the floor back on Chloe's desk. "C," he read, thinking, I shouldn't be reading this, the whole time he was switching on the desk lamp and continuing to read. "Why don't you ever write back? Too good for your old hubby? Cat got your tongue ha ha? . . ."

FLASH! BOOM! The desk light went out and the unusually loud refrigerator motor died.

"Piet?" Chloe was standing naked in the doorway. Without her lenses it was hard to bring her into focus, her eyes a watery noncolor. "What're you doing?"

"Shutting the window," he said, and when she pointed out that the window was on the other side of the room, he explained that he'd been returning the sheet of paper to the desk.

"I was watching you," Chloe said. "Besides, you dropped it."

She didn't move or make an attempt to cover herself. She just stood there, her features still out of focus and without color, though the overall effect of her, her shape and substance, was strangely iconic, like a recently unearthed artifact. "You should be more careful," Chloe went on. "When people snoop sometimes they find out things they don't want to know."

Then all of a sudden the power came back, restoring the warm cheerful glow of the desk lamp. Motors began humming; life kept marching on. The friendliest of the two cats, the little gray tiger cat with extra toes, leapt to the floor from the chair where it had been asleep on Chloe's hockey jersey. Lady Panthers, number 10. The cat's name was Gigi, and the other one, the white one that clawed and bit and was stone-deaf, was Mignonette. Chloe tugged the jersey in place over her head. Her eyes were actually hazel.

"I'm sorry," Piet said.

"It's okay." Chloe walked over and put her arms around him. "Forget it." She gave him a kiss; she was very good at kissing.

"I'm a compulsive reader," Piet said. "I see words, and I can't help myself. You know what I'm like in the car."

"I said forget it," Chloe said. "What time is it, anyway?"

All of the clocks were flashing 12:00, as if despite everyone's best efforts, it really could happen, time could actually stop. We stopped using gears and cogs to measure its passage and switched to electricity, and then because to know the clock is to know the clock maker, we also watched God devolve into amperage.

"My watch is on the bedside table," Piet said. "But I think it's about four-thirty."

He wanted to get back into bed. He wanted Chloe to wrap her arms and legs around him like a bear climbing a tree. He wanted to forget how frightening she had looked, standing there in the doorway, and the closer she was to him, the easier it would be to do that. Though you'd never mistake what he wanted for intimacy.

"Come on," he said, pulling her behind him down the hall.

In the bedroom Gigi had assumed her muffin position on the pillow that the man thought of as his own when he was there but which any fool could see belonged to Gigi. It was dented by her body, the feathers pressed into a perfect nest that the man's head fruitlessly tried to enlarge. Gigi was Queen. Gigi knew the Girl understood this, which was why Gigi stayed with her despite the fact that the Girl had stopped giving her Fancy Feast, even though Gigi could have told her the vet was wrong and that the momentary indisposition had nothing to do with canned food but was from a bad mouse.

"Time's up," Piet said, trying to tip Gigi off the pillow like a ball or a shoe, something without claws.

"What're you doing?" Chloe demanded.

Of course Gigi didn't want to be picked up and moved to the foot of the bed, but it was better than being dumped on the floor. The Girl was her ally, she could tell. As for the purring — it just happened. If she could control it, she wouldn't have started purring at this precise moment, when it was crucial to establish Eminent Domain.

"I don't like the way he's looking at me," Piet said.

"*Gigi,*" said Chloe. "She."

He did seem a little like a mouse. Pointy nose, dark beady eyes. Too big to hunt down, toy with, kill. Snap off the head and remove the liver and entrails, depositing them near the Girl's shoes, where she couldn't fail to find them. She wouldn't be pleased.

"Mmmmm," she was saying. "Mmmmm, that's nice."

Meanwhile Mignonette was sitting in the living-room window seat, watching the world go by. This had become her place ever since a week ago, when her nice woolen bed had mysteriously disappeared from the floor of the hall closet, only to reappear three days later on a hanger, wrapped in plastic.

The porch roof protected the windows from the rain, and from where she sat Mignonette had an excellent view of Summer Street. Some leaves blew by. *Très intéressant!* A group of young humans appeared, turning onto Main Street, headed for the vacant lot behind the church. Two young men and a young woman. Mimi, the rector's daughter. Of course Mignonette didn't know this was who it was or that a drug deal was in progress, but she knew something bad was about to happen — she could detect a stale electric smell in the air, the smell humans gave off when they were scared and looking for trouble. More leaves. *Ooo la la!* A car drove past with its window rolled down and its radio loud enough for Mignonette to feel the *thump thump thump* of the bass. *Thump thump thump,* and then a news update, likewise full blast, but without the bass Mignonette felt nothing. It didn't matter, though. Mostly she liked to watch things move. Number one: round or cylindrical things like styrofoam cups. Number two: paper bags when the wind got inside them. Number three: leaves. Not counting things to eat like birds or mice and so forth.

"Civilian casualties," the radio hollered and kept hollering — "chief of staff could not be called upon to . . ."

In the bedroom Piet rose onto one elbow, leaned over, and slammed down the window. What was it with people and their car radios? "I don't believe it," he said.

"Relax, baby," Chloe murmured drowsily, making herself a spoon against his back. "It's out of our hands. Go back to sleep."

"That's what people always say. That's just another way of letting jerks like that off the hook."

"Not *these* hands," Chloe said, snaking them through the slots between Piet's upper arms and his torso. "Watch out, here they come." She played with his chest hair, curling it around her fingers, making nests. The air smelled fresh; birds were starting to sing, lots of them, which meant that at least for the moment the rain was ending or had ended, the rising sun invisible on the other side of the street behind a radiant wall of mist. "It's in our nature," she said. "Face it, baby, we're animals."

"I don't see the cats doing things like that."

"That's because you're not here. They fight all the time."

"You don't see me making that jerk listen to *my* music."

"Huh?"

The phone rang; Chloe rolled away from Piet to answer it. "Not now," she said, and sat up. "I'm busy." She listened for several seconds, staring quizzically across the room at her face in the mirror above the mahogany dresser, then said, "Did you hear me?" She paused, laughed. "No, not that one." Of course without her lenses she couldn't see a thing. "Later, okay?" Then she hung up and turned back to Piet.

"I thought you meant the war," she said. "I thought you were talking about the invasion."

"If I was talking about the war, I wouldn't have said *jerk*."

How could she possibly get it so wrong? She knew he'd been opposed to the war from the beginning. At some point you had to say *enough* to a woman, Piet thought, especially a woman who seemed to put you on the scale somewhere between Thai food and Bikram yoga and definitely below ice hockey and talking on the phone with her girlfriends at all hours of the day and night. She was half his age; she didn't even know who Nina Simone was. He took out his frustration on Gigi, trying to displace her by giving her a firm nudge from beneath the covers with his foot, though the transaction proved to be more complicated than expected.

Gigi began kneading; Chloe cast a reproachful glance in Piet's direction. "Look how nice she is to you," she said, "and you treat her like dirt."

Sunday morning — in the steeple of the Catholic church on Elm Street, the bells started ringing. Four bells, quite impressive! That is, until you realized it was a recording. The sky was blue, then it was gray. Then it was raining again. A car alarm went off near the deli. Gigi settled in for a good long knead.

A lot of claw in each squeeze of the paw — that was the feline way! The Girl meanwhile climbed out of bed and began to brush her long golden hair. Sparks were flying. It was only a matter of time, Gigi knew, before she'd have the Girl all to herself again.

Soon enough the man would be gone. The Girl would figure out a way to get rid of him. He was clueless, like a dog, whereas the Girl had her secrets. Gigi knew she was up to something. She had her eye on something and she could sit still as a statue for hours if she had to, like Gigi watching a mouse. Sit there with her teeth daintily achitter and the very tip of her tail atwitch with pent-up excitement.

In 1873, the year of the Sunday School Outing Disaster, every family in the St. Luke's congregation had their own private pew, a place where they could stow their hymnals and prayer books and embroidered kneelers, as well as their horehound drops, spectacles, handkerchiefs, and fans, not to mention the ubiquitous bottle of smelling salts for the ladies. If the family was prosperous, they might have endowed a window, a set of vestments, a font. In 1873 the members of the St. Luke's congregation had thought there were some things in their lives that would stay the same forever.

You could still see the holes on the sides of the pews where the brass plaques used to be screwed in. Number 4: Bliss. Two children lost on that fateful afternoon, the youngest not much more than a toddler. Number 7: Webb. A seven-year-old boy, and his older sister, recently betrothed. Number 10: Mayhew. Two children, identical twins, both asthmatic. Number 19: Fair. A new chapel window had been commissioned in their memory: Suffer the Little Children to Come Unto Me. Originally the stained-glass artist had attempted likenesses, but they'd proved too heartbreaking, and he'd been asked to replace them with a more generic set of faces.

In the absence of plaques, the seating system at St. Luke's was now first come, first served, though among the faithful it was understood that certain members of the congregation had come to prefer certain pews and to have established something resembling squatter's rights. Mrs. Quill, for instance, as Billie Carpenter had discovered three weeks earlier, liked to sit on the left side of the church in the very back, where she could spy on everyone during the passing of the collection plates and see who the skinflints were. The Brackneys — the young couple who always tiptoed in late with their wailing and recently baptized baby, Emma — usually sat in the pew across the aisle from Mrs. Quill, and the large mismatched group of people from the Terrace Street neighborhood, who for some reason arrived all at once and out of breath, dispersed themselves throughout the section in front of the Brackneys, but as far from the central aisle as possible.

When she felt up to leaving her room at the Crockett Home, Helen Zeebrugge sat with her son, Piet, in the first pew on the left, immediately in front of the pulpit, where she had the best chance of seeing what was going on, and behind her sat the splendidly turned-out Crocketts, where they had the best chance of being seen. Behind them, Marjory Mason and her son George. Behind them, a family of Romanian refugees, shrouded in black shawls and silence. Ever since his near-death experience, Mr. Banner had laid claim to the first pew on the right, immediately adjacent to the choir and Mrs. Banner, and two pews ahead of Billie Carpenter, who liked to sit near the organ and watch the organist, but not if it was one of the Sundays when Dr. Christine Stokes was already sitting there with her huge Mexican reticule, ready to regale Billie with stories of her blessed namesake, who had been known to soar to the roof of the parish church in Liège, Belgium, on more than one occasion. Dr. Stokes was said to be some kind of naturopath and her bag to be full of dried plant life.

Chloe Brock never sat in the same place twice, nor did she

ever sit anywhere near Piet Zeebrugge, as if no one knew what was going on between them. James Trumbell tended to stand near the vestry door and pace. The rector's wife, Mary, and their younger daughter, Pam, only came to the eight o'clock service; their other daughter, Mimi, hadn't been inside the church since she was twelve. There were two Seeing Eye dogs, Barney and Zephyr, a black Lab and a shepherd-husky mix, attached to members of the choir. You weren't supposed to pet them, though once Billie saw the rector slip Zephyr a Communion wafer.

Today the church was almost full. In addition to the regulars, a larger-than-usual number of visitors and walk-ins were present. Marjory Mason's ne'er-do-well brother from Salt Lake City. Mr. Brackney's former college roommate. All year long it was cool and shady in the church, a great virtue during the dog days of summer but seductive even on a muggy day in early June. The kazoo-playing man with the top hat and Hawaiian shirt who lived in the supermarket bus shelter had taken a seat across the aisle from the Crocketts, who had brought along Sunny's friends Mees and Lorna, as well as Kathy Crockett's tan, shriveled parents, recently back from Florida. Four long-limbed Jamaicans with dreads who came north every summer to work the market gardens of Hebron stretched their bare legs into what would have been the transept aisle if St. Luke's had possessed a transept.

"Holy, Holy, Holy, merciful and mighty, God in three persons, Blessed Trinity." The sequence hymn ended, followed by the Gospel. "They shall take up serpents; and if they drink any deadly thing, it shall not hurt them." A sparrow had gotten into the church and after flying madly from one end of the nave to the other came to rest atop the rood screen. Richard Jenkins mounted the pulpit, adjusted his reading glasses. A small thin bald creature in a ruffled pink blouse and camou-flage pants scooted into the pew in front of Billie.

June 8, Ascension Day, the day Jesus bade the apostles fare-well and rose on a cloud to heaven, leaving them alone after two precious and unprecedented months in His company. All of the excitement of the liturgical year was essentially over, having been crammed into less than half of it: Advent, Christ-mas, Epiphany, Lent, Palm Sunday, Good Friday, Easter. The Child who had been so eagerly awaited, born in a stable and worshiped, then reviled and crucified and resurrected from the dead, was gone. Judas was soon to fall headlong onto the field he'd bought with his blood money, where he would spectacu-larly burst asunder and all his bowels gush out, an event followed shortly thereafter by the rushing winds and fiery tongues of Pentecost.

And then? Richard Jenkins paused for a moment, letting the question sink in.

And then, he answered himself, nothing. And then week after week after week of the same old thing. The First Sunday after Trinity, the Second Sunday after Trinity, the Twenty-fifth Sunday after Trinity, the Millionth Sunday after Trinity. And then all those weeks after Trinity known as the Propers, blend-ing together into an undifferentiated, boring lump.

"Takes one to know one," said the bald creature in front of Billie. "Cocksucker."

It turned around and smiled at her, stuck out its tongue and spat. No teeth, but Billie could see two breasts lifting the ruf-fled pink front of the blouse. Definitely a woman.

Over the heads of the three girls, Kathy Crockett gave Billie a look. *Do something.* Her pretty daughter was bent down, try-ing not to laugh, the tall skinny girl intent upon the sermon, and the little black-haired one scowling and swinging her legs.

"So here we find ourselves, poised on the brink of abandonment and boredom," said Richard Jenkins. "Not unlike the poet Anthony Hecht, confronting his vision of a hill, 'mole-colored and bare. It was very cold.'"

"Fuck you," said the bald woman.

"Shh," said Mr. Banner, over his shoulder.

"Shh yourself," said the bald woman. "Shithead."

Of course Richard Jenkins had brought this on himself. He liked to think of his church as a safe haven. No matter how avidly the vestry militated against it, he'd leave the small side door unlocked all through the night, and in the morning something invariably would be missing. The rector of the church Billie attended as a girl would never have allowed such a thing. He would have fixed the bald woman with such a look of Old Testament wrath that she would have slunk off, never to darken the door of the church again.

She's frightened, Billie thought. If she started up again, she would try to reassure her. A reassuring touch on the shoulder, the way you'd calm a frightened animal. Of course *shush*ing her wouldn't do any good. The poor thing was frightened out of her wits, as who wouldn't be by this world we'd never asked to be born into, with its weapons hidden here and there throughout it like Easter eggs under sofas.

"Poised on the brink of abandonment and boredom," Richard Jenkins was saying, "each one of us sees his or her life looming ahead like Hecht's hill, like the Propers, vast and featureless and . . ."

"Hypocrite," said the bald woman. "Cocksucker."

"It's all right," Billie said. She reached forward and patted the woman's back. Under the pink blouse it was humped and lacking in resilience like a cheap sofa cushion.

And then suddenly the sparrow took off from the rood

screen and flew into the sanctuary, where it lit on the altar cloth between two huge arrangements of forsythia. "Take your hands off me!" the bald woman was yelling. "Take your hands off me, you pervert!" Whirling around to face Billie, revealing the hole of her mouth, out of which flew dark winds of outrage and decay. "You think I'm not wise to your tricks?"

She grabbed a handful of Billie's hair and yanked it hard, pulling several strands loose at the roots. She pinched Billie's side, the thin skin above the rib cage.

Meanwhile, those members of the congregation who were in a position to see what was going on were doing their best to ignore it.

The walkie-talkie system wasn't up and running yet or Richard Jenkins might have used it to alert the ushers, one of whom was James Trumbell. He was sitting at the very back of the church, near Mrs. Quill, who smelled like mothballs and folding money. Alone, so alone.

Mr. Banner had his eye on Mees Kipp.

Police Log — Sunday, June 8

2:02 a.m. Water bubbling out of ground near Perry Street business.

4:30 a.m. Alarm activated at Mountain View Circle residence.

5:40 a.m. Drug activity behind River Street church.

8:13 a.m. Accident reported on East Main Street.

11:18 a.m. Accident reported on Route 10.

12:28 p.m. Bridge out over Canton Brook.

1:15 p.m. Out-of-control teenager on Maplewood Avenue.

3:33 p.m. Tires slashed on vehicle in Terrace Street driveway.

5:00 p.m. Flooding on County Road between elementary school and Hebron Hill.

5:11 p.m. Black and white cat "Beulah" missing from Cummings Street residence.

8:56 p.m. Loud music reported at Summer Street residence.

11:01 p.m. Rear-end accident on County Road.

Just a little flood, not a big one. Nothing requiring an ark, animals two by two, and a hole in the ark's roof for the giraffes' heads to stick out of. Cloaked in clouds, and darkness, the rain once again made its appearance, ferried on a cold front from the Canadian Maritimes, where Daniel Murdock's floatplane was soon to splash down. A little flood — nor did it have its origins in God's wish to wipe clean the slate but in an unstable pressure system and contending air masses.

Overnight, the low-lying cornfields on either side of the Canton River turned to immense, still pools, the water a pale creamy brown with scallops of scum at the edges. The corn had grown about four inches tall, and in some places you could see the bright green tips of it poking out of the floodwaters, though whether the crop would survive the storm was anybody's guess. By now each plant had a fairly well-developed root network, and the corn, to the extent that it *knew* what it was doing, knew that it should pin its hopes on its roots until the sun came out, though if worse came to worse, all that would happen was that it would rot and return to the soil a little sooner than usual, before it had a chance to experience the singular thrill of cross-pollination.

In terms of its consciousness, corn isn't particularly evolved, endlessly preening itself for having once been used as legal tender in place of gold and silver. Like most feed crops it's fascist at heart, taking strength from numbers. It started out as grass. It doesn't know how to talk.

Lichen, on the other hand, lives to be very old and can survive the worst the world has to offer. Storms and wars, fires and floods. Lichen speaks a language like some music, repetitive and incantatory: *manna star fold star. star star fold reindeer. fold fold fold fold. starlight starlight.* It kept up a running commentary around the base of Daniel Murdock's tent, though he didn't know that's what he was hearing. The ever-present wind, he thought, caught in the tent fly. The little yellow pebbles on the beach, scooped up and discarded by the sea. He didn't know the lichen was explaining how a recent storm had abandoned Labrador for Varennes, exchanging north for south, husband for wife.

So many things are alive: lichen, moss, grass. Also people. So many things are alive and *that's* what's strange, not that things like stones aren't, especially when you consider how everything's made from the same materials.

Heading home from Montreal in the driving rain, her windshield wipers flapping back and forth like mad, Andrea Murdock was also talking. She'd spent two nights in the hotel, rather than the one night she'd anticipated, due in part to the fact that the border crossing took longer than usual. That damn gun! Of course Danny needed a gun to protect himself from polar bears, but if only he would remember from one year to the next to bring the appropriate forms.

The rain was wild, out of control, and the sight of it made Andrea blush over her recent indiscretion. *Si j'avais une femme comme toi . . .* The man had been heavy, his features thick and debauched. He wore jewelry, and he smelled oversweet, his breath like fruit, his skin like lilies, the piano bar lapped with red tongues of light. *Chérie,* he'd said, his accent forced, taking her for a native. *Chérie.*

So many things were alive at that precise moment. Beulah, a little black-and-white cat, had lost her head while chasing a mouse and found herself far from home when the rain began to come down in earnest, sending her across River Street to the church, where she sat for a while on the side porch, licking herself dry. Between the toes, the tops of the paws. How disgusting to be wet! How like a dog! There was a puddle on the church lawn getting bigger and bigger, night crawlers oozing from it onto the sidewalk. Rainwater leaping from a gutter into a lilac bush, making the flowers heavy, bending their heavy wet heads to the ground.

And then the side door creaked open on its immense hinges. A person looked out, saw the rain, and cursed. *Cocksucker!* A foot shot forth, but Beulah was too quick for it, running into the church, under the pews and out of reach. A service leaflet, a handful of change. An action figure, a crumpled piece of Kleenex. Nothing of interest except possibly the green jelly bean wedged between two kneelers. *Pat pat. Pat pat.*

The door slammed shut; for a moment it was perfectly dark, perfectly still. If the moon had been shining, the stained-glass windows might have let in a trickle of weak, watery light, but the moon wasn't shining. And if it were, just let those windows try to let in the least trickle of light, and the next thing you knew it would be gone, swallowed by the heavy wood of the pews, their deep red cushions, the cold slate floor, the great corbeled arches of the nave.

A church wants to generate its own light; this is why churches are full of things made of gold. A thing made of gold doesn't hoard the light it swallows but exudes it. God from God, Light from Light.

Even in the pitch darkness the little black-and-white cat could see the gold tracery on the front of the pulpit, the gold candlesticks on the altar, the huge gold cross. She poked her nose out from under the pew where Helen Zeebrugge usually sat, and looked around; though the person who had tried to kick her was nowhere in sight, she knew she wasn't alone. Nor did Beulah think she'd suddenly stumbled into God's presence, since like most animals she dwelt there all the time in happy oblivion. No, this was something else entirely, a tiny voice coming from high above her head.

Tseet! Tseet!

It was the sparrow: now that the congregation had left the church, he was once again perched on the rood screen, pleased to be dry. Pleased to see a wet cat on the slate floor far below him. *Lost* was a concept foreign to the sparrow, since unlike Beulah, he belonged to no one. A fowl of the air who neither sowed nor did he reap, yet his heavenly Father made sure he had plenty of food — though of course he didn't know that either.

Everything alive: the sparrow, the cat, the corn, the lichen. On Pitsulak Island Daniel Murdock slid into his sleeping bag and adjusted his flashlight to read over his notes: *Red paint burial; surprising quantities of Ramah chert.* Based on his findings he was developing a paradigm for the way the people whose bones and artifacts he was in the process of uncovering had lived their lives. Though "uncovering" was a bit misleading, since nothing was exactly buried, due to the permafrost. A red paint burial, probably signifying an important member of the community, maybe even a religious sacrifice, though the skeleton appeared to be that of a young boy.

It was never easy, developing a paradigm. Andrea refused to accept what he was doing as science. Why don't you admit it? she would say. It's fiction. You're making up stories. But Daniel knew the evidence was real; it was merely a matter of knowing how to read it. A young boy who'd died over one thousand years ago had been granted a chief's burial, the ground around him strewn with mysterious artifacts that came all the way from the northernmost tip of the Labrador peninsula. From Ramah Bay, where the Torngat Mountains rose straight out of the sea, over five thousand feet. Where according to legend, the wind was born.

Moonlight filtered through the greenish-blue fabric of the tent, dreamy, aquatic. *fold spin fold fold. reindeer. starburst.* The greenish-blue veil of the lichen, draped across the big yellow stones: caribou often fed on it, turning it in their intestines to spring salad, a delicacy prized by Inuit hunters. Outside the tent the air was thick with bugs; the blackflies of Pitsulak Island made the blackflies of Varennes seem like a picnic. Andrea would lose her mind.

Andrea, Daniel thought. What was she doing now? Probably sleeping — back home it was well past midnight, one and a half time zones away. He pictured her thick black curls, her soft white body, her beautiful round breasts. Her moles. Her pajama pants. The way she sometimes sat bolt upright, then banged her head against her pillow while she slept. Snoring, grinding her molars to dust. No doubt about it, she'd taken some getting used to.

Not that Daniel didn't love his wife, but he loved her so much more when he was away from her. He loved her with all his heart; he loved her like a lovesick swain. The truth is, though, he also loved being in a tent all by himself. If he wanted a cigarette, for instance, no big deal. No big brown eyes following his hand's movement toward his breast pocket with censure and concern. He could smoke his brains out right now if he wanted, except for the undeniable fact that once he traded the interior of the highly flammable tent for the fly-infested outdoors he'd be eaten alive in two seconds flat.

Daniel sighed and turned off the flashlight. Just a young boy, he thought, a young boy buried facedown with a rock on his back to hold him in place, and for some reason he found himself remembering his second-year Latin teacher, who'd broken into tears over a classmate's botched translation of Catullus. It was the last thing he thought of before falling asleep.

All through the night the solar wind blew, sending immense yellow-green waves of light across the sky above Pitsulak Island, flooding the far-off telephone wires and power lines of the North American continent with a torrent of wild electrons. Aurora borealis, in her ever-changing cloak: from time to time someone will try whistling her down to earth, and they're never seen again.

Meanwhile Andrea Murdock was speeding along Route 10, steering with one hand while with the other she attempted to bring in a radio station that didn't keep turning to static . . . *back someday come what may to zzzzzz just in, reports of zzzzzz and He walks with me and He talks with zzzzzz closed until further notice between exits nine and zzzzzz* . . . Only five miles to go, and then she'd be safe inside her house, the door firmly slammed shut on the thread of the journey between Montreal and Varennes, snipping it in two and forever severing the connection with that oleaginous faux Frenchman. *zzzzzz hits your eye like a big pizza pie* . . .

She crossed North Street, the town on her left and not a light to be seen, meaning the power must be out. Great. Around the new rotary, the construction of which had driven

Danny to write letter after letter to the local paper, and onto the Lower Road, which was fast turning to a stream. *Could* it be raining any harder? Andrea rummaged in the bag in her lap for one last Goldfish. Just one lousy Goldfish, was that asking too much? At the blinking light she made the turn onto the County Road and took a deep breath. Almost. Almost. . . . *stars make you drool just like pasta fazool . . . !* What a fabulous song.

The car hydroplaned slightly, but Andrea was quick to bring it back under control. For a careless driver she was surprisingly competent, the few accidents she'd been involved in mere fender benders. On her left the Canton River, foam-flecked and surging from its bed, the black willows along its far bank whipping their tresses side to side like madwomen. On her right the town forest, darker than dark, deeper than deep. *You secret, black, and midnight hags! Aroint thee, witch, aroint thee!*

The road began its long curve around the clearing for the elementary school. *SLOW CHILDREN* playing their slow games at the foot of a giant tree, though of course not in this weather nor at this hour. Hansel and Gretel? Maybe there was one last little Goldfish. Maybe there was one dear little Goldfish that had escaped her notice by falling from the bag. Andrea felt around with her right hand, then glanced down at the floor.

Which is why what she was seeing when she crashed into the back of the blue Volvo stopped at the roadblock was her damp gray floor mat and not the Volvo's red flashers, the trooper waving an orange lantern, the black road lapped in a billowing sheet of water.

"I trust we're all in agreement?" George Mason looked around the Banners' dining-room table, his expression expectant yet stern. Like the sixth-grade teacher he in fact was, peppering his speech with his listeners' names, just like a teacher. "I trust you don't appreciate your wife having to hear that kind of talk any more than I do, do you, Carl Banner? Am I right, James Trumbell? Am I right, Bobbie Carpenter?"

"Billie," Billie said, but she didn't care. She'd come to the meeting because she hoped Piet Zeebrugge might be there, church security being among the proposed subjects under discussion, and he wasn't. Of course he wasn't there — the whole idea was idiotic. This was just one more of the many choices she'd made in her life because she was hoping some man would take notice, or some boy, starting with the Louisville Slugger she'd used all her birthday money to buy instead of that Ginny Doll outfit complete with little magenta ice skates, just so she could play ball in the middle of Hartwell Lane with Ricky Rosenfeld, when she couldn't hit the broad side of a barn.

Billie found it hard to believe that she was sitting in the Banners' dark, airless dining room on her day off, which also happened to be one of the most beautiful days of the year, morning cobwebs on the grass having betokened fair weather, the rain finally over, and the river more or less back where it belonged, the mist evaporated, everything unnaturally bright, sparkling, radiant, a perfect day to take a long walk along the lake or canoe across it or just lie on the dock in the sun in her blue lawn chair, tempting fate, drinking a sugary tropical drink with a name like Skull Smasher.

"Billie?" George Mason prompted. "Are you with us?"

It was two in the afternoon, a clever choice in that it not only excluded people with real jobs and insufficient time on their hands to become the first-class meddlers key to the plan's success but also avoided the problem of food, though a little snack of some kind would certainly have helped mitigate the truly wretched decaf coffee Carl Banner was dispensing from an urn on the sideboard.

Answer, Billie told herself. Answer. "I guess I'm not sure," she said.

"Well then, what are you doing here?" Mrs. Quill swelled from her seat like a genie from its bottle.

"It's all right, Florence," said Glenda Banner, patting her down. "Billie hasn't lived in Varennes for as long as the rest of us, but she's a member of the St. Luke's flock just the same."

"Sir!" A small man with wild eyebrows and wearing a short-sleeved white dress shirt buttoned to the neck raised his hand.

George Mason nodded. "Russell?"

"Russell Mackey," the small man said. "I hope I'm not out of line, but I was under the impression that the flock was the very thing we were here to discuss. The St. Luke's flock. 'He that enters by the door is the shepherd of the sheep.' John, ten. I come from a long line of sheep farmers. From the Shetland Isles, if you must know, where everyone is born recognizing the value of a good sheepdog." He looked around the group with a pleased grin, as if he'd just scored a point.

"Thank you, Russell," Carl Banner said, scribbling on a notepad. "I couldn't have put it better myself."

What on earth were they talking about? There had been a Shetland sheepdog long ago living on Hartwell Lane in the house across from Billie's. Pepper, the sheepdog, who herded himself to an early grave, barking without cease and chasing everything that came within his ken: cars, falling leaves, shadows, ghosts. When she knew her mother wasn't watching, Billie used to let Pepper hump her, which she'd thought was his way of letting her know he liked her better than everyone else.

And then to her alarm she saw Carl Banner lean toward her confidingly across the table, the light leaking in over the sideboard turning his glasses into big yellow and black-rimmed lemur eyes. He smiled. "Billie? You were saying?"

"I'm sorry," Billie said. "I'm afraid I lost the thread."

"Wolves in sheep's clothing," prompted Florence Quill.

"Real dangers," Glenda Banner added. "We were talking about real dangers."

"That's right, Billie." James Trumbell bowed his head, shook it sadly from side to side. "As much as I hate to say it, this is a different world from the one we all grew up in. There are things abroad in the land, dangerous things, things that don't even bear thinking about."

"But we have to think about them," Glenda Banner said.

"We have to think about them," said James Trumbell.

"That freak," Glenda went on. "Warren Hommeyer let her into the choir. He made her first soprano."

"Otter sheep," said Russell Mackey. "The ones with the wee little legs that don't belong."

There was a quick knock on the front door, and before anyone had a chance to get up and see who it was, the door had flown open, discharging traffic noise and sunlight and Kathy Crockett into the house. Elegant, harried, wearing a beige linen sheath, Kathy strode right up to the edge of the arched entryway into the dining room and not a step farther, coming to a dramatic halt between the two snake plants. "I only have a few minutes," Kathy said. "It's nap time at the Home — they're all out like lights. How's it going?"

The mood in the room changed. Thickened, like that moment in chemistry class when you added the last crucial drop of something or other, and the separate elements finally and mysteriously came together, bonding in a sense of common purpose.

Conversation stopped. Everyone looked expectantly at Kathy, and Billie was interested to see that Carl Banner seemed simultaneously annoyed and relieved, his wife relaxed and cheerful, smiling as she handed round a plate of gingersnaps no doubt left over from Halloween. Of course, Billie thought — *Glenda* was the woman in the oil painting over the piano, though she found it impossible to imagine Glenda so much as removing her popcorn-stitch cardigan, let alone posing nude.

"Not bad," Carl Banner said. "Not bad at all, Kathy." He adjusted his glasses, read from his notepad: "'We the undersigned do hereby respectfully urge the timely eviction from the premises of St. Luke's church any and all persons hostile to or disruptive of our right to worship God as we see fit. At this time we urge our rector, Richard Jenkins, to act more forcefully on our behalf, rising to the occasion when his flock is threatened like a good sheepdog.'"

"Huh?" Kathy Crockett furrowed her brow and snuck another quick look at her watch. "I was with you right up to the end."

"It's as if he condones it," explained George Mason.

"He that enters by the door," James Trumbell added help-fully.

Kathy stared at him for a moment, hooked a sleek strand of hair behind one shell-like pearl-studded ear. "Whatever," she said, a locution she'd picked up from her daughter. Then she stuck out her hand. "Okay, give it here," she said. "If I'm not on the scene when they wake up, they're all on the phone to their lawyers. Do you have a pen?"

A flurry of signing followed, during which Billie tried to look involved while managing never to actually put her name on the paper. Three-fifteen, she thought. Not too late for a paddle, maybe even a quick dip. Check out the beavers' latest activity. Who needed Piet Zeebrugge? Piet Zeebrugge and his crummy Danish book bag. Kathy Crockett seemed headed for the front door — maybe Billie could sneak out in her wake.

But just as she was starting to do so, Kathy once again came to a halt, taking Billie's hand. "I don't know if you heard," she said, lowering her voice. "One of our neighbors was in a bad accident last night. Andrea Murdock."

"Andrea?" Billie said. "Oh no." She'd learned after Dougie died: the worse the news, the harder to decide which piece of it to deliver first. "What happened?"

"She drove into the back of another car," said Kathy. "On the County Road. They say she's in critical condition." She took another look at her watch. "Call me later, okay? I've got to get going. Good-bye everyone. Good-bye and good luck." Once again the door flew open, letting in sunlight and traffic noise, and then Kathy was gone.

"Mrs. Murdock," mused James Trumbell. "Didn't she bind those 1927 hymnals for us? She was such a nice woman."

"That's the one," said George Mason. He walked over to Billie, so close that she could feel his breath on her cheek.

"*Some* people," he said into Billie's ear, "might not say she's so nice."

"What?"

"Our host," George said, indicating Carl Banner, who stood in the kitchen doorway holding a plate of cookies. "Your friend accused our host of — well, let's say, *improper* behavior." George's breath was oddly milky, like a child's. "I know you're here to spy on us." He poked Billie's arm with his long pointy finger and added, "Don't worry, I'm not going to blow your cover. As long as you behave yourself."

"What are you talking about?"

"What do you think? I want you to sign the petition. You think I didn't notice?"

"I'm not a spy!" Billie said, louder than she intended, whereupon Mrs. Quill once again swelled like a genie from her bottle.

"You're a naughty girl," she said. "Very naughty indeed."

Everyone was watching, including nude Mrs. Banner and the dispassionate Indian maidens in the mahogany breakfront. George Mason crossed his thin arms over his narrow chest; Carl Banner sighed. James Trumbell nudged the plate of gingersnaps in her direction, giving her a quick little smile, and it suddenly occurred to Billie that he had a crush on her.

"I give up," she said, but she didn't mean it. Nor did she sign the petition. She merely snatched a gingersnap and raced from the house.

Outside the world was sun-dappled, and a sweet mild breeze was blowing. Andrea, Billie thought. Andrea Murdock. She paused for traffic at the corner of Main and Summer. The sidewalks were dry, but there was still a thin stream of rainwater in the gutters, and when she finally crossed the street, she could see how dark and wet the dirt looked in the flower beds outside the post office. Impatiens. Why did everyone plant impatiens? Petunias, too, with their petals like the skin of a dead person.

She'd parked in the lot where Main Street met Route 10, and she began walking briskly toward it. Walking briskly down Main Street toward the slowly descending sun, which was shining brightly in a cloudless sky above the traffic lights strung like big charms across the intersection. Walking, blinking. Past the deli, out of which strode a pair of teenage girls in cutoffs and sleeveless cotton blouses and flip-flops, who would have been exactly like normal teenage girls were it not for the impossibly elaborate hairdos — hairdos worthy of Marie Antoinette! — towering above their girlish heads. Past the overpriced used-clothing store where she thought she recognized one of the dresses in the window, the teal number with the gigantic lace collar — she could swear she'd seen it once on Mees Kipp's mother, Sophy.

Walking faster, past the bench in front of the library, where a third young woman in cutoffs and a sleeveless blouse and an even more elaborate hairdo sat reading. Tonight was prom night, of course.

How *dare* George Mason! How *dare* he!

A very unbecoming shade of blue, teal. Billie stuck the cookie in her mouth and began to chew when a shadow fell across her path and —

"Well, hi there," said Piet Zeebrugge.

In nineteenth-century Varennes, if your house was infested with rats, it was common practice to write the rats a letter telling them what you were planning to do to them if they failed to depart, where you wanted them to go (ideally to the house of someone you despised), and what route they ought to take to get there. You would write the letter on good paper made from linen rags, so it would last, and you would grease the letter with bacon fat, to both protect it and make it more attractive to the rats, and then you would ball it up and stick it into the rat hole.

Dear Rats, you would write, I have borne with you till I can bear with you no longer. Dear Rats, I cannot find words to express the horror I feel when I hear you gnawing on our trace corn while we sleep. Black devils with your black devil claws and your white devil teeth! Spirits of the bottomless pit, begone! Begone!

Helen Zeebrugge sat up late Wednesday night in her handsome English lounge chair in her room on the second floor of the Crockett Home, reviving this custom. She was using her expensive fine-wove stationery, next to impossible to obtain now that almost all correspondence was conducted electronically, but which Piet had managed to track down for her in the town's one depressing gifte shoppe, which would explain why the paper reeked of bayberry and vanilla. The smell drove Helen mad, but she figured it couldn't fail to attract the attention of Kathy Crockett, who not only went in for scented candles in a big way but also happened to be the very rat Helen hoped to trap.

"Dear Rat," Helen wrote, "I have endured your mean and petty ways long enough. I cannot find words to express the horror I feel when I hear your little feet squeaking down the hall toward my door, the scratching of your nails on my doorknob . . ."

Really, there *were* no words to express Helen's horror, and while *vengeance is mine, sayeth the Lord* had once been her firm belief, it seemed to her that nowadays evildoers always got away with murder, as if the world had deviated so grotesquely from God's original plan for it, like a watercolor turned first to mud and then to no color, to the end of color and light and hope, that He'd at last given up. Balled the world up, jammed it in one of those rat holes in the space-time continuum you were always hearing about on the news. Dear Rats, go to hell. The outer dark, the weeping and gnashing of teeth.

Where we live now, Helen thought, though you could be tricked into forgetting. You could be tricked by little things, the dawning of a new day for example, the latest chef (doomed already by his use of alarming and unfamiliar ingredients) producing basil-and-shiitake-mushroom omelettes for breakfast, followed by a leisurely walk with Janet Peake to the foot of the garden, where they'd whiled away the hour the moron from the Arts Council was inside strumming on his banjo, sitting outside in the gazebo, playing Ghost.

The sun had been shining brightly, the round white buds of the peonies along the back fence crawling with ants. Only yesterday Helen had watched Crockett frantically trying to pick them off, until she, Helen, explained that if it weren't for the ants, the peonies would never open. The peony buds had to feel those little feet walking around on them or they would become hard as rocks and die . . . And wasn't that a lesson for all of us? Crockett had replied. Really, the way that woman could take the simplest fact and transform it into a homily in nothing flat was truly amazing.

"P," Helen said to Janet, thinking of the pipe vine turning the gazebo to a rippling green tent. A beautiful day: the peonies getting ready to bloom, the irises already blooming. Ben, the handyman, was running the mower along the side of the building, and on the porch of the Locust Inn next door, a mother was reading aloud to her child. *SOME PIG!!!*

"L," Janet appended, swatting at a fly. "Crockett's problem is she never got over being teacher's pet. Abigail Andrews, fourth grade. I don't think her hand went down the entire year."

The mower approached; Helen could see the look of fierce concentration on Ben's face, as if he were computing an algorithm. "U," she said.

"What about me?"

"No, the letter."

When Janet laughed you could see how wonderful her teeth were: perfectly rectangular, practically translucent, small and perfect Ming teeth. Her tongue was also perfect, pink and small, like the tongue of a kitten lapping cream from a perfect Ming saucer, and for a moment Helen was so overcome with rage at the thought that a woman could have managed to keep her body in one piece for all of these years only to have it drop like a Ming saucer from the careless hands of Kathy Crockett onto the concrete floor of the exercise room that she could hardly catch her breath. This was how people had apoplectic seizures.

Because Crockett *knew* the treadmill wasn't working properly; it had been a "gift," which usually meant a piece of junk some relative decided to donate to the Home as a tax write-off, like the automatic bread machine that exploded one midnight while kneading anadama dough or the electric wheelchair with a mind of its own. Helen had overheard Ben telling Crockett the treadmill needed an adjustment before it would be safe enough to use, but as Crockett would have been quick to point out, she had a master's degree in sociology, whereas Ben hadn't even finished high school. The banjo player was just winding up with a sing-along chorus. "O my darlin', o my darlin', o my daaaarlin' Clementine, thou art lost and gone forever..." A roomful of women at death's door singing a song in honor of a girl who died young — it didn't bear thinking about. Crockett linked arms with Helen and Janet. "Come on, you two," she'd said, herding them out of the sunroom and into the elevator, where she'd pushed B, for Bowels of the Earth.

I should have stopped her, Helen thought. She was like a scientist with a brand-new maze to try out, and poor Janet the ideal subject, so agreeable, so game, so (literally) unable to stand up for herself.

Later, at dinner, everyone had been told "a little accident" had occurred, to squelch whatever rumors had been circulating since the surprising appearance in the front hall of two paramedics and a stretcher. "An exercise mishap," Crockett had actually had the nerve to call it, but Helen had seen Janet's face as they lifted her from the floor, the gray color of her skin, the look in her eyes, which was no look at all.

"Dear Rat," Helen wrote.

"If you knew as much as I do, you would run and hide. I will keep nothing to myself. I am preparing water to drown you, fire to roast you, cats to maul you."

Also a legal suit, Helen thought.

She'd tried calling the hospital, but since she'd made the mistake of being honest with the receptionist and telling her that she wasn't kin, she'd gotten nowhere. Janet's kin were probably on their way to Upper Valley Hospital, if not already there, but Helen had seen for herself how weary Janet became after each of their visits to the Home, how melancholy after one or the other of her sons deposited a kiss on her lucent brow and hightailed it out of her room, bored grandchildren in tow. Plus, her ex-husband was a worm.

Moonlight over the Locust Inn, black sky, twinkling stars. This used to be enough to make me happy, Helen thought, and she began to sob the way she had when she was a young girl and her heart was broken, the deep sobs of youth that well up out of the apparently bottomless black pit of what passes for utter hopelessness but which is nothing — *nothing* — compared with the dead hope of old age.

The traps had been blind set along the southern edge of Black Lake, partially submerged in the water near the beaver slide and camouflaged with rocks and mud. There were five of them, three to the left of the dam, two to the right, their steel jaws open wide and baited with young aspen boughs scraped to show their tender white insides — five traps just waiting to be sprung, just dying to snap down on any curious, hungry beaver that swam too close, holding it fast until it drowned. When Carla Fine had asked if that wasn't terribly cruel, Beau O'Brien had said, no, not really. The traps worked fast, he'd reassured her, and were much less cruel in the long run than the ones in which you caught the animal alive, drove it miles away to some other pond or lake, to some other ecosystem, only to let it get torn to pieces and eaten alive by the resident beaver population, beavers being only slightly less xenophobic than humans.

Now the men were going to check the traps, Henry Fine and Roy Diamond having persuaded Beau O'Brien to take them along with him, though he'd advised otherwise. "I still haven't gotten used to it," he said, "and I've been trapping since I was a boy. What you see, I mean."

A boy. Lorna Fine's long sallow face blushed bright red. In her book he had already kissed her — kissed Mary MacDonald that is. On the stone stairs leading to the beach, under the rowan tree. Conjurer's tree, tree of mystery. *Her* boy.

It was late Friday afternoon, and the workweek was finally over. Lorna's father had exchanged the linen suit he usually wore when he had to appear in court for a pair of madras plaid shorts and a T-shirt, whereas Mrs. Diamond's husband was still in his blue postal-worker uniform. "Don't even think about it," Carla Fine had said, when Lorna expressed what she hoped sounded like offhand interest in being included in the expedition. Then Carla had turned to Beau O'Brien, who was lounging back against the Fines' kitchen counter in a pair of cutoffs, his long tan legs crossed at the ankle with all the inbred elegance of a true man of the world, and explained that Lorna was the last person in the world who ought to be looking at dead beavers. She was so suggestible, Carla said, so sensitive. When she was six she hadn't been able to eat or sleep for days after watching a documentary about life on the Serengeti Plain.

"I think that's a nice quality in a person," Beau O'Brien said, and Sunny gave Lorna a quick jab in the ribs.

"Do the traps break their necks?" Mees asked. She'd only just arrived, slipping in her usual stealthy way through the porch door, and now stood smack in the middle of the kitchen, staring up at Beau, who towered above her.

"No," he said, clearly taken aback.

"I just wondered," Mees said, without taking her eyes off him.

It was so terrible to be stared at by Mees, as if you were being stared at by something condensed and inanimate, something full of occult meaning like a fetish. To be stared at by Mees was to feel as if your own life was utterly meaningless, though whatever judgment there was in the stare seemed not to come from Mees but from the place where meaning itself came from, immense, vigilant, indifferent.

The porch door sprang open again, slammed shut — Margaret trotted in, holding her plumed tail aloft. She'd been in this room once or twice before, but there'd never been so many bodies together in it, so much human excitement mixed with little bursts of something else. Not exactly danger, but on the verge. Margaret held her ears back, her nostrils open, making sure. There she was, that girl of hers! Also Buddy's girl, and the other one. Also many divine smells such as beaver, also bacon, also blood. Where to sniff first? The rule was: No crotches! But Margaret couldn't help herself.

"Hey, cut it out!" said Sunny, swatting at Margaret's nose. "Can't you make her stop?" she hissed, but it was obvious, even when Mees ordered Margaret to sit, whose side she was on.

Beau pushed himself off the counter, looked from one to the other of the two men, his hazel eyes sliding across the top of Lorna's head in the process. "You're going to have to do something with that dog of yours," he said, addressing Mees, though his eyes remained on Henry Fine, and Lorna was surprised to feel her adoration waver slightly, to feel the formerly boundless sea of it ripple for just a fraction of a second with disappointment. *That dog of yours.* It was almost as if Beau were relishing his chance to regain the upper hand, throwing his weight around like some stupid boy. "We can't have it following us to the lake," he explained sternly, covering the distance between the counter and the porch door in three long strides.

"Don't worry," Carla reassured him. "I'll make certain."

When you are ruled by curiosity, as Margaret was, you are rarely affronted. Even when a human woman fills a bowl with things you've never eaten before and puts it on the floor for you. You sniff the things, you push them around with your nose, you open your mouth and pick one up and close your mouth around it. If you don't like it you open your mouth and drop the thing back onto the floor. Practically good as new — no one will ever know the difference.

"*She*," said Mees. "Not *it*."

She made her private kissing noise and Margaret came to her side, wagging her tail.

"Margaret hates bananas," Mees said.

The men set out through the side yard along the empty mill-race, Beau in the lead, closely followed by Henry Fine, with Ron Diamond bringing up the rear. "Did you hear the one about the man?" Henry Fine was saying. "The man who wanted to know the meaning of life?" If it weren't for the beavers there would have been a torrent of bright water leaping and shining in the late-afternoon sun, but as it was — even despite all the recent rain — there was only a thin muddy trickle, scarcely enough to keep the bed moist or the tadpoles alive.

From the porch, where they were sucking on Carla Fine's homemade juice pops and pretending to lounge in Henry Fine's homebuilt Adirondack chairs, the three girls could see Mr. Diamond wildly flail his arms, swatting at every pale exposed inch of himself as he disappeared into the alder swale at the edge of the Fines' property. Blackfly season used to begin on Memorial Day and end on the Fourth of July, but that was before a hole had been ripped in the heavens, letting the hell-fire loose. Now the flies arrived on Mother's Day, though they were still at their worst toward evening.

"Yuck," Sunny said, as Lorna smeared herself with fly dope. "You smell like ham." In the Fine household, fly dope was the repellent of choice, whereas the Crocketts preferred a highly perfumed skin softener that obviously smelled as repulsive to blackflies as it did to Lorna. Mees, on the other hand, claimed immunity.

"I do not," Lorna said.

"I think Lorna smells good," Mees said, twisting to look over her shoulder and into the kitchen. "Like a boardwalk." Margaret was curled in a ball under the table, returning her look, albeit sadly, the white tip of her beautiful plumed tail resting delicately atop her nose.

"A boardwalk? When have you ever been on a boardwalk?"

"In Brighton," Mees said. "To visit Gran. Before we moved here."

Sunny sighed. It was a sigh meant to be heard — her mother's sigh, in fact — and would have signaled to an adult woman, had one been there to listen, a girl's subtle, all but imperceptible, shift of alignment toward womanhood. Some girls put up less of a fight than others. Some embrace the shift, opening like flowers. "Just wait," Sunny said to Mees. "Wait till you get your period."

Lorna, who hated this subject more than any other subject in the world, leaned over and looked at her toes, which were very long and flexible like fingers. She picked up a cigarette butt. Who had been here, smoking? No one smoked anymore, least of all the people who came to visit her parents. She stuck the butt in her shorts' pocket. A clue of some sort? But what was the mystery?

"My period," said Mees, and burst out laughing.

Inside the kitchen the radio came on — a terse male voice speaking quickly, trying to make himself heard above the sound of sirens.

"If we don't leave right away," Lorna said, "we'll be too late."

"Too late for what?" Mees said, still doubled over laughing.

"Besides," said Sunny. As usual she was following her own train of thought, sleek and silver and impenetrable, an express train, a Metroliner, shooting through the landscape. "It's bad to chase after a guy," Sunny told Lorna. "You've got to play hard to get. Then he has to chase after you." Her advice notwithstanding, she hauled herself out of the chair and stretched, displaying her newly developed body parts like credentials. "Of course, if a person wanted to walk another person home, I don't see what would be so wrong with that, do you? And if a person wanted to take a little detour on the way, I don't see what would be so wrong with that, either."

They set off across the yard, arms linked, their shadows sprawling long and thin and identical, all the way over the bright green lawn to where the tops of their heads hit the far bank of the millrace. Mrs. Diamond was sitting on her front porch with Doozie in her lap and drinking beer from a can. Mrs. Diamond, just sitting there in a white sundress, surrounded by hanging baskets full of purple petunias, doing nothing except drinking beer! They had to wait at the Dump Road while a log truck came rattling through, taking the turn for Canton much too fast, followed by a Payless cab, of all things, also speeding. Pay *less*. Merely cheap, not free.

"That looked like Mr. Murdock," Sunny said, breaking the link with Lorna to shade her eyes. "In back."

Everyone knew he'd been fetched home from the far north because his wife was in a coma, though naturally many rumors were circulating, both about his reason for going north in the first place, as well as about his wife's condition.

"The poor man," Lorna said, pointedly relinking with Sunny.

"It was almost exactly a month ago we used her phone," Sunny said. "She looked fine."

Mees unlinked her arm from Sunny's and came to a halt. "Of course she looked fine. It's not like she was *sick*. It's not like you can tell by looking at someone that they're going to have an *accident*."

"Hey," Lorna said. "Hey, Measle. Calm down."

"What would be the *point?*" Mees said. But she too relinked her arm with Sunny's, and the three of them kept walking toward the lake.

Three girls, arms linked, shadows misleadingly alike — Lorna had been right earlier when she'd said it was too late. Though she hadn't been right in the way she'd meant it. Of course it wasn't too late to catch up with the men. The girls could see them through the alder branches, the lake water sparkling golden-blue behind them like a backdrop, Beau O'Brien squatting on his lean tan haunches, Mr. Fine and Mr. Diamond stooping above him, all of them regarding whatever it was they were looking at with the utmost seriousness.

No, what was too late was any hope of staying linked. The friendship they'd formed when they had first met one another in kindergarten — three little girls drawn together by a mysterious alchemical process involving pheromones and geography as well as a shared love of their teacher, Mrs. Mahoney, and a shared terror of the milk they were given to drink at snack time, which was never cold enough and tasted waxy like the pint containers it came in — this friendship was about to come unlinked forever. Sunny's arms, with their downy golden hair, with their smell of perfumed skin softener and their strong, competent hands, Sunny's arms were about to let go of Lorna's long skinny arms, of Mees's short ones, forever.

Not quite yet. But soon.

It almost always happens this way.

In order to approach the men, they had to let go of one another.

"Gentlemen, we have company," said Mr. Diamond, the first to notice the girls and, not being a father, not quite sure how to handle the situation.

"Jesus Christ." Mr. Fine wiped his hands on his knees and straightened. "Lorna, what did your mother tell you?" His face had an unwholesome tint to it that didn't seem entirely due to the dappled greenish light that dripped onto him from the alders.

Beau continued doing whatever he was doing. "Get them out of here," he said, and Lorna could see a streak of blood on his cheek.

She could see the streak of blood and smell the lake, the particular smell it gave off near shore, of frog spawn and algae and rot and mud. Pinpoints of sun were jumping crazily off the water, arrows of sun shooting through the alder leaves and hitting her all up and down her left side. Not a breath of wind anywhere and blackflies everywhere. Buzzing, buzzing — and then all at once there was a horrible dull clank as the sprung trap's huge teeth bit down on themselves.

"Whatever," Sunny said, backing up into a shrub. "Oops," she said, "excuse me," and Lorna could hear her draw a deep breath to regain her composure before breaking into a run, taking her golden hair and her golden breasts and her golden pragmatic brain with her. "See you tomorrow?" Sunny called over her shoulder. "Oh, wait, I forgot? I have rehearsal . . ."

"*Hasta la vista,* baby." Mees's voice seemed to be coming from deep within the thicket, but she was nowhere to be seen.

Meanwhile Lorna crept closer. What was she thinking? But she couldn't stop herself. Lorna was fated to need to know the truth about the people she gave her heart to, which is why she was also fated to live most of her life alone. It's hard to mate with another living creature who refuses to let you dissemble from time to time. Unless you're an animal, that is.

The beaver was lying on its back in the muck. It was bloated, its belly distended, one of its forepaws folded protectively over its chest, the other resting in the muck near its tail, the empty armhole where it had once been attached still oozing water and blood. The beaver's eyes were open and translucent like marbles.

Lorna looked across the beaver and straight into the hazel eyes of Beau O'Brien, who looked straight back at her, frankly, with a glimmer of interest, and for a moment — for a fraction of a second even briefer than the one that had passed earlier in the kitchen when she'd felt that swift ripple of disappointment — Lorna felt something she'd never felt before. Her legs weakened; she thought she would swoon.

"I warned you," Beau said cheerfully, returning to his work, springing a second trap, releasing another dense, waterlogged body. A kit this time, born the previous spring.

He was too preoccupied to see Mees standing off to his left, her dark little eyes shut, her fists clenching, unclenching at her sides. Talking to herself.

"What do you do with them now?" Henry Fine asked.

Beau shrugged. "Their pelts are worthless this time of year. Haven't bushed out yet." He tapped the kit with his toe. "It's up to you, really. You paid for 'em, they're yours."

In the far north, the world is shaped like a hill and floats upon the water. Fingers of sun break through the thick canopy of clouds, pointing at animals tucked in the tundra like prizes. In order of importance: a caribou, a bear, a beaver, an otter. A fox, trotting through the cotton grass and yellow poppies, heading for her den when *snap!* goes the trap. This is her destiny. In the far north, the animals have souls, and their souls are reasonable. Treat the possessor of the soul with respect, and there will be more foxes in your future. Whereas profane the fox after killing her, throw her bones to a dog, and word will get out. No more foxes for you. You will freeze, you will starve. You will be as good as dead, and your own soul will go out like a spark, drifting black and lifeless across the tundra, perhaps as far as the distant land where the caribou live under an immense white tent made of their own hair.

But what does that mean, distant? It's still part of the same world, only farther off. It's the place where the caribou come from, mysterious yet actual, like those places in the body where fluids originate, the islets of Langerhans, for instance. Only in a season when the caribou hunt goes poorly does a northern hunter find himself wondering what exactly is going on in that distant white tent, though he'd never dream of going there to find out. Cast-off antlers form an impenetrable wall for miles around it — you might just as well try reaching through your rib cage to get a look at your heart.

Of course no one in Varennes thought the world was a hill floating on water, nor had a single one of them aside from Daniel Murdock ever seen a caribou except in a movie or a zoo, and when Daniel did see one — gazing down at him with an oddly doting expression on its face as he knelt brushing dirt from a Paleo-Indian thigh bone — he certainly didn't stop to wonder where the caribou came from.

Just as Beau O'Brien hadn't bothered elevating the beaver kit's skull on a stick or returning her bones and her eyes and the piece of gristle behind her paunch to the lake, as a mark of tribute to her soul. He'd never done anything like that, and he'd been trapping beaver for years. When you kill a beaver in twenty-first-century Varennes and you want to live to do more trapping, you aren't expected to eat the beaver in a special bowl made of bark or abstain from the use of a knife. In twenty-first-century Varennes, you aren't expected to pay for a transgression that belongs to another world. Or you are, but only if you're at war with it.

Though how could they be so different, the rules governing souls?

Space and time are made out of strings the universe conceived when it was still a baby, little and fierce. The strings wove together; they collided with other strings, releasing even smaller strings, which were the new dimensions, humming, humming, humming. If a human being had been there to hear that music, it would have killed him. Eventually the strings made waves, some smaller than the smallest thing we've discovered so far, some greater than the distance between our world and the farthest star. The fox languished, her leg caught, bleeding to death.

Then the dry land appeared.

According to Helen Zeebrugge, the intensive-care unit of the Upper Valley Hospital was situated on the fourth floor because it was closest to heaven. You didn't want the souls of the newly dead drifting through the nursery or, worse, the psychiatric ward. The emergency room was different — it had to be on the ground floor for two reasons. One: the elevators were fatally slow. Two: it was closest to hell.

The skinny middle-aged nurse who'd come to check Janet Peake's vital signs tolerated these reflections with good humor, despite the fact that she found them offensive on both religious and scientific grounds.

"You'd be surprised how few we actually lose up here," the nurse said to Helen, tossing back her yellow corkscrew curls and sticking a thermometer in Janet's ear. When had this practice started?

"I guess that's good news," Janet murmured.

The nurse removed the thermometer and smiled at it tenderly. The hair was ridiculous but seemed to be her own.

"You're very thin," she said. "Kitchen tells me you're not eating."

"Kitchen?" Helen said. "*Kitchen* tells you?" She put the crossword puzzle book she'd brought for Janet on the bed tray, beside her untouched supper.

"I'm not very hungry," Janet explained.

Which was true: ever since she'd awakened in this strange hard bed on this plastic-coated mattress in this windowless room surrounded by gauges and dials and clear bags of liquid suspended from silver trolleys, Janet had had no appetite whatsoever. At one point not long after she'd been admitted, she'd heard Crockett telling someone how much she, Janet, loved fish sticks, and if she hadn't been so doped up, so, frankly, at the very threshold of death's door, she would have burst out laughing.

In intensive care the visiting hours were less flexible than in maternity, and the ancient volunteers who manned the reception desk were unbudgeable on this point. Intensive-care visiting hours also didn't overlap with gift-shop hours, since heart-shaped balloons and Beanie Babies and boxed candy and arrangements of unnaturally dyed carnations tended to elude the interest of the critically ill, who were too busy studying the shifting shoreline deep within themselves, looking for the best place to embark from it in their little boats, to even say hello.

Andrea Murdock, for instance — after depositing Helen on a chair at Janet's bedside, Billie Carpenter had tried getting into Andrea Murdock's room but had been turned away at the door by an attractive young male nurse wearing a tiny diamond earring and trendy dark-rimmed spectacles. Mrs. Murdock wasn't to be disturbed, he informed her, but he'd see to it that she got Billie's bouquet, which he deemed uncommonly nice. On the other hand, Mrs. Peake's condition seemed to have stabilized, though there was some question about whether she'd be able to return to the Crockett Home immediately, if ever. When you were long past menopause and fractured your pelvis, as Mrs. Peake had, it automatically aged you by at least ten years, and that wasn't even taking into account the damage the Parkinson's had wrought.

A high-pitched beeping noise started up at the other end of the hall, and the young nurse excused himself. Then the elevator doors opened, letting out two doctors, followed by Billie's neighbor Henry Fine, of all people, who consulted the palm of his hand like a soothsayer, mouthed something — a room number no doubt — and headed around the nurses' station in her direction. Walking on the tips of his toes as if he were sneaking up on her or had been with the ballet in a past life.

"Billie," Henry said, "what are you doing here?"

"The same as you, I guess," she said, and then, because he was already staring past her, no longer interested and ready to move on, she added, "I came to visit Andrea Murdock. But you can't get in her room."

If Billie were pretty would Henry's expression be different? Even her late husband, Dougie, had often failed to find her interesting, though he'd loved her dearly. She'd never doubted that for a minute, even though everything else about Dougie had turned out to be a lie. He wasn't even named Doug.

"In fact, I came to see Mrs. Peake," Henry Fine said, inclining his head toward Janet's door.

"How do *you* know Janet?" Billie asked, and Henry shook his head. He was almost completely bald, balder by far than Piet Zeebrugge and not only swarthy by nature but also unfashionably tanned, his eyebrows pitch-black and tilting slightly toward the bridge of his nose, giving him the appearance of a stage devil.

"I'm here in an official capacity," Henry explained, holding his briefcase aloft.

Together they walked into the room, where Janet Peake was still lying on her back, though her eyes were now closed and her lips parted as she softly, musically, snored. Meanwhile

Helen was busy eating Janet's mashed potatoes and working on one of her crossword puzzles.

"Maybe we should just leave her?" Billie whispered, but Henry Fine was tapping on Janet's arm in an empty place between the hospital bracelet and the intravenous bandage. "Mrs. Peake?" He cleared his throat, tapped again as if on a door.

"Ma," Janet said. "Ma."

She was trying to catch the attention of a tall young woman wearing around her neck a skinny brown fur piece with shoe-button eyes, some kind of weasel-like animal furiously biting its own tail, meaning the young woman had turned her back, was walking away. No, not walking. Running. It was Janet's mother, and she was running down a long flight of red-carpeted stairs, busy doing something with her hands, her arms. Evening gloves! *Ma!* Janet could smell the heavy animal smells of attar of rose, of kidskin, and could see how the hilarious cartoon face of the full moon completely filled the round window above the landing, pushing against it, making it bulge. *Get back in bed this instant, Jennie! Get back in bed or I'm going to have to call the paper hanger!* But my name is Janet, Janet tried to tell her.

She opened her eyes, gasping. Nothing like this had ever happened: Janet's mother had rarely gone anywhere and would never have forgotten her daughter's name. She'd been a good mother, an exemplary mother — too attentive, if anything. Nor had the front staircase ever been carpeted in red. The fur piece was familiar, though. And where had these three people come from?

"Mrs. Peake," Henry Fine was saying. "I didn't mean to startle you." He looked around, making room on the bed tray for his briefcase. Then he pushed the call button for the nurse and stood back, staring into space with his arms crossed, waiting.

"I don't think we're supposed to do that except in an emergency," Billie said.

"So?" Henry continued to stare into space until the nurse appeared — the same attractive male nurse who'd steered Billie away from Andrea's door. "Do you think we could have some chairs in here?" Henry asked with excessive, ironic politesse.

Well, at least they had in common a desire to sit.

How close and still Janet's room was, how clammy and almost hot, despite the air-conditioning. From time to time certain machines sprang into action: the blood-pressure cuff, for example, would suddenly decide to tighten itself around Janet's upper arm and an attendant gauge would beep, or the inflatable cushion used to prevent bedsores would suddenly start puffing and puffing and puffing itself up like the wolf trying to blow down the house around the three little pigs and then, just as suddenly, let out a huge sigh and go perfectly flat. Henry Fine once again consulted his palm and also let out a sigh, less dramatic than the cushion's.

"Okay," he said. "Okay. I guess I'll have to do this standing. Mrs. Peake, my name is Henry Fine. Your son contacted me; I'm an attorney."

"Go away," Janet said. She closed her eyes; there was nothing else she could do, really. "Tell Edmund to stop pestering me." She opened one eye and took a quick peek at Henry. "It *is* Edmund, isn't it? Philip would never dare. Tell Edmund to sit tight. All he has to do is wait. Tell him I'll be dead soon enough, but until then what I do with my money is none of his business."

An enormous woman stormed into the room clutching two folding chairs, set them up with a rapidity that could only have been born of rage, and stormed out again.

Was it catching? Billie suddenly wanted to kill Henry Fine, who was snapping open his briefcase and removing a yellow legal pad and a silver fountain pen before taking a seat. A PalmPilot *and* a fountain pen — so technologically advanced and yet so quaintly old-fashioned, Henry Fine, like a farmer sitting to milk his herd of cloned cows at a milking stool.

"I think there's been some misunderstanding," Henry said, uncapping the pen, preparing to write. "Your son hired me to look into the unfortunate event that landed you where you are now."

"Birth?" said Helen.

He missed everything. Sitting there on the beige folding chair with his legs spread apart because his thighs were too thick to cross. "The events of Wednesday last," he prompted. "When Mrs. David Crockett suggested you join her in the exercise facility."

"David," Helen said.

"What are you laughing at?" Henry asked.

"Nothing," Billie replied.

Meanwhile, at the other end of the hall, Andrea Murdock was busy binding a book. It was the size of a twin bed, and she was using a sheet of vellum that had been folded many more times than the six we're told is the limit for folding a sheet of *anything,* whether gossamer thin or grossly thick, a fairy's wing or an elephant's hide. The vellum had been folded more than a hundred times into a cube so small Andrea could barely see it, though it was also so heavy she could barely lift it, complicating her task. *We're going to need to use the winch,* someone said, and Andrea tried to warn them that the winch would be a terrible mistake, given the condition of the vellum, which already showed signs of a violent form of red decay — the least pressure, the least touch of a fingertip, and it would flake into dust.

Besides, it was still alive, she could hear it bleating. If she could just unfold it, she would let it go. It could scamper off, join its brothers and sisters, sheep, goats, whatever. She began picking at the edge of the cube, peeling it back, little by little. *We're losing her,* someone said. *Andrea. Mrs. Murdock, can you hear me?*

It was very hard work; for a while she stopped breathing, which made things easier.

And in any case the cube wasn't vellum after all. It was her old self, Andy Aikman!

All throughout the intensive-care ward there was a lot of similar activity going on, much of it involving situations where scale ran counter to expectation: there was a wedding dress in Room 413 too big to see in its entirety, and it had to be got into before the guests gave up and left the church, as well as a pair of shoes too small to be seen at all. In Room 400 there was a wave that kept growing taller and taller and taller, growing and growing until it had taken up all the room there was in the world and would keep on growing until it had been coaxed into a cobalt blue eyecup.

Humans can't live without projects.

Police Log — Sunday, June 15

3:11 a.m. Bag of mail found outside North Street garage.

4:30 a.m. Bear reported in Terrace Street yard.

6:08 a.m. Neighbor pounding on wall at Summer Street residence.

8:45 a.m. Male in jeans and vest relieving himself on church porch.

10:02 a.m. Woman sweeping in rotary.

10:13 a.m. Sheepdog barking for an hour on Skyline Drive.

12:47 p.m. Gray tiger cat "Gigi" missing from Summer Street residence.

2:15 p.m. Armed robbery at Route 10 Quik Mart.

4:50 p.m. Very disturbed female reported at River Street business.

7:01 p.m. Damage to flower boxes outside post office.

9:30 p.m. Accident reported on Canton Road.

11:22 p.m. Gunshots reported on French Hill.

Mees Kipp was sitting in the heart of the woods at the base of the smallest of the Five Erratics, her favorite, a perfect round ball that even if you leaned against it wouldn't start rolling. Margaret lay at her side, her head in Mees's lap, panting hard following a fruitless chase after a porcupine. They didn't play fair, porcupines, climbing trees. *Tell me!* Mees said, and Margaret rolled her dark brown eyes, making white crescent moons at their bottoms. *You have to tell the rules!* Mees folded her hands and bowed her head. *Please, Jesus.*

She knew He was close by: the trees were trees, the ferns were ferns. The squirrels were squirrels, the birds, birds. A very soft wind was blowing through her hair, touching her scalp, which was a part of her body she usually wasn't aware of. This was always how it happened when He appeared. The sky was blue, also it was the sky.

"What is it like?" Lorna kept asking Mees; but it wasn't *like* anything.

"Stop asking," Mees would reply, scowling, kicking at what she took to be the nearest inanimate object, which often turned out to be a human shin. "Just open your eyes," she'd tell Lorna. "Shut up."

Mees Kipp, so small and dense and tempestuous — you might think she was the least spiritually evolved child imaginable, the least likely candidate for such a gift. The truth is, she couldn't even remember when she'd first put it to use, except in the way we remember events in our lives that have been reported to us by older family members, stories no different really from *Alice in Wonderland* or *Mary Poppins,* despite the fact that the central character has our name. Mees had been three years old at the time, an unexceptional child, an average child in fact, learning to walk and talk a little late, though not so late as to cause alarm, her first word, predictably, "Mommy," unlike her older sister, Mersey, who'd uttered an entire sentence and then never shut up. Both sisters had been named for rivers, their father being an avid kayaker. He died somewhere off an island in the Outer Hebrides that wasn't even on a map.

But the first time Mees exercised her gift, Trevor Kipp was still very much alive and had taken his family to England for Easter to visit his mother, who lived by herself in a quaint stone cottage not far from the sea, where she spent most of her waking hours reading the Bible and knitting sweaters for those less fortunate than herself, which according to Sophy Kipp had to be a truly immense population once you took into account not only the great number of sweaters but also the very high esteem in which old Mrs. Kipp held herself.

The trip hadn't been a success: Sophy was a rabid atheist and too nervous for needlework, and she'd found herself hard-pressed to get along with her mother-in-law, deeply resenting the fact that she'd forced them to get out of their none-too-comfortable beds and walk to church at a truly ungodly hour on Easter Sunday, after which there was no egg hunt or baked ham or canned peach trifle or *any*thing, really, to commemorate the day aside from having had to stand and kneel and sit and kneel and stand and kneel and sip some dreadful wine in a dark cold building that reeked of lilies. It was as if Sophy were bracing herself in advance, devising a mood equal to the terrible loss she was to sustain only two years later, an elaborate fortress with flags of many colors snapping in the breeze at the turrets — so beautiful, Sophy, the opposite of stone, with her river of black hair and her moist dark eyes and her skin like milk.

Mersey took after her mother, whereas Mees took after her father, at least insofar as her brushlike black hair was concerned and her sturdy physique. She loved to swim; she could stay underwater almost as long as a beaver. Also, she loved her grandmother, who'd once gathered Mees onto her lap when she was fuming because Mersey wouldn't play with her and informed her that after God made the world He gave us Jesus, so that He, God, and we, the world, wouldn't be lonely. Jesus was the vine, and we were the vine's branches, her grandmother explained. We were that close to Him, and when we bore fruit, it was His body and blood that gave it life. Then her grandmother taught her a prayer, which Mees learned by heart and which she would recite every night for the rest of her life — or at least until *that* life no longer mattered. *Keep us, Lord Jesus, as the apple of your eye. Hide us under the shadow of your wings. Amen.* Her grandmother also gave her a Bible that closed with a zipper and had colored pictures in it, but the Bible didn't come till later. DAD, Mees printed on the page marked *DEATHS*.

After church and Easter dinner, which had turned out, amazingly, to be macaroni and cheese, and which they'd eaten at noon at the kitchen table on mismatched plates that Sophy Kipp later told them were worth a king's ransom, old Mrs. Kipp said she thought she'd like a "lie-down" and began to head upstairs in that very slow way of the very old, almost as if she were dragging the banister and the attached steps down to her own level rather than rising to meet them.

"At least let's take the girls to the boardwalk," Sophy said, her voice louder than Mees thought was nice or even polite. "It's Easter, for Christ's sake!"

An early Easter, that year — barely the end of March, and the afternoon sky was colorless and swarming with thin gray clouds, a cold wind bringing with it from across the Channel intermittent handfuls of sharp little raindrops, squalling gulls, the smell of creosote and bilge. Despite the weather, though, the Kipps were hardly alone on the boardwalk, and like them, most of the other families strolling there were still dressed in the clothes they'd worn to church. God may have fallen into disfavor in the latter years of the twentieth century, our feeling of abandonment and wounded pride having turned our need to worship something, anything, back on our ceaselessly busy, endlessly acquisitive selves, but old habits die hard. The new spring outfits, the uplifting hymns, the promise of rebirth — what was not to like about church at Easter? Besides, as Sophy Kipp was quick to remind them, Easter was originally a pagan festival, named for a heathen goddess.

All along the boardwalk there were vendors selling souvenirs, ice lollies, balloons, T-shirts. Sophy and Trevor Kipp walked holding hands, her bad mood a thing of the past the minute she shut the door of her mother-in-law's house behind her. Now, even though the sky remained overcast, it was as if the sun shone; Sophy thought she wasn't so very different from the teenage girls stopping in full sight of everyone to French kiss their spotty boyfriends. "What's got into *you*?" Trevor had asked, but of course he didn't really want an answer. "Wait for your sister," Sophy called after Mersey, who had gone racing on ahead.

They finally caught up with the girls near the entrance to the Ferris wheel, between a booth where a toothless old man sat crouched over a sewing machine, stitching names onto hats, and a crate full of baby chicks dyed all the colors of the rainbow, presided over by a handsome young man. The chicks had been marked down, since it was too late to buy one for Easter morning — Mersey was making a great show of her delight, squatting to run her fingertips over the tiny soft bodies and then suddenly standing, sending her bright curtain of hair into intoxicating motion. "Oh please? Oh please?" she begged, and Sophy knew what her daughter really wanted wasn't a lime-green chick, but the vendor himself, with his blond hair and blue eyes and a tattoo of a death's-head on his biceps.

Mees meanwhile had plunked herself down on the board-walk in front of the crate, her hands planted on either side of her stout little body, her stout little legs stuck out straight ahead. She was yet to make known her love of the color pink, and so was wearing a yellow dress appliquéd with daisies, and held a pair of wax lips upside-down between her teeth.

According to the family story, Mees's attention had been caught by a lavender chick near the front of the crate which wasn't cheeping and marching about like the other chicks in that strangely heavy-footed way of infant poultry but had top-pled over onto its side and was perfectly silent, its eyes tight shut and with a large black ant crawling across its breast. "Oh no! The poor thing!" Mersey cried when she saw what her sister was looking at. "Is it dead?"

Mees didn't answer, merely screwed her own eyes shut and leaned in closer. "Does the little girl need help?" asked a plump woman wearing the white cap and dark blue cloak of a profes-sional nurse. "Her color doesn't look good," the woman ex-plained, but just as she was reaching down to feel Mees's forehead, and the young man was reaching into the crate to remove the dead chick, Mees jerked away her head. "Don't!" she yelled, the wax lips popping from her mouth like a cork.

The surprising thing is that both the nurse and the young man stopped in their tracks or, as Trevor Kipp would later amend, maybe not so surprising given the way his three-year-old daughter tended to take command. You didn't cross Mees — that was a family joke.

Everything stopped: the Ferris wheel, the sewing machine, the chatter of passersby. The squalling of the gulls. A cloud. A wave. The pole of the heavens stood still; the lavender chick opened its eyes. It got up, puffed out its feathers. It opened its little yellow beak and said *cheep,* immediately following which the world went back to normal, whatever that means. "Hats all around!" Trevor Kipp decreed. The Ferris wheel inched forward a notch. The waves smashed against the pilings. Things moved onward in their course. *Miss,* stitched the toothless old man. *Mercy. Sofa. Trevor.* You couldn't ask him to tear out what he'd written.

"He's too old," Sophy said. "Too shaky," added Mees. "What lies quaking at the bottom of the ocean?" Trevor said. "Give up? Give up? A nervous wreck."

Years went by. The hats became another family joke, including the fact that for some reason the old man got *Trevor* right. Mersey, who refused to throw anything away, still had hers hanging on her closet door, though she never wore it; Sophy's became, briefly, a favorite article of apparel until it got stolen. Mees's claim that the wind blew hers off her head was a lie; Sophy knew she kept it hidden under her mattress.

But was the Chick and the Dead, as Trevor liked to refer to it, merely another family joke? They'd tended to treat it that way, even Mees herself, eventually arriving at a plausible explanation. The unfortunate chick had been suffering from toxic shock due to the lavender dye, and the fact that it chose that precise moment to open its eyes and stand was nothing more than a coincidence. If the young man hadn't pronounced it a miracle, and if the nurse hadn't decided to faint, that would have been the end of it. A simple coincidence, and nothing more.

And yet for the next year or so, when she was about to fall asleep at night, Mees would sometimes get caught up in thinking about the hideous snarl of black thread the bobbin left on the underside of her hat. *Find the loose end,* a voice would say, and the snarl would catch. There would be a spark, as abrupt and infinitesimal and short-lived as a dust speck catching sun.

Jesus Jesus Jesus, Mees said. She was sitting on the damp cool earth in the shade cast by the erratic, Margaret's nose cupped in the palm of her hand. Wet nose, breathing nose — it was impossible for Mees to keep her fingers out of the noseholes.

You couldn't do anything, Jesus said. He came to sit beside her, shifting the weight of the light, letting His breath enter the woods and stirring the trees from their crowns to their roots. *Your father was too far away. They never found his body.*

That was the rule: you had to have a body. Even Jesus Himself, deposited in Joseph of Arimathea's rock tomb with His legs and arms broken, His lungs collapsed, His right flank slit wide — the Resurrection would never have worked if there hadn't been a body. The body was the point. In the tomb all opening began, for whereas pure spirit can do whatever it wants, drifting among clouds or diving to the very bottom of the ocean where the bones of the drowned make their melancholic music, once the spirit has taken up residence in a body, it's stuck there until the body lets it go, which it only does reluctantly, since once it has done so, the body's dead.

What about those beavers? Mees asked.

In the picture in the Bible her grandmother gave her, Jesus was a slender bearded man standing in a tempest-tossed boat, though over time Mees had come to think of Him as being more like her father, less insubstantial, less willowy, yet with a similarly kind, watchful expression on His face. Seated in the boat, not standing, the twin-bladed paddle lightly balanced in his hands, dripping saltwater back where it had come from. He was in the eye of the storm.

He *was* the eye.

Of course these days the psychological explanation trumps all others, with the scientific explanation running a close second. If your father drowns when you are five years old, a wound is inflicted on the psyche. If a man stops breathing, at some point he is pronounced dead. The question of measurement remains; you might even say that the ability to measure, to count heartbeats, to assign pattern only reinforces the mystery.

Margaret had no inkling of Jesus' presence, though despite the blackflies buzzing around her head, landing to bite the pink silk insides of her ears, she seemed unusually calm. Midday — all around them the woods were dark and cool, silvery hemlocks climbing the hillside to Adder Ridge, spilling shade into the valley like dark, cool water. All around them the smell of moss and dirt, and faintly, faintly, from high above, the smell of cut grass. A tractor engine getting loud, louder, impossibly noisy, then softer, soft, a whisper, a memory. High above on Adder Ridge the sun was shining. Ellen Fair's hired man was making the first cutting of hay, the sun beating down on him, turning his neck red. Making hay while the sun shines. Steering the tractor around and around the field, leaving behind a wide swath of mown hay and with it the occasional beheaded woodchuck.

Okay, Mees conceded, there had to be a body. But how were you supposed to choose among them? There were millions of bodies in the insect world alone, all the blackflies and ants and the little green caterpillars that hung from their invisible thread like question marks, and who knew what else she was in the process of crushing to death or suffocating under her butt at that very instant? Leafhoppers? Ticks? Those tiny black worms that curled themselves into perfect tight spirals? Did it matter how long ago their spirit had departed? Also, what about severed body parts? Worse yet, eaten?

Mees recalled being told by Trudy O'Hara, a Catholic girl who had recently moved to Varennes, that if there was a nuclear war and you lived at ground zero, your body would turn to vapor, and your soul would vaporize with it, leaving you with no way to get to heaven. That was why Trudy's parents had left Washington, D.C.

It wasn't exactly an elbow in the ribs — you couldn't exactly feel Him. But Jesus was like a boy sometimes. *Vaporize,* He said. He found some words funny.

Bone unto bone in joints, sinew, nerves, flesh and skin and hair thereon . . .

The tractor stopped, sputtered, started up again. A woodpecker began drumming on a nearby tree.

It's not your choice, Measle, He said. *It's never your choice. There was nothing you could do. The beavers were out of your hands. Likewise the fowl of the air and the creatures that swim in the sea, wild beasts and four-footed cattle of the field, weasels, too, and mice . . .*

It was just Mees and Margaret. Just Mees and Margaret and — Mees couldn't quite believe her eyes, so she rubbed them the way people did in movies — Dad. Dad waving from a tiny door. The quilt turned down in his beautiful blue and gold room.

*Tues April 2 — At home. Snowed and blowed all day. Sewed on
my print. Have not felt the best.*

*Wed April 3 — At home sewed on my print. Ma read to me out of
book "Fighting Joe."*

*Thurs April 4 — At home sewed on my print dress. Went in the
afternoon to Mrs Corners made a call. Still dont feel the best.*

*Fri April 5 — At home sewed on my pink apron. Wrote to V a long
letter.*

Sat April 6 —

At home. Andrea Murdock was at home, sitting by the
kitchen window of the Fair homestead, writing in her diary.
Snowing tonight. Cold. Oh how lonely. Her thin little wrist, eye
of a needle threaded with blood and bone. There was an Inuit
word for the way she was feeling: she-who-tries-on-a-garment-
she-knows-will-be-too-small. Danny taught it to her a million years ago, back when she used to hang on his every word.
Now the tables were turned. Now he was sitting at her bedside in the Upper Valley Hospital, hanging on her silence
like the fly hanging above him on the vast expanse of white
ceiling.

Daniel Murdock was sitting at his wife's bedside, watching
her, his eyes on her skin like a light breeze, like a little zephyr,
moving over her as she, in turn, deftly made her way from the
kitchen to the parlor, though all he could see of her was her

white motionless face, the white bandage where her curls used to be. Both her eyes were black-and-blue, as if she'd been in a fight. The surgeon said it was going to be touch-and-go for the next few days. The longer Mrs. Murdock remained in the coma, the worse her chances of making a complete recovery. On the other hand, her pupils responded to light stimulus, which was a good sign and meant her brain stem was still functioning. "Talk to her," Dr. Bloom suggested, and when Daniel looked at him like he was crazy, he'd added brightly, "Nothing wrong with her ears."

Daniel cleared his throat. "Andy?" he whispered. Something on squeaky wheels passed the partly opened door, a woman laughed, and a bell chimed. Under the circumstances it was ridiculous to be embarrassed. "The sky above Pitsulak Island had been dark for weeks," Daniel said softly. "Probably due to a forest fire burning out of control in Quebec. Thousands of acres of trees up in flames." Was Andy going to die? But then wasn't this what had brought them together in the first place, a shared preference for the company of the dead, their mutely suggestive artifacts? "The Paleo-Indian experienced nature phenomenologically," Daniel whispered, positioning his mouth against the bandages close to what he hoped was his wife's ear. "Cause and effect coexisted." He glanced over his shoulder. "I'm sorry," he said, though for the life of him he couldn't remember what they'd been fighting about before he left. His camp stove, which she'd "hidden" on a shelf in the cellar, after he'd purposely left it on the coffee table so he wouldn't forget to take it with him? "I love you," he said.

She was nineteen when they met, already living in the commune on French Hill, where he would finally track her down, having been unable to get her out of his head ever since he'd first discovered her in a back corridor of the Smithsonian. She was studying the museum guide, he was carrying a bear skull. "This is the worst map I've ever seen," she'd complained, flirting. In those days she was quite thin and wore her black hair very short, a cap of curls so shiny they made you blink. Her minidress was lime green, her lace-up boots brown suede. "Does that look like a ladies' room to you?" she'd asked, pointing at a case full of atlatl weights. "Come with me," he'd replied, then drew her through the door he'd just emerged from and into that part of the museum the public never gets to see, a rat's maze of ill-lit narrow corridors containing everything that wasn't currently on display, shelf upon shelf of weapons and pots and bones, as well as the staff bathroom.

Of course if a person looked at his life from above, he could see the whole thing for what it was; he'd only feel lost while he was living it, when he still hadn't figured out that it was in fact a maze and that both the way in and the way out led to the same enormous empty place surrounding it.

At twenty-five Daniel Murdock was not an unattractive young man, but his romantic history had suffered from a fear that he was, given the extreme pallor of his skin and hair, his practically white eyebrows and eyelashes, not to mention his deaf ear. While Andrea busied herself behind the closed bathroom door, he'd waited outside, holding on to his bear skull for dear life. The toilet-paper dispenser squeaked; the toilet flushed. It was probably too late to ask a woman her name, let alone her phone number, after you'd overheard such things. He fixed his attention on the skull, which still showed traces of the vermilion paint it had been decorated with before being raised high on a lopstick, a bark-wrapped plug of tobacco inserted between its jaws. A cigarette — that was what he needed. Back then you could smoke anywhere. Daniel had just started fumbling for his pack in his shirt pocket, the skull gingerly tucked beneath his arm, when Andrea threw the door open so carelessly, with such heedless exuberance, that it smashed against the wall. "Thanks, man," she said. "I thought I'd die." She handed him her museum guide, and before he even had a chance to say, "You're welcome," she was striding majestically down the hall exactly like someone who'd been working there for years, except in the wrong direction.

Only later did he realize she'd written her name and phone number on the guide, but since she'd left out the area code, it took what seemed like forever before he finally located her high on a northern hilltop surrounded by goats. He could hear them bleating in the background as she gave directions. No, she hadn't left the area code out by accident, she'd told him. She'd left it out on purpose, as a little test. When he asked how he'd done, there was a pause. "That remains to be seen," she'd said.

"The inhabitants of Pitsulak Island were terrified that they had offended the spirits," Daniel continued. "There were lots of them to offend: Day Sky, East Wind, Thunder, Heart of Tree."

Maybe he was still being tested. Maybe he'd offended a spirit — certainly things couldn't be much worse. He looked around the room as if to catch one of the spirits scuttling from its hiding place. Maybe he'd made a fatal mistake, removing the rock from the boy's back. Though he'd trained as a scientist, like many archaeologists Daniel was a poet at heart, his relation to the objects of this world allusive, greedy, superstitious. He leaned over to get a better look at his wife, at the feathery curve of her brows, the way her lips parted to reveal the telltale gap between her two front teeth that was supposed to signify a lusty nature. No damage there, plus he could feel her breath, soft and warm and smelling faintly of sugar water and vitamins. He knew she was sometimes unfaithful — it was okay with him, really, giving him leeway, as it did, to live alone in a tent.

The corkscrew-curled nurse reappeared, checked the level of the liquid in Andrea's IV bag, stared at the monitor, adjusted the blinds. Night seemed to have fallen; the lights in the parking lot were surrounded by moths, the stars were out. Summer night, mid-June, practically the solstice. Nothing — nothing! — connected him to the island where he'd just been; on both sides of the window, the wages of civilization flourished. Eighteen-wheelers plunged along the interstate; the elevator doors opened and closed. Down the hall flat-chested Billie Carpenter was reading a *Reader's Digest* article about the perils of breast augmentation to stacked Janet Peake, who was sound asleep.

"Any change?" The nurse came to stand beside Daniel, staring down with him at Andrea's indurate face, and the nurse's genuine concern, combined with the fact that she was standing there alive and capable of speech, capable of having adorned her corkscrewing yellow hair with daisy-shaped barrettes, was almost more than he could bear. Who cared about the stupid camp stove?

Daniel shook his head, and the nurse touched his shoulder. "Don't worry," she said. "I've seen them come out of worse than this. I've seen them open their eyes and blink just like waking from a nap." She leaned over and delicately adjusted the blanket, covering Andrea's shoulder.

A little rustling noise, the sound of fabric brushing against leaves. Feet moving, feeling their way across an uncertain surface . . .

Mon April 8 — At home. Sewed on my dress. Done some house-
work. V been gone a month last Saturday.
Tues April 9 — I sewed on my black dress in the forenoon. Rode
out in woods without my hearing from him only asking my for-
giveness for the wrong he has done me . . .

At home — which is to say, in the Fair homestead on Adder
Ridge. Andrea was at home in the clock room, winding the
clocks. There were twenty-three of them, their ticking a constant immeasurable stream of sound, nor did their chimes
sound in unison. Danny had been gone for a week. Seven days,
one hundred sixty-eight hours, ten thousand eighty minutes.
The stream plunged over the falls and into a churning pool of
notes at the bottom. When you wound the banjo clock too
tight, the key spun the other way, mad with release, and if you
tried to grab it and stop it, it cut your fingers.

"Sweetheart, is that you?"

Andrea stiffened; Danny's shadow fell across her face.

Unrequited romantic love is like the love of the soul for the
body. The body never adequately returns the love, since the
body thinks, being the container, it's more important than
the soul and thus owes the soul very little, if anything. Whereas
the soul owes the body everything, or at least something like
rent, not to mention gratitude, for giving it shelter.

Naturally the Fairs, being no-nonsense Yankees, never would
admit to it, but with the exception of Inez, they all found the
clock room disturbing. The Curfew Clock, with its black bell
hanging from a bent finger bone. Rosalinda. York Steeple.
Two-Faced Vixen, with her big round face above and her little
round face flicking from side to side on the pendulum. The
school clock that moved in jerks exactly like time in a school-
room. Grandfather. Grandmother. The phases of the moon.

There was a shared sense among the Fairs that the air in the clock room wasn't quite right, that there were places where it seemed to have coagulated, where you felt yourself brushing against something thick and substantial yet utterly invisible, like when you swam in Black Lake and a fish — or something even more unspeakable — slipped past you underwater.

This is because souls are attracted to measuring devices, those places where things as purely noncorporeal as themselves, which is to say numbers, are made to serve material ends.

Turn the key, wind the clock. When she was a girl, Inez Fair had thought trees shook to make wind, but you wouldn't catch Andrea Murdock making a mistake like that. She felt her soul yearning for her body, a palpable anguished aching that made her eyeballs roll from side to side and caused Daniel to call out "Look!"

Then the sun came up; then it was another day. The created world can be both reliable and surprising. A bull moose was sauntering in the laid-back loose-limbed way of its kind along the boggy verge of Goneaway Lake, pausing from time to time to take a bite out of a leatherleaf bush. Clouds of blackflies swarmed around him, landed on him, in the tender places inside his ears or in the corners of his eyes or on his exposed furless underbelly, but he didn't mind. The day was warm and the ground under his hooves mucky and moist. The cotton grass was just starting to open. He had mated two months earlier, and though he had no memory of this event, it had left him with a deep sense of well-being, of things having happened the way they were supposed to happen, like the muck underfoot, and the tender new shoots of the leatherleaf, and even the flies biting his belly.

Pink buds of bog rosemary, gaping mouths of sundew — everything was happening the way it was supposed to happen, the sun rising over his humped left shoulder, its heat just starting to penetrate his thick hide and warm his blood. He was headed more or less southwest, into a dense thicket of Labrador tea.

Of course the moose's vocabulary was less detailed; it consisted of a single (for want of a better word) *word,* that underwent constant modification, alternately stretching and shrinking. Were things not to happen as they were supposed to happen, which is to say, the way they happened year after year, as if repetition were somehow synonymous with cosmic design — if, for example, the designated mate failed to appear, having gotten involved in a collision with a pair of opera lovers in a black Saab on their way home from Montreal, or if she'd ended up languishing in a suburban backyard, having fallen victim to a snail infected with the brain-fever parasite, or if she ended up as a pile of shrink-wrapped packages in a hunter's freezer — a new word wouldn't form in the moose's brain to express surprise or dismay or sorrow.

Among other things the ability to think like a human is predicated on a need to anticipate change, not for the better. Maybe this is how we came up with the idea of progress.

Meanwhile the moose continued to amble along, browsing on this and that. It was a Thursday in June. June 19, in fact, the same date when, more than two hundred years earlier, a freak hole had appeared in the hardpan-and-marl crust that formed the southwestern tip of Lake Lonely, the precise place, more or less, where the moose was now ambling, and down which the entire lake, anticipating its current name, had "gone away," taking with it over two billion gallons of water. The hole had been small to begin with, but as more water disappeared down it, it started growing bigger and bigger, creating a channel a thousand feet wide and over two hundred feet deep, into which entire forests and glacial erratics and human dwelling places crashed, leaving behind a huge muddy socket dotted with flopping dying fish and large quantities of eggs, some light green, some yellow, some dark gray, some nearly as large as hens' eggs and others very very small. At first it smelled terrible, and then, after a while, in the manner of bogs, it began to smell sweet.

Now there was a stone marker, barely visible from Route 10

if you knew it was there, commemorating the event, which it referred to as "cataclysmic."

"Can't we get out?" Billie Carpenter asked, as Piet Zeebrugge slowed his Land Rover to a crawl.

"I don't see the point. It's just a lot of moss and trees." He took a covert look at his wrist. Chloe was going to be pissed if he wasn't back in time for lunch, since she'd invited Mary Holst-Jenkins and Richard (assuming he didn't get called away by an errant or declining member of his flock) to discuss what she referred to as the Banner Situation. Also Gigi was missing — had been since Sunday, when she slipped through Piet's legs as he was leaving to pick up the papers, and though she routinely left the house whenever she felt like it, this time for some reason Chloe had decided to blame him. Later, when he was out looking for her — calling, "Gigi, Gigi," so softly it was no wonder she didn't come running — he'd seen the bald woman from the summer choir, the one who'd pulled Billie Carpenter's hair and bent Glenda Banner's nose out of joint, standing in the middle of the rotary with a push broom in one hand and a bottle of beer in the other. And then he'd run into Billie herself, coming out of the AP office, looking so bright and unscathed and irrepressible that when he had asked her what she was up to and she told him she was headed to some lake just over the Canadian border where she intended to release a beaver she'd caught in her Havahart trap, he'd suggested they take his Rover. Women and their little projects — unlike men, who seemed happier breasting the occasional flood or stamping out the occasional fire as the occasion arose.

"Moose country," Piet said, pulling the car onto the shoulder and cutting the engine. "There isn't any water here," he reminded her, because the beaver was still with them.

It had refused to leave the trap when Billie tried tipping it out onto the lakeshore earlier that morning. The day was chill, the beach rocky and strewn with hundreds of dead fish and the worst human leavings, dirty diapers and used condoms and bloody tampons, the wind tearing at them savagely straight from the north — it was a landscape that so far exceeded any romantic notion of desolation, that so purely desolated the spirit without providing even a hint of that romantic frisson that is, in the face of utter desolation, the equivalent of hope, that Piet couldn't blame the little creature, which was now dozing companionably on the backseat safe inside its trap.

He resisted the thought, but the beaver did look cute.

It did not look to Piet like the powerful creature the Inuit said could disappear by penetrating the ground or rising aloft in the air in any shape it chose or by diving into the depths of a desolate northern lake and remaining as long as it wanted. The caged beaver didn't look like a powerful creature who could only be caught with its own amiable consent. Though the difference wasn't in the beaver, or in beavers in general.

"Could it happen again?" Billie asked, testing the ground before setting off along the narrow path that led away from the marker, across a narrow clearing and into the bog. The floor of the clearing was bright yellow-green, sprigged with shrubs that turned out to be cranberry bushes.

"No," Piet said. "It's like lightning." He looked at his watch again. "Billie," he said. "I've really got to get going. I told Chloe I'd be back ten minutes ago."

"My late husband was hit twice," Billie said.

"You're kidding."

"I wish. And then he was murdered." She came to a halt near the edge of the bog, gracelessly swatting at flies. There was no way to make sense of her, really, in her flannel-lined jeans and her yellow old-lady cardigan, her pale blue Alice in

Wonderland hair ribbon, and her gigantic multitiered earrings, like a Mexican hooker.

"In a bank," she added.

"I'm sorry," Piet said, and Billie shrugged.

"It was ages ago," she said. She looked him in the eye, then down at the ground. He was very good-looking, no denying the fact. "You work in a bank, don't you?" she asked. A dark implacable eye, set with a single glint of light like the diamond in the jet locket she'd inherited from her mother but never wore because it frightened her. *Ruinous god, leave me be!* Billie prayed. *Two-faced savage god, look at me! I'm too old!*

"Not *in*," Piet said. "I don't work inside a bank building."

"Oh," Billie cleared her throat. "Speaking of husbands," she said. "When you met me in town? I'd just been filing a story off the AP wire. About Chloe's ex-husband."

Piet was torn: he wanted to know what Billie was talking about, but even more than that he wanted to know what she *was*. Curiosity, curiosity — you never knew where it would lead you. A question here, a question there, followed sometimes by the removal of clothes, and then rarely (and certainly never with Chloe), the slipping of the soul from the skin. "Chloe's ex-husband?" Piet said. "What about him?"

"He's wanted by the law." Billie lifted a foot and stamped. "Are you sure it's okay? The ground feels funny."

"That's the moss. We're on a thick mat of moss. What did he do?"

"Something. I can't remember." Mail fraud? Maybe it was some kind of civil disobedience. Billie felt the wind going out of her sails. "Is she your girlfriend?"

"Who?"

"You know." Billie considered imitating Chloe's way of staring, cross-eyed like a Siamese cat, but thought better of it.

Piet shrugged. "I'm not sure 'girlfriend' is the right word."

"Then what is?"

Now it was Piet's turn to look Billie in the eye. "We have sex."

"Oh."

They were interrupted by a noise from the Rover — a loud, metallic bang, as if the beaver might have been trying to open the trap and in moving around had caused the trap to fall off the seat.

They both turned to look. A rust-colored Dart shot past, headed south toward Varennes, going much too fast for either the speed limit or the condition of its suspension system. "Idiot," Piet said.

It was like being served a warning. As Billie and Piet walked together to the Rover, he took his key from his pocket and pressed a button, making the parking lights flash and all the locks release. It was like being tapped on the shoulder just when you thought your life might be about to take a turn for the better. As it happened, the cage had indeed fallen to the floor.

"What are you going to do now?" Piet asked, returning the cage — which was hard to handle — to the seat. "You can't keep a beaver in your house."

"I know," Billie said. "And if I try putting it back where I caught it, that trapper will skin it alive."

Even though they'd left the windows open, the inside of the Rover smelled terrible, a little like wet dog but with a lewd and slightly decomposed undercurrent. The beaver was working away at the bars of its cage, chewing with a viciousness and intensity of purpose that was hard to overlook — its teeth were huge and sharp and seemed, suddenly, dangerous.

"I wish I could see a moose," Billie said, and just then a little brown mouse ran right across the road in front of them.

Curiosity. Its oldest roots in *cura,* meaning "care."

Over time its meaning has undergone a succession of meta-morphoses, from scrupulousness to ingenuity to attention unduly bestowed on matters of inferior moment (curiosity about meats and drinks for example) to the desire to learn or know about anything, trifles or matters that are none of one's business, such as a curiosity to know the faults and imperfections in other men. . . .

Also, it killed the cat.

There can be no question about it — curiosity also happens to be one of the prime traits we have in common with animals.

On Sunday morning, after scooting through the door between Piet's legs, Gigi had headed into the lilac hedge bordering Chloe's front yard. The lilacs were fully leafed out, leaving shady patches of dirt on the ground beneath them, with warm sunny patches between. Best to lie in a warm patch, with the tip of your nose in the shade. Who knows how long she lay there? After a while a robin sat on a branch above her — a robin with his plump juicy breast, keeping an eye out for worms. Gigi's teeth chattered with excitement. It didn't so much matter whether she caught the robin, the tooth-chatter alone being thrill enough. Then the bird had taken off, landing on the Wexlers' lawn across the street, and Gigi had followed.

Of the cats, the white cats are most ferocious, the orange

cats most sweet, the black-and-white cats most elusive, the tiger cats most curious.

"You don't understand," said a girl, walking past on the sidewalk. She was unfashionably plump and wore her jeans low on her hips, her gold belly-button ring just barely visible within two creamy folds of skin. "I can't go home now. They think I'm at Project Graduation."

There was a tubular bird feeder hanging from a silver maple in the Wexlers' backyard, and as the robin perched on the lawn beneath it, scavenging sunflower seeds, Gigi took cover in the peony bed and watched. The storm had left the peonies lying like postulants, their shattered faces flat on the ground; a few goldfinches landed on the feeder, and then a few more, and then they all took off at once in the way of birds, as if something had startled them. The sound of Jill Wexler's clarinet drifted through an open window. *Liebestraum*. Love Dream.

Life has nowhere to move, being everywhere, doesn't move though it's always in motion, is the leaf is the trash is the girl's pierced navel the worm the cat's paw the lengthening shadows.

Gigi followed the shadow of a goldfinch through the fence separating the Wexlers' yard from the Sanbournes'. She couldn't help herself. Ever since old Mr. Sanbourne passed away that spring, the grass had remained unmowed, and the long blades and wildflower stems felt good against Gigi's fur as she slunk through. Moles and voles and mice were hiding in their holes under her paws. *Yes, Gigi. Yes.*

When Thomas thrust his hand into Jesus' side, what he really wanted to feel was his own flesh and marrow. That's curiosity: the wish to know exactly what we're made of and to determine how fragile we are, or mortal, or even — clinging to that most romantic version of hope that's nothing more than wishful thinking — immortal.

God isn't curious. Being everything, He has no need to be.

The day wore on. Seven days from the solstice, the sun appearing to stand still in the sky. If we lived in a finite universe, the day's light would eventually travel back to us, and with it an image of ourselves on that very same day.

Helen Zeebrugge was sitting with Piet in the gazebo behind the Crockett Home, eating a coffee ice-cream cone and watching him smoke one of the rare cigarettes he permitted himself. "You wouldn't need family albums," Piet was saying, "in a finite universe." Sunday supper, always a depressing affair, was over; the moon was just beginning to show above the locust trees next door. Deviled ham on white bread, cream of celery soup. No one *ate* cream of celery soup — everyone knew it was meant to be used as an ingredient in something else. And the news about Janet was even more depressing. As soon as she could be moved, her eldest son was planning to place her in a level-three facility, which everyone also knew was an antechamber to the grave.

"Here, kitty kitty kitty," said Piet, and Gigi crept out from behind a rosebush and cautiously approached his outstretched hand. "What a pretty kitty," he said as Helen reached down to pet the little cat, and the top of Gigi's neat striped skull rose to meet her fingers. "Where did you come from?" He didn't recognize her — the truth is, he'd never paid that much attention to either of Chloe's cats or to animals in general.

"No collar," Helen said.

It was the black and pearl time. Gigi was rubbing up against her leg and purring loudly, her eye on the ice cream. "Poor thing," said Helen, giving Piet a look — head demurely cocked to one side, eyelids lowered — that he remembered from childhood and knew was anything but demure. "Come on," Helen said. "Help me sneak her in."

Black and pearl — the black limbs of the locust trees two-dimensional against the pearl-colored sky. Chloe's cats never wore collars or tags because it was Chloe's contention that you could never really own another living being. Behind Piet's head, behind the locust trees, the sky proposed an unprecedented color. As if a dream might be real, Helen thought, and it *is,* it *is.* Something like a foretaste of death or the chance to get a little practice before the fact.

A car alarm went off; the wind picked up, tossing the branches of the locusts, all those threadlike twigs identical in design to the air tubes in the gill of a mayfly. A bat swept past.

Just as Gigi was about to take off to investigate, Piet reached down and scooped her up.

Piet's beating heart was loud and trapped with Gigi under his jacket; there wasn't much fat on him to muffle the noise. It's a terrible thing to be scooped up by strange hands and tucked away like that. A door swung open; a door closed. There was a smell like cooked meat and human sweat and urine. An accident in the dining room? Then another door opened, and Gigi felt the floor begin to lift. "You'll never get away with this," Piet said to Helen. A bell dinged, very faint, like a belled cat stalking a bird. "I wash my hands of the whole thing," he said, and he was laughing. Then a light came on.

In her room Helen let what was left of her ice cream melt into a porcelain saucer that had been a gift to her mother from the emperor of Japan and should have been in a museum. As soon as Piet was gone, she set the saucer down on the far side of her bed, where it couldn't be seen from the door, and sat in her English lounge chair. Soon she could hear the sound of a little pink tongue, lapping, lapping, lapping melted ice cream.

I have been loved. I have been old and alone . . .

Sometimes it happened almost the way Piet had been

describing it, but not exactly: all the Helens Helen had ever been would suddenly be present in the Helen of today. The first lapping notes, and light would vanish from the west, the sun no longer visible yet still the sun. Thick round branches radiating against the slightly paler sky. Wind, the music stirring. How can it be? Real trees, the trees against the sky, the lapping noise, yet where does it come from if not your own dream of yourself, watching the world as it proposes itself to you, so beautiful, the notes swelling. It could ALL be this, Helen told herself. Just what you're feeling at this moment. Helen. Helen. Everything you've ever dreamed, the trees, the black branches, the paler sky, the wind making its sound, something is happening, your life is happening, and the music is what's happening, a wind of notes, pink tongue lapping cream, nothing more, thank God, nothing more.

Gigi stayed at the Crockett Home with Helen for three days and two nights, until Marjory Mason complained to Kathy Crockett about an unpleasant smell in the hallway.

"You can't keep a cat in your room," Kathy patiently instructed Helen, gleeful to have at last caught the old woman doing something she could be punished for.

"I pay enough for the room," Helen said. "I should be able to keep an elephant in it if I want to." Gigi was curled in Helen's lap, and the voice in Helen's ears was still going on about the Forsytes, describing how the waters of change were foaming in for them, carrying the promise of new forms only when their destructive flood should have passed its full. What next, now that she was almost finished with the Forsytes?

Kathy was also gleeful about the situation at church. Insurrection intoxicated her; she never cast herself in the role of loser. Evidently Richard Jenkins had laughed out loud when he read Carl Banner's petition, and rumor had it there was to be a lunch meeting with Piet Zeebrugge and Chloe Brock and who knew who else? Meanwhile the world was getting more and more dangerous — anyone could strap a bomb to himself and blow innocent people away. Vigilance, Kathy thought. Vigilance was the key.

And really, if Chloe Brock had been a little more vigilant, Gigi would still be home on Summer Street, where she belonged, instead of riding along Main Street in the back of Kathy Crockett's white SUV. Kathy made sure the windows were all rolled shut while she tried crashing the meeting at the rectory, where she was deflected at the door by the rector's daughter Mimi.

"My father can't be disturbed," Mimi told Kathy. She lounged like an odalisque against the doorframe, her small eyes amused, hooded in turquoise.

"That's ridiculous," Kathy replied. "He's at lunch. I know it. I can hear them eating."

"Who is it, Meem?" Pam, the good daughter, peered down the staircase, wearing a pink towel like a turban. "If it's Mr. Hommeyer, tell him the music's in the box under the stairs."

But Mimi merely shrugged, and when Kathy said it was an emergency, she offered to convey a message to her father to that effect.

"Don't bother," Kathy said.

When the cat's away, the mice will play.

It was Thursday, the nineteenth day of June. It was to be the last full day of Gigi's life, but she didn't know that. *Last full day.* She didn't even know such a thing existed. She was sound asleep, curled in a ball on the floor of the SUV's cargo area, when Kathy activated the garage door opener and pulled into the garage, but she woke fast enough when Kathy clicked open the hatch, and the next thing she knew there was a big brown

DOG face looking in at her. Dog nose, dog teeth, dog tongue, dog drool. That smell. So excrementitious, dogs! Gigi took off, skirting the edge of the garage, slinking along behind the immense cans of driveway sealer Mr. Crockett planned to get around to using one of these days. Beyond the open garage door, a to-be-avoided-at-all-costs road, and beyond the road, a to-be-avoided-at-all-costs expanse of water.

Still light out. "Come back here, you!" Kathy said, but her heart wasn't in it. The little cat slipped out the open garage door and was gone.

Billie caught a glimpse of her moving through the alder thicket toward Murdocks', the house dark and empty and expectant. MISSING. FEMALE TIGER CAT, ANSWERS TO THE NAME OF GIGI. She'd noticed the signs in town the other day. "Gigi?" Billie tried, but the cat ignored her. It was getting late. Piet Zeebrugge approached from the south, clad in his running togs and only slightly out of breath, and when she called hello he nodded his head once, creating the illusion that he was too preoccupied with moving forward to let on that he was looking her way, and continued toward the Knoll.

Just a little tiger cat, nothing so very important in the grand scheme of things.

In the Bible dogs are mentioned sixteen times, cats zero.

The earth tipped on its axis; the stars came out. If the universe is infinite, the sky should be infinitely filled with stars. It should be like what Gigi saw, moving through the alder thicket: a dense thicket of stars with only the most minuscule dark flecks intervening. It should be a sweeping brightness, the face of God.

A fisher-cat appearing out of nowhere.

The policemen were onstage, about to be surprised by the pirates. General William Stanley's flower-bedizened daughters were crowded together in the girls' bathroom, waiting for their cue, which would come in the form of a rapping on the wall above the stalls.

"With catlike tread, upon our prey we steal," sang the pirates, their voices trailing faintly across the hallway, drowned out by the comic stamping of their feet.

"I look dreadful," Sunny said, and Lorna thought she was right, she did, though you could tell Sunny didn't think so herself and was merely waiting for someone to contradict her. Not I, Lorna thought. We all look like clowns. She leaned back against a stall door and watched as Sunny bent forward to examine her face in the long mirror that ran above the sinks: Miss Kowicki had really piled on the makeup, but what did she know? She was the gym teacher and probably a lesbian. The bathroom smelled of disinfectant, everything swabbed mercilessly with it every single afternoon by the toothless psycho janitor, except for the area above your head, where you couldn't even see the corners of the ceiling anymore because of cobwebs.

"Mason had a fit during Kevin's solo," Brittany Bliss informed Lorna, looking straight at her, though in the mirror. "Did you see?" Kevin Funk was the "smart boy" and presumed by most of the sixth grade to be romantically linked with Lorna, the "smart girl." He was also Major General Stanley, by virtue of the fact that his part had the most lines and Kevin could be counted on to remember them, though he couldn't carry a tune to save his life.

Lorna stared back at Brittany but without the mirror's intervention. It wasn't as if Brittany was dangerous like a basilisk. Lorna let her mouth drop open *just a little* to indicate disdain. She said nothing, though she was thinking *Beau wouldn't stand for this,* as if he were actually her boyfriend. Beau. Thank God he couldn't see her — she looked like the doll on the toilet tank in Grammy Steiner's powder room who had a roll of toilet paper instead of legs. Except of course he couldn't see her — he wasn't there! Duh. Meanwhile she could hear the policemen singing about their unwillingness to tangle with the pirates and the sound of the audience laughing. *Tarantara tarantara tarantara . . .*

Though they'd been ordered not to, Lorna had snuck a look during the first act, so she knew who was out there: Mr. and Ms. Crockett and the three Crockett boys, somberly attired as if for a funeral, seated in the middle of the first row, in the place of honor, between homespun Mr. and Mrs. Byrd on one side, whose dependents included not only Frederick and a trio of little girls but also a barnful of dairy cows, and on the other, orange-haired Mrs. Mason, Mr. Mason's ancient mother, all of them flanked by Mr. Couture, the Pirate King's depressed single dad, and Mr. and Mrs. Funk, who would appear at your door when least expected, handing out free copies of the *Watchtower,* which Lorna secretly couldn't get enough of. Her own parents, each wearing linen, her mother dress-up black, her father summer courtroom white, sat three rows behind the Crocketts, and directly behind them the Kipps, Mersey and Mees and Sophy, the latter two attired as usual like homeless people. Until as late as last Wednesday, Mees had still been one of Major Stanley's daughters, but her behavior at dress rehearsal — her inability to stop laughing at the sight of the first-act backdrop, a Cornish seascape that happened to be Mr. Mason's own handiwork — had caused him to drop her from the cast like a hot potato. Now, Lorna knew, Mees was no doubt banging her foot over and over again into the back of Lorna's father's chair, driving him nuts. Soon he wouldn't be able to contain his anger, whirling around and giving Mees a piece of his mind.

A piece of his mind, Lorna thought. He did that so often, no wonder it sometimes seemed like there wasn't any left.

It was Saturday, June 21. Seven o'clock at night and not yet dark out — summer solstice, the longest day of the year. Time of the Egg Moon, also called the Dyad Moon, in honor of the celestial twins, who for the time being held sway over the solstice but who hadn't two thousand years ago and who wouldn't again, thousands of years in the future. The great belt of the zodiac undergoes continual minute adjustment — Mercury in retrograde, the war on terror going badly.

"The Time Being," a poet wrote. "The most trying time of all." In periods of crisis belief in astrology is always on the increase.

"Mees, stop that right now," Sophy Kipp said tersely, under her breath. "If I see you so much as brush the back of Mr. Fine's seat one more time, we're out of here."

Inside the auditorium it was hot, the day's heat still hanging around as was its wont in all the things that were, themselves, hanging — the giant American flag with its gold fringe and the more modest Union Jack (brought out of mothballs for the occasion), as well as in the faded red-velvet curtains and the audience's trouser legs and skirts and shirts and blouses. Many members of the audience were fanning themselves with their programs. Blackfly season was finally over, its swarms of specklike biting insects having been replaced almost overnight by suicidal deerflies the size of raisins and mosquitoes, with their constant passive-aggressive whining and their cargo of West Nile virus. A mosquito landed on the nape of Kathy Crockett's neck, and she smacked it dead.

"Look, Kath! Here she comes!" said her husband, a smitten expression on his face, and sure enough, there was Sunny, poised and — even Mr. Crockett would have to admit — a trifle wooden, fixing the dairy farmer's son with a wooden look of love. At least she was pretty (unlike poor Lorna Fine), and she had a nice voice. "Take heart of grace, thy steps retrace . . ." But would Sunny remember this night for the rest of her life or would it get swallowed up, as so many of Kathy's own memories had, by that penchant for order and niceness that had so far served to distract almost everyone from her overwhelming, and anything but orderly or nice, appetite for power?

Mees slammed her foot for the last time into the back of Mr. Fine's seat.

Next Wednesday, Lorna was thinking, swaying from side to side more or less in harmony with the rest of the Daughters. Next Wednesday, school — which had gone on a little longer than usual due to all the snow days — would be out. There would be sixth grade graduation. She would have to stand up in front of everyone and read that stupid Dr. Seuss book Mr. Mason was so enamored of. When she was little, Lorna had read a biography of Anna Pavlova and decided she wanted to be a ballerina, until it turned out she had two left feet. In any case, you didn't see Dr. Seuss standing up in front of everyone making a fool out of himself. That was the advantage of being a writer.

"Lorna!" Becky Stroup jabbed her in the ribs. Time to move to the front of the stage.

Soon this would be over.

Though why wish for time to move more quickly when all it was already doing was propelling you faster and faster into a future you weren't even sure you wanted to inhabit? Next year they'd be starting middle school at Varennes High; they'd be on the bottom of the heap all over again, just like kindergartners. They'd be in different homerooms, they'd be separated. Sunny would make a whole new set of friends, good-looking and sophisticated. She would continue to do well in school, while Lorna would flounder around in some classes and flourish startlingly in others, but always in ways that would serve to undermine rather than enhance her popularity. Worse, there had been some talk about Mees needing an individual classroom aide. Like she was one of the slow students. Mees!

Now every pirate and every policeman was claiming one of Major General Stanley's daughters for his own. Such an out-of-whack group of lovers, most of the girls still towering over the boys. Lorna was paired with Bobby Chan, whose mother was the accompanist. Bobby Chan, who reminded her of an acorn.

"Peers will be peers," sang Kevin Funk, "and youth will have its fling . . ."

Mr. Mason looked like he was going to have a heart attack, he was so happy.

This is it, Lorna thought. Me and Sunny and Mees — after tonight we'll never spend the night together again. Not the three of us, not at the Crocketts'.

Though how could you know? How could anyone ever know?

How could you be expected to predict, for example, that Sunny Crockett would become president of middle school student council, star of the junior musical, *Bye Bye Birdie,* and class valedictorian before heading off to Vassar, where she would momentarily get swept into the arms of the radical feminist movement and flirt briefly with the idea of moving to France with a woman named Odile before suddenly changing course for Ottawa, where she would meet and marry an earnest young man, the two of them raising three healthy children and running a very successful mail-order exercise-equipment business, getting older together and maybe at some point along the way each of them having a halfhearted affair, but also remaining essentially devoted to each other and dying in their sleep four months apart in their late eighties?

Because it *could* happen like that — assuming that in so many years nothing will change. Assuming that meaning will continue to inhere in "mail order," "Ottawa," "sleep."

And if not? What then?

What about Lorna, lost in Labyrinth XI under the Pan-Asian continent, finally beautiful after so many years as an ugly duckling, and now her beauty, ironically, impossible to see, the darkness having swallowed everything up in the early teens of the twenty-first century, following the incineration of the Cradle of Civilization and leaving everyone wandering sleepless (sleep having been rendered unnecessary by the implantation of "slumber nodes" in the pineal gland) — what about Lorna? Lorna dying in childbirth somewhere near the intersection of Labyrinth XI and the Burmese Corridor.

Mees dead, too.

Also Sophy and Mersey and Kathy and Mr. Mason and his mother and the Byrds and the Funks and the Fines and the

Coutures and Margaret and Buddy and Gigi and Beulah and the beavers and the moose and the deerflies and . . .

Because of course that's the one thing you can reasonably predict.

The curtains drew closed — Billy Ainsworth tugging madly on the ropes like someone milking a cow. Applause. More applause. The curtain once more inching open — Sunny taking a bow. Sunny being pelted with cheap bouquets of flowers from the supermarket, mostly white carnations dyed green and blue. Bravo! Bravo! (Sunny and Justin Byrd inviting Mr. Mason and Ms. Chan onto the stage.) The audience was standing. It felt like the end of everything. Never again would they come back to Varennes Elementary, where if nothing else you could count on finding Mrs. Diamond lodged in her dark little office, smiling her mysterious horsey smile, protecting them all from harm. Lorna was going to have to give back the ancient leather-bound copy of *Kidnapped* Mrs. Diamond had lent her from her own personal library at the beginning of sixth grade, and though it put Lorna to sleep every time she tried to read it, she'd nonetheless hoarded it all year long like a talisman.

"Do you have a tissue?" Sunny hissed over her shoulder, and for one surprised moment Lorna thought Sunny might be crying, succumbing to the same hollow terrified heartsick feeling she was experiencing herself, like when you've accidentally swallowed water while swimming. Like being in love. Though as it turned out, Sunny merely needed to blow her nose. And who could say which, as a physical object, Lorna loved more — a book or Beau O'Brien? If you want to avoid romantic triangles, never marry a writer.

Thirty-two children on the stage. Seven pirates, eight policemen, thirteen daughters, plus the principals.

Of course children have no idea what it is their parents are feeling at a time like this. It's one thing to know, as Lorna Fine did, that your life is about to change and to suspect that as terrifying as that change will be, it will also be thrilling to find yourself plunging more or less headlong into your own future, and it's another to watch, as Sophy Kipp did, your own mortality hurtling at you like a cinema meteorite to annihilate everything on the planet.

Having returned to her seat after planting Mees firmly in a chair in front of the terrarium in Mr. Mason's classroom and having ordered her to stay put and keep an eye on the snake, Sophy was herself seeking a tissue in the pocket of her dress. *Poor wandering one,* she heard twelve-year-old Sophy singing inside her head; she was lying on the living-room floor in her blue sailor suit, listening to the record player. *Though thou has surely strayed. Take heart of grace. Thy steps retrace* . . . It didn't matter that the song was sentimental or that the extended belcanto passage it ended with was intended as a spoof. Her lifelong love story had only just been getting started then, was still in its earliest stages, all sweetness and yearning and not as yet ruined by actual contact with a lover.

You got that moment — once! — and then it was done. Like Major Stanley's daughters, singing their hearts out at this very moment on the stage, and her daughter not among them.

Eventually the sun went all the way down. The moon and the stars came out. From the feet of the white birch trees grew long black shadows. Spangled is the earth with her crowns, said Sappho; that part never changes. Also the pond, the birds.

Everything stopped. Margaret was stretched across the hall floor, her head near the door to the cellar, where some of last year's air was still trapped, leaking from under the crack and smelling like winter. Smelling like snow. Like rolling in snow. The house was dark, locked up tight, front door and back, all of the windows open just a couple of inches. "What have you got in your house, lady, a lion?" the man in the hardware store asked Sophy the last time she took a pile of screens to be repaired. On one side of Margaret a long steep staircase led to the second floor, with clouds of fur in the corners. Margaret's own fur — she was almost done shedding, and once the fur came out, she had nothing to do with it. It wasn't *her* any longer.

Margaret had a dream of moving, moving her legs as she dreamed, and then she woke, and her legs were still moving. She got up, stiffly. There was almost too much room in the house. It was too empty, with too many possible directions in which to go. Hills upon hills upon hills upon hills, and the hills, too, empty.

Spangled is the earth with her crowns.

Is there anyone who watches the sun go down and thinks they're seeing the world move? Anyone who looks at the night sky and thinks they're seeing galaxies racing away from the world and from each other, going slower and slower but never stopping, the universe growing colder and darker as the stars burn out one by one?

The house was empty of people, but also of their residue. When a person left, there was usually something left behind, a placeholder, here and there, like a little round head perched on a big fat body, a knob of smell.

Margaret began to whine, pawing at the floor.

Something was wrong. Something having to do with Mees. The sound of yipping started up, not too far off. The red wolves were coming down from Canada to mate with the local coyotes, creating hybrid pups with bigger, sharper teeth and forcing the fisher-cats south, where they'd already penetrated the gated communities, snatching beloved house pets out of backyards right before their horrified owners' eyes. Also the hawk population was on the rise. Hawks were roosting in suburban shade trees, keeping an eye on the bird feeders. For the hawks they were like drive-in restaurants, fast food, very nice.

A key turned in the door — Sophy Kipp reached her arm through the opening and turned on the light over the sink. Mersey was at a party at her friend Dede's, and since the culture decreed that it was okay for teenagers to get drunk as long as they didn't climb into cars and drive a hundred miles an hour into trees or guardrails or one another's cars, Sophy knew Mersey would be spending the night there. Mees was at Sunny Crockett's.

It was too late to get a movie, too late to call anyone. Margaret was whining; Sophy snapped the leash onto her collar and opened the door. "Want to go?" Sophy said, though she had no way of knowing that this was Margaret's favorite sentence in the world. There wasn't a lit window anywhere, the grass white in the moonlight. Margaret's ears were pricked, her hackles up. She pulled Sophy down the road toward the Fines' house. "What is it, girl?" Sophy asked, trying to sound like her daughter. Mees never used the leash; when Sophy thought about Mees, she started to cry. It isn't fair, Sophy told herself, but what was so desirable about a normal life? Had her own life been normal?

At the first intersection Margaret abruptly squatted to pee, looked back over her shoulder at Sophy, then continued pulling her along the road past Fines' and toward Diamonds'. She was very excited. WANT TO GO! There was a rustling sound in the brush bordering Canton Brook, a pair of eyes. Sunflowers were sprouting under Dorothy Diamond's bird feeder, the starlings and finches having dropped seed there all winter long. "Margaret!" Sophy said, as loud as she dared. "Cut it out!" Then a light appeared in a second-story window, and Sophy could see a face veiled by a lace curtain peering down at her.

"Is everything all right?"

Sophy could hear Mr. Diamond saying, "Come back to bed, Dotty."

It was hard to imagine the two of them in bed together. Like a horse in bed with a possum. Mr. Diamond would end up with a concussion, kicked in the head by a flailing hoof.

Whatever Margaret was after, it had to be something unsavory. Something dead. Something rotting. Something wild, with bared teeth.

There are sixteen references to dogs in the Bible, none of them good.

And would I rather Mees had a boyfriend, Sophy asked herself, like her sister? Who says romantic love guarantees happiness? Do I really want her life to be like mine?

Margaret was straining hard on the leash, trying to pull Sophy off the road and across the ditch into Fair's Woods, where she could smell, what? A beaver? A moose? A bear?

Gardener's Almanac — June 21

Midsummer's eve, summer solstice, the moon full. *Body and soul estranged amid the strangeness of themselves, caught up in contemplation* . . . Now is the time to cut your hair, take care of your teeth, prune your shrubs and slaughter your chickens. The sun rises today at 5:05 A.M. and sets at 8:38 P.M.; the moon rises at 5:15 P.M. and sets at 2:47 A.M. Mars is five hundred times brighter than Uranus, which can barely be seen floating above it.

Because plants are largely composed of water, they respond to the tidal pull of the moon. As the moon grows full it draws plants up, enhancing their growth. Gemini, a barren sign, gives way to Cancer, fertile and moist. This is the time to gather herbs and fruit, to make a second planting of lettuce, chard, and rocket. As the moon once again prepares to wane, all is changed, and the soul remembers nothing — nothing!

When she first came back to Varennes, Chloe Brock told herself it would be temporary. It had been hard enough to get away to begin with, hard enough to yank loose the roots, and then, having done so, to accept the fact and stop feeling like a thinned seedling shriveling in the compost pile. She'd waited to come back until her parents didn't live there anymore. They broke her heart — especially her father, who also made her furious, since the more someone broke her heart, meaning the more obvious their weakness was, the more infuriating Chloe found them.

This was why she preferred cats.

"Come here," Chloe said, lifting Mignonette to her lap. Not only did cats not like it when you paid attention to them, but they also didn't like paying attention to you. If Chloe forced Mignonette to sit there longer than she wanted, Mignonette would bite her, hard, on the hand.

In the winter a human being's lap generated heat and was, hence, desirable. In the winter a human being's stomach and thighs made an ideal bed. Tonight was too warm. The windows were open, letting in the smell of squirrels and tunneling rodents. Also a whiff of something else — something large and to be avoided. Mignonette jumped from Chloe's lap, landing heavily in the middle of the carpet like the Sunday paper. For a second or two she stood motionless, then suddenly sprang, light as a fairy, onto the window seat facing Summer Street. Moonlight everywhere! Mignonette was troubled by the Gigi-shaped hole in the house. Like when the sofa got sent off to be reupholstered, only more disturbing.

It was nine o'clock, the full moon suspended in the sky above the Wexlers' roof peak. Chloe lifted the phone, looked at it, put it back down. She and Piet were supposed to have gone to the Thai restaurant for dinner — he was usually so reliable. The glider on the Wexlers' front porch squeaked. Okay, Chloe thought. So this is what it's like to be stood up. *Tant pis.* Whereas unpopular Jill Wexler finally seemed to have found herself a boyfriend at Project Graduation and the two of them to have become entwined on the glider, chastely kissing like old-fashioned sweethearts while June bugs banged themselves senseless against the porch light.

As if the twentieth century had never happened. As if you could turn your back on history and while it was turned atrocities would continue being committed, millions and millions of murdered bodies swept under the rug and the planet manhandled, every spare inch of it, and even the encompassing heavens crammed with human waste as the let vein of polar ice continued dripping blue-green into the world's oceans, raising their level little by little until eventually waves would come crashing against the feet of skyscrapers, submerging shrubs, trees, houses, whole cities, all of them little by little, the way everything happens, little by little, and by the time you noticed, it would be too late.

Piet was supposed to have arrived around eight, but his reliability could be tiring, like any changeless thing, despite the fact that Chloe liked having sex with him.

Men and women, men and women — whatever went on between them was becoming harder for Chloe to ignore. Though the room had grown dark, she didn't bother turning on the lamp. Someone rode a bicycle very fast down Summer Street; a car pulled into the driveway of Linegangs' house next door and left the engine idling and the Jesus station playing. *Praise the Lord! Praise the Lord!* Once, when Chloe was ten years old, her father hadn't dropped her off outside the Canton ice rink as he usually did but had come inside to watch. Harold Fair — he'd been considered handsome in his day, and she could tell from the way Mrs. Comeau skated over to where he stood leaning against the boards drinking cocoa and bent toward him to take a sip from his cup that he still was, at least to women his own age. For a woman her age, Mrs. Comeau happened to be a fairly accomplished figure skater, and she wore competition-style outfits, which is to say she had on a formfitting aqua dress with a short skirt that flew up and showed her matching underpants when she did a sit spin.

Chloe meanwhile was standing by the vending machine. A boy whose name she didn't know but whom she thought was cute was hip checking another boy, and she remembered watching him as she put in her money and not paying any attention as the machine dispensed her cocoa, so when she took her first sip (all the while watching the boy, who was the lean and rat-like type that would always appeal to her), it seemed fitting that the machine had put in too much water and too little cocoa, and the only thing she could taste was the cardboard cup, as if that was all her system could absorb as she watched the boy skate toward her, a really cute daredevil in a T-shirt that said FATE in red letters outlined in black. It had been so exciting! Anything could have happened!

The phone rang. "This better be good," Chloe remarked to Mignonette. "Well?" she said into the receiver.

But it wasn't Piet.

In fact Piet had completely forgotten that he'd agreed to meet Chloe for dinner and was at that very moment sitting on Billie's dock in the light of the full moon with his pant legs rolled up and his feet in the water, the beaver beside him in the Havahart trap, dismantling a slice of Nova Scotia salmon. As Piet watched, interested, the beaver held pieces of fish very close to its bright little eyes, its expression dismissive, as if it had seen better. Beavers are, in any case, vegetarian. Billie was floating on her back in the middle of the lake, looking up at the moon and stars.

"Guess where I am?" laughed the voice on the other end, and Chloe almost dropped the phone.

"Malcolm? Where *are* you?"

"Where do you think?" But it was a spurious question — no one ever knew where Malcolm was, least of all his friends. "Okay," he said. "Give up?"

She remembered the last time she'd seen him. His hair had been in two long pigtails that hung to his waist, and his skin had been the color of polished mahogany. You could see more of it than you wanted because he hadn't been wearing a shirt or pants — only a sort of chamois loincloth, even though it was late October, Halloween almost. He also had thrown away his eyeglasses, standards of "goodness" for vision being purely relative.

This wasn't long after Chloe's first attempt at leaving Varennes and Malcolm behind forever. He'd been her high-school boyfriend and then vanished during the college years, reappearing the day she moved into her first apartment only to vanish again, and then reappear, then vanish, then reappear, and so forth and so on. At the time she'd been living in Iowa and had just driven home from her job teaching conversational French to farmers at Sioux City Community College when she found Malcolm lounging on her porch, surrounded by jars of home-canned cherry tomatoes. He had a cat with him — a gray shorthair cat named Fidel that was dense and hard as a muscle and pretty much totally feral, since Malcolm didn't believe in commercial cat food. Whatever Fidel ate, he had to catch himself. Fidel's digestive system also harbored every parasite in the book, but Chloe didn't discover this until later, after Malcolm disappeared in the middle of the night, leaving her with the cat and the canned tomatoes and, in a shared moment of insanity, his surname and a ring.

Occasionally thereafter she would hear from him. Sometimes he needed money or wanted her to give shelter to some shady-looking friend, some fellow revolutionary, though Chloe was rarely clear on Malcolm's politics, which often seemed more self-serving than idealistic. Recently she'd seen the article about him Billie picked up from the wire service. He'd fled the country after the coast guard caught him engaged in an act of supposed environmental terrorism in Narragansett Bay — something having to do with codfish.

Malcolm Brock. So in love with the natural world was he that he couldn't bear to let a single cherry tomato wither on the vine, nor could he drive a single stray cat from his door, the only hitch being that he didn't really *have* a door of his own, which meant that he had to count on his friends to be tender-hearted in his stead.

"No, Malcolm," Chloe said. "I don't *want* to know where you are."

Midnight, White Sunday. Even the clearest water is less transparent than air, and more than seven hundred times heavier, its surface stronger than that of any other fluid except mercury. Springtails can spring on it, water striders stride, their six minuscule feet dimpling it without breaking through, as hydras hang their heads downward from it, and planarians glide noiselessly along its underside.

Not human beings, though — we're too heavy.

Like Billie Carpenter, floating on her back toward the middle of Black Lake, while above her head the full moon continued dipping toward Adder Ridge, taking with it the Harp, the Shield, the Little Fox, and all the other summer constellations. Billie was wearing the black two-piece bathing suit she'd had since college. Only a small part of her body was exposed to the air: her face, her collarbones, the palms of her hands, her hip bones, her toes.

As the lake surface cooled, the top layer of water dropped slightly, a shift that was of enormous importance to the animals and plants living there. Water fleas, mosquito larvae, fairy shrimp, algae — the closer Billie drifted to them, the more of them she displaced, at the same time sending bigger creatures, minnows, frogs, and water beetles, diving deeper for cover.

The wind picked up; Piet Zeebrugge put on his sweater and thought about going indoors. He could still see Billie's limbs like a light cast on the lake by a star-shaped heavenly body, drifting away from him in the direction of the town beach. The question wasn't whether Billie knew what she was doing — she'd already told him not to worry. The one thing she was really good at, she'd confided ruefully (following their first attempt at a kiss), was swimming, especially distance. She'd even considered having a shot at the English Channel.

No, the question wasn't whether Billie knew what she was doing, but whether Piet did.

Out on the open surface of Black Lake, the wind blew unhindered; there were great areas of water where the littlest creatures could find no place to hide. The lake surface harbored a huge population of them, being born or being eaten or getting blown onto the town beach, where their bodies would be found the next morning — caddis worms and mayfly nymphs, whose skins routinely got washed up into windrows. Others drifted down past the place where the fish lived, into the lonesome reach of water where nothing lived at all really, eventually hitting the deep soft ooze of the bottom.

A pike swam directly under Billie's floating body, at a depth of about five feet. Pikes have been known to pull swimming ducks underwater, but Billie was too big for it.

The pike's mind was tuned to one thought. *Kill,* it was thinking, and would always be thinking, *Kill, Kill, Kill* — except, that is, in the early spring, when it would once again thrash its way into a flooded field to spawn, and then it would be thinking, *Sex!*

Unlike the tadpoles, schooling near Piet's toes in the shallows under the dock — the tadpoles were in a state of terrific confusion. Practically overnight they'd changed from herbivores to meat eaters, their intestinal tracks from elegantly coiled watch springs to crude food canals. What had become of their appetite for algae and diatoms? Of course now they could get back at the hydras, who used to eat them.

They hem me in, sang David the Psalmist, alternately exhilarated and depressed by the world. *They hem me in on every side. In the name of the Lord I will repel them.*

At some point Billie raised her head and waved. Then she turned and began to swim back toward shore. Piet could see her arms lifting and lowering; she was doing the Australian crawl, shining spangles of lake water dripping from her elbows like jewels. "She's good," Piet told the beaver, who wasn't paying attention. The beaver was asleep, in fact, snoring.

What were they going to do with it?

What were they going to do?

Under the water lived creatures big and little, nimble and graceless, strong and weak, swift and slow, all born to feed and grow and reproduce, to eat and to be eaten.

Water has more properties that are beneficial to human beings than any other substance. Also it can drown you.

TOWN PLUNGED INTO MOURNING

On Sunday afternoon last a shocking accident occurred on what is known as Black Lake in Varennes, which resulted in the deaths of eight children, all of whom were members of the Varennes First Congregational Sunday School class taught by Miss Inez Fair of Adder Ridge, and all but one of them under the age of twelve.

Miss Fair and her thirteen charges were having a picnic party that afternoon at White Birch Point, when according to an unidentified eyewitness, Miss Fair proposed a boat ride across the lake to the Inn at Canton Brook. The boat in question was constructed of two small boats placed alongside and decked over with seats, with a railing built around it. It was the property of Miss Fair's father, Clark Fair, who claimed he'd never given his daughter leave to use the boat, which was unfit.

The boat started to tip over immediately. There was a pump on board which Willie Ainsworth attempted to use, calling upon Miss Fair to "back the boat as one of them was filling." She replied that it would be all right if some of the passengers changed their positions to the other side. The children, now frightened, moved so quickly that it caused the boat to careen in the opposite direction, and Samuel Webb and three others were thrown overboard. His older sister, Alice, seeing the accident, plunged in after Samuel, tipping the boat the other way and throwing out three more (Bessie *and Justin Bliss and Lawrence Mayhew). Those who remained upon the boat were safe, as it sank only about two feet under the water.*

The names of those drowned were as follows: Mr. Lawrence Mayhew, age seven; Miss Laura Mayhew, age seven; Miss Elizabeth Bliss, age three; Mr. Justin Bliss, age ten; Miss Alice Webb, age sixteen; Mr. Samuel Webb, age seven; Mr. David Danvers, age eleven; Miss Caroline Sprague, age nine.

Miss Webb was a strong young woman and a good swimmer and lost her life trying to save her brother as well as Miss Sprague, seizing one in each hand and struggling until she strangled to keep them above water, when all three sank together. Miss Mayhew and Miss Bliss did not sink at all, being supported by their clothing, but had fallen in head downward and, when reached, were dead. Miss Fair fell into a faint and apparently hit her head against the railing, rendering her unconscious for the duration of the event.

Six of the bodies were recovered that evening. The body of Miss Webb was found Monday forenoon, while that of Miss Sprague was not found until Tuesday afternoon. The water at this point was fifty feet deep, with a muddy bottom.

The entire community is plunged into the deepest grief at this sad calamity, and a great deal of sympathy is expressed for those who by this misfortune are called upon to mourn the loss of those lives dearer to them by far than their own.

The excitement over this event is intense, and various stories and rumors are afloat about the matter.

Three in the morning, and Lorna was wide awake. She wasn't the only one: Mr. Crockett had just padded down the hall in his Black Watch pajama pants, followed by Buddy, the two of them headed who knew where but certainly not to the bathroom, since the master bedroom had a bathroom attached to it. You could never feel as lonely as you did spending the night at someone else's house, Lorna thought, hearing the sounds of people sleeping around you and the house opening around you fold by fold as if there was no end to it, like an origami flower coming undone. Every now and then there'd be a thump, but never where there were thumps in your own house, plus the Crocketts' house had central air-conditioning, which made you feel like a droid held in suspended animation, waiting to be granted the gift of human life.

Mees was talking in her sleep, her fingers clenched, gripping the sheet as if it were a weapon. Lorna couldn't understand a word she was saying. Sunny was in her own bedroom, from which every trace of her pink-and-white girlhood — with the exception of her many dolls, who'd been consigned for all eternity to a Louis Quinze curio cabinet — had been recently expunged. The three girls had spent the evening in Sunny's bedroom, playing Hearts the way they used to and trying to act as if they were enjoying themselves, but Mees and Lorna had been forced to leave when it was time to go to bed, since Sunny claimed she could no longer sleep with other people in the room. Also her Hearts game had lacked its former intensity — Lorna couldn't remember a time when Sunny didn't try shooting the moon almost every hand, but tonight, not even once.

"Hey!" said Mees. "Hey! Where are you going with that?"

Lorna leaned across the bed and studied Mees's face. She had to fight the temptation to shake her awake — never a good idea with Mees. You might get spit at or punched in the nose. Alone, alone, I am oh so alone, thought Lorna. Even her good friend the moon had abandoned her, having moved into some part of the sky you couldn't see from either of the guest-bedroom windows, both of which were impossible to open. "Going with what?" Lorna asked, and Mees chuckled as if the answer were hilariously self-evident. "*You* know," she said.

At the party after the play, Sunny had danced with Justin Byrd's older brother, Nelson, who was an eighth-grader, and Lorna had watched, fascinated, as Nelson put his hand on Sunny's rear end like it was something he did every day, and Sunny hadn't batted an eye. Lorna figured she could ally herself with Sunny, and there might be some dancing with boys in her future, or she could ally herself with Mees, who'd spent the entire party watching Mr. Perkins, the sixth grade's pet horn snake, swallow a mouse whole.

The moon wasn't visible, but the entire outdoors was lit almost as if it had just snowed, and there was a great tail of silver ripples fanning open toward the beach on the far side of the lake. Lorna could see a man and a woman sleeping together under what looked like a white bedsheet on the dock below Crocketts'. Or maybe they weren't sleeping, since the shapes under the sheet kept moving around and changing. Maybe they were having sex.

Lorna was dying to touch herself and think about it, but the idea of waking Mees was too frightening.

She could hear Buddy returning alone down the hall without Mr. Crockett, his toenails clicking past the room where Sunny's three little brothers had finally conked out and circling just outside the door to the master bedroom, flattening a bed in the high grass for himself, as Mees had explained it to her, before landing all at once in a heap and falling asleep.

The more sleeping bodies around her, the wider awake Lorna became.

At least Mr. Crockett seemed to be in the same boat, pacing around the yard in his Black Watch pajama bottoms. He looked better this way than when he was dressed in a suit, unlike Lorna's father, whose entire torso was covered with curly dark hair like an ape. Mr. Crockett was holding a phone to his ear, his mouth opening and closing rapidly, talking fast. Lorna renewed her efforts to get the window open; eventually she located the latch, recessed into the side of the frame.

"You're crazy, baby," Mr. Crockett was saying. "You're driving me nuts. . . ."

Lorna had kept her eye on him at the party, though chiefly to monitor his interaction with Mr. Mason. As far as Lorna could tell, there was no bad blood between the two men, despite Sunny's claim that her parents had caught Mr. Mason stealing. In fact, once Mrs. Crockett had left the party, Mr. Crockett seemed chiefly interested in Ms. Bamberger, the art teacher, who had put peacock feathers in her hair for the occasion. Maybe all that was happening was that the old people at the Home were stealing from one another, bearing out Grammy Steiner's conviction that we turn into thieves in our old age, which also happened to be why she said she would rather die than enter the perfectly nice retirement community Lorna's parents had gone to a lot of trouble to find for her.

I'm hungry, Lorna realized. If only I could eat something, then I could fall asleep, though going downstairs to the kitchen meant running the risk of bumping into Mr. Crockett, who would immediately know that she'd been spying on him.

She needed an ally. "Mees," Lorna said softly, bracing herself.

But Mees just rolled onto her side, facing Lorna, smiled, and let out a sigh. There was a big pillow crease in her left cheek, and her breath smelled minty from toothpaste. Her eyes were squeezed shut.

"Are you awake?" Lorna asked.

"No, I'm a cake," Mees said, and burst out laughing. Then she curled herself up in a little ball. "Go back to sleep, Lorna," she said. "It's the middle of the night."

"I can't go back to sleep," Lorna said. "You can't go *back* to sleep if you haven't been asleep to begin with." She could feel the familiar panic, the sense of literally nauseating isolation that she would confuse until the end of her life with homesickness. It was as if there was a place called "home" that had nothing to do with where she lived and if only she could find it, she could finally sleep like a normal person. "Come on, Measle," Lorna begged. "Please? Let's go get something to eat."

But Mees was once again lying on her back, gripping the sheet for dear life and softly snoring.

Okay, Lorna thought. I give up.

She rolled out of bed and tiptoed into the hallway and down the stairs, Buddy at her heels. Mr. Crockett seemed to be sitting in the living room with the lights off, staring out the window at the lake, drinking a short glass of what Lorna was pretty sure was whiskey, given the color and the presence in it of ice cubes. She could only see the back of his head, but something about the position of it, the slight tilt forward, made her think he was in a pensive mood.

"Buddy, is that you?" he said. "C'mon up, pal," he said, patting his knee. "Buddy?"

There would be cupcakes left over from the party, Lorna figured. A cupcake with yellow icing would be just what she needed, the next best thing to a friend.

She was lifting the cake cover when she heard footsteps behind her.

"Jesus Christ, Lorna. You want to scare a person to death?"

Naturally there was no good answer to that question.

"I'm sorry, Mr. Crockett."

"Well . . ." He planted both hands on the counter and leaned forward, propping himself on his forearms and staring glassy-eyed at nothing. "I guess us insomniacs have to stick together." Then he roused himself and fixed her with the same glassy-eyed stare. "I don't suppose you'd care for a drink? No, of course not."

Lorna selected her cupcake, considered it for a moment, its smear of yellow frosting, and put it back. This was how the Evil One got his hooks in you. You took a little bite and you were his forever.

"I guess I'm not hungry after all," Lorna said.

But Mr. Crockett had once again returned his gaze to nothing, which now seemed located a little above and to the right of Buddy's head. "What gets me," he said, "is I was only trying to be nice. You try being nice to some people, and where does it get you? Nowadays everyone's a fucking lawyer."

Had he forgotten what Lorna's father did for a living? Meanwhile Buddy was angling for a cupcake, lying on his back, wagging his tail and doing everything in his power to look adorable.

All Lorna really wanted to do was leave the Crocketts' house and go home. Her own house was less than half a mile away — but even so, she knew that if she picked up and left, everyone would have a fit. When you spent the night at someone's house, it was like being in prison.

Worse than prison here, because even if you made it through the night, you had to eat Sunday breakfast with the whole Crockett family, which always included soft-boiled eggs that hadn't boiled long enough so you could see the string that may have grown up to be a chick if only you hadn't eaten it, and then you had to go to church and pretend to believe in God.

But how else could it have happened?

Can it really be an accident that there are as many stars in the Milky Way as there are neurons in the brain?

And in the members of the body the heavenly signs arranged, viz. the Ram in the head, the Bull in the neck, the Twins in the arms, the Crab in the heart, etc.?

The Fiend had a visage like a young man's, said Julian of Norwich, and he thrust it close to her face. She was lying in her bed unable to sleep, the English fens stretching out on either side. The Fiend's hair was red as rust, clipped in front, with locks hanging down over the temples. His paws gripped her by the throat and tried to strangle her, and from him came a human jabbering as if there were two people, and it seemed to Julian that both of them were jabbering at the same time, as if they were having a very tense discussion.

The darkness is eternal, the Fiend would have it understood, and out of it came the ruler of this world. The sower of seeds was sloppy. Much was said about the principle of moist things and the principle of fire: the Fiend would have it understood that all good things happen in the world not by the power of God but by contrivance or art.

Consider the shield fern, the Labrador duck, the narrow-flippered penguin, the archaeopteryx — every living thing that didn't just die its own small death but vanished forever from the face of the earth. Not a single one of them was contrived or artificial; even the Fiend can't make another Labrador duck.

Consider the souls of the extinct creatures.

Suppose there are many universes, each one called into being at the slightest touch, an action no stronger than a flower? Suppose our galaxy and all the others, instead of drifting more and more slowly, reluctantly even, away from one another, with heavy hearts and a lingering backward glance, are instead speeding up, as if the process isn't a long drawn-out endgame but an excited rush toward something? As if the end itself could be the exciting goal, even if that something is the complete extinction of space and time?

Would there be anything left over?

Helen Zeebrugge was climbing a long steep staircase leading to an open door, behind which she hoped she would find her husband. It had been many years since she'd last seen him, and she knew she probably wouldn't recognize him. What happened to a person after they died? Would they continue to look the way they did the last time you saw them alive? If that were the case, he would never have been able to make it to the top of that long steep staircase, since the last time she'd seen him alive he'd been lying in the hospital bed in Italy, where they'd been on vacation when he had the second (and as it proved, fatal) of his heart attacks.

It had just rained. The sea was dark green and wild, hurling itself at the Ligurian coast like an inconsolable lover. The steps were made of stone and brick, many small segments intricately pieced together, covered with moss, very steep, very slippery. There was also a handrail, but it was positioned at a level more hospitable to dwarves than to normal-sized people, and John was unusually tall.

"Johnny," Helen had cried, watching him lose his grip.

No, probably he wouldn't look the same.

And he probably wouldn't have been restored to his buoyant young manhood, or tender youth, or squalling infancy, either.

Something completely different, then, Helen thought, that was what she would find waiting in the room at the top of the stairs. Something that couldn't be contained in a body. Something large and seemingly inanimate, mineral even, like a rock or a hill, but also without any form at all, as if it were made of air, and just when you thought you were on the verge of seeing it for what it really was, it would suddenly dissolve into a pool of water and run down a hole in the floor the way an eel might or a snake, with bone-chilling, unknowable purpose.

Helen sat bolt upright in bed. It was Sunday morning, June 22, but still early, the sun not yet risen, though the sky was beginning to brighten a little between the branches of the locust trees next door. Going to be a hot one, the night nurse had said when she gave Helen her blood-pressure medicine and checked her pulse. As if there was anything to make it race these days.

June 22 — John would have been ninety-six.

You slept and you woke and you slept and you woke and your head hurt and there was a small, insufficiently banked fire smoldering at the doorway to your esophagus and really the only thing that changed from day to day was that the hand in front of your face grew harder and harder to see.

Helen leaned back into her pillows and stared at her hand. Try as she might, she couldn't remember a younger version of it, at least not attached *there*, to that wrist. As for her wedding ring — even if she wanted to remove it, good luck. She tried to remember John putting the ring on her finger. Twenty-eight-year-old Helen's hand boldly extended for all to see in a church; if it weren't for the photograph, she'd probably remember nothing. Her dress, for instance, which had subsequently been worn by two of Piet's brides, the others having deemed it hopelessly old-fashioned, though the truth is they were too fat to get into it. Now her dress was in storage, awaiting bride number five.

Johnny. All those mornings I woke next to him, Helen

thought. You'd think I could remember at least one of them, but the best she could come up with was the bedroom window in the apartment on Riverside Drive, where they'd spent the last years of their marriage, on its sill a single stem of flowering plum in a Mei Ping vase and the organdy curtains moving in that enchanted, heart-wrenching way of curtains in a summer breeze, and (here it got harder to *apprehend,* exactly) some sense of Helen's brain considering the day ahead and what she was going to do in it, as if there were choices to be made, which book to read now that she'd finished, what? *The Forsyte Saga* no doubt, and which markets to visit and happiness — yes, *happiness,* not too strong a word! — when she thought of what could be done with the things she might discover out there in the world, fresh chervil or Amish peaches or an insanely beautiful piece of fish, as from the bathroom came the sound of John's bare feet on the tiles as he paced in front of the mirror, brushing his teeth.

Johnny would be ninety-six years old today, and the altar flowers at church were to be in his memory. Helen sighed, a sound she profoundly disliked. As if being helped into one of the pastel garments Crockett bulk ordered from a catalog weren't indignity enough, and having to inch along on Piet's arm down the hall past the kitchen and out the back door of the Crockett Home and then to be shoved into the passenger seat of his car only to be yanked forth moments later into the blazing sun like a reluctant newborn and once again to suffer the indignity of inching along, this time across the gaping crevasses of the church parking lot and up the handicap-access ramp and into the dark church. She knew she had no choice in the matter. You couldn't order altar flowers and not show up for the service.

Pink and gold light filled the east-facing window. Helen's blinds were never drawn — this was a fight she had bitterly fought and finally won shortly after being moved into the Crockett Home, earning her the undying animus of Kathy Crockett, though as far as Helen was concerned, anyone who had time to waste watching a ninety-three-year-old woman getting undressed wasn't worth worrying about.

The sky brightened. It sent a patch of its brightness across Helen's room and onto her Hokusai print of a woman combing another woman's hair. Soon the morning noises would start, doors banging, toilets flushing, as well as every conceivable sound a human body could make, including howling and groaning.

Helen threw off her sheets.

Suddenly she remembered with ghostly clarity the feel of Piet's hair under her fingers, how cool his hair had always felt, even when his scalp was warm, and how soft and sleek it was, and how it was a very light brown, just like his father's. She could feel the hot weight of him in her lap as she stroked his head and held him.

He must have been about three years old and unhappy about something or he wouldn't have been there — Piet had never been an affectionate child. He was more affectionate now that he was a grown man, an old man. When he came later this morning to pick Helen up for church he would almost certainly give her a big hug and a kiss and the hair he had left would be gray and the texture of shredded wheat. Unlike ghost-Piet, so smooth and cool he could slip through her fingers . . .

There came a hesitant tapping at the door.

"Come in," Helen said, and then, as the knocking continued, growing louder and more peremptory, frantic even, she raised her voice and repeated, "Come in!"

It was the woman from New Jersey, wearing her pink flowered housecoat inside out and carrying a sewing basket. "I've been working on it all night," the woman told Helen, and she reached into the basket and removed something that at first glance looked like a Portuguese man-of-war but that on closer inspection turned out to be a snarled mass of thread with spools and bobbins hanging from it.

"Yes?" Helen said, wary yet neutral.

"All night," the woman repeated, her shoe-button eyes darting around and around the room. "Didn't you used to have a little kitty cat in here?"

Helen knew she was going to have to lie, because if she were to tell the truth, she was going to start crying, and the last thing in the world she wanted was to have Crockett suddenly materialize in her room and find her crying. "No," she said.

"Yes you did," said the woman. She walked right up to Helen and shook the mass of thread in her face. "Help me," she said. "Please?"

The sky grew brighter still.

From down the hall came the sound of someone coughing, a sound so prolonged and so deep and so violent it was as if she were bringing up her eternal soul.

"I don't know what to do," the woman from New Jersey said, setting her sewing basket down on the mattress.

"Throw it away," Helen told her.

The bell rang, meaning it was time for breakfast.

By now the sun was already high in the sky above Pitsulak Island, heating the big golden stones. Three metal tent pegs belonging to Daniel Murdock remained stuck in the sand, and there were also twelve piles of smaller stones known as deadmen that he'd arranged at intervals and in a circle, to provide anchorage and make the pegs stay put.

The cotton grass was just coming up, the weather warmer than usual. The yellow poppies were in bloom. One and a half meters due east of the circle of deadmen, a raised hearth could be found, everything in it, with the exception of two paper clips, a fourth tent peg, a foil package that used to contain freeze-dried beef Stroganoff, and a crumpled piece of paper with ANDREA written on it and emphatically crossed out, long since consumed by fire. In addition, nineteen matchsticks lay scattered around the perimeter of the hearth, the tip of only one of them unused and red.

A heavy rain two days earlier had washed away almost all cigarette ash in the vicinity of the tent site, though not the butts of three cigarettes.

Clearly Daniel Murdock left the island in a hurry, otherwise he would have been more careful.

The wind was from the west. The flies were bad, also the mosquitoes. Though "bad" is a relative term, meaningless in the absence of human inhabitants. In fact the only living creatures on the island that might find the flies and mosquitoes bothersome were a family of foxes, the vixen tending to her litter of new cubs while her mate scavenged mice for dinner.

The sea was calm, the sun shining. An iceberg drifted past to the east, the sunlight turning it to a world that seemed not only possible but also irresistible to enter, a shade of aquamarine verging on no color at all, crystal clear, like heaven. In the water, capelin and seals. In the air, razorbills and gannets.

Archaeology is a particular Western notion of knowing about the past; it assumes a dominant materialist bias. As a scientific paradigm it purports to be impartial and rigorous in its search for the truth.

The man who left Pitsulak Island in a hurry was a smoker and a carnivore. While on the island, he lived in a tent and cooked his food over an open fire, though he may also have slept in the open air and used a portable stove on occasion. He had some knowledge of camp craft. One of the last things on his mind before he left the island was his wife.

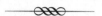

June 22, Pentecost. Also called White Sunday, though traditionally the priest's vestments are red, symbolizing the Holy Ghost's descent upon the apostles in tongues of fire. According to the story, the apostles were in Jerusalem, sitting together in an upstairs room when this happened, after which they began to speak in tongues as the spirit gave them utterance, while at the same time men from every nation under heaven (Medes and Parthians and Elamites and the dwellers in Mesopotamia, and in Judea, and Cappadocia, etc. etc.) who were also in Jerusalem found that they could understand one another as if they all spoke the same language. Wine was blamed, but Peter was quick to point out that it was only the third hour of the day.

In Italy rose petals are scattered from the church ceiling on Pentecost; in France, trumpets are blown. In England, for some reason, Pentecost is celebrated with horse races.

Richard Jenkins sat in his study on the third floor of the St. Luke's rectory, reading over his sermon. He'd worked on it until two in the morning and arisen at six to finish it. Now seven o'clock had come and gone, and he had to be in his vestments and in the church in less than an hour for the early service, but he still wasn't happy with what he'd written. The last sentence — *As much as we differ from one another in the smallest particulars of the flesh, we are the same body in spirit* — wasn't striking the exact note he'd been going for of relief verging on admonition.

The rectory was a three-story Victorian of no special charm: it was made of brown brick, and its trim was mustard yellow. Richard's study was on the top floor at the rear of the building; from it he looked out over an untended yard that extended level for a short distance before rising steeply up a sumac-covered hill to meet the perfect gardens of Mountain View Circle high above. He'd originally chosen the room because it was protected from the traffic noise of River Street, but over the years it proved to be cold in winter and hot in summer, as well as dark all the time and with a depressing view to the right of the parking lot, where on more than one occasion, he'd seen his eldest daughter, Mimi, conducting business of a questionable nature.

Mary Holst-Jenkins said Mimi was coming around, it was only a matter of time. He should be more patient. But she hadn't always been like this, Richard thought, not when she was a little girl. He liked to remember Mimi as having been sweet and tractable, though to be perfectly honest, she'd always had a mind of her own, which is to say, she'd been stubborn as a mule. Pretty, though. The boys liked her. She was with one of them now. The stocky fellow with the shaved head who kept trying to engage Richard in philosophical discussion. Arthur something. Watch out, Arthur, Richard thought. She'll eat you alive.

"And the wolf shall dwell with the lamb, and the leopard shall lie down with the kid; and the calf and the young lion and the fatling together; and a little child shall lead them." Isaiah 11. The lesson for the day.

Richard could hear the anguished moaning of the pipes from the second floor as his wife turned on the shower, followed by a wild outpouring of water and then a tempering of the sound as she stepped into the tub. A cool shower, he thought — Mary would be taking a cool shower because the day was already hot. Mary's cool, wet body; he wished he didn't have to leave the house, let alone preach a sermon. It was only seven-thirty, and the study was like an oven, his hair like an animal sitting on his head.

Richard removed his reading glasses and rubbed the bridge of his nose; then he put them back on and returned his attention to what he'd written.

The problem isn't animals, the problem is people, he read.

Of course animals routinely ate other animals; it was in their nature. A wolf ate a lamb and thought nothing of it. When a wolf ate a lamb, it wasn't treating the lamb like something it wasn't. For a wolf to dwell with a lamb was merely the opposite side of the same coin: the key difference being that the wolf's appetite hadn't been activated.

Whereas human beings since the dawn of time had continually used all of the resources at their disposal to treat other human beings like something they weren't, that is, not human. Human beings turned their young into walking bombs and sent them forth to destroy places of human habitation. Human beings wrapped other human beings in pitch and set them alight and mounted them like torches in gardens; they sewed them in the skins of wild animals and set hunting dogs on them. They scraped them with pincers, they tore out their eyes, they cut off parts of their bodies and roasted them. They gassed them, they starved them, they turned their bones to radium. There was no other side to that coin.

Richard looked out the window; two thin arms of sunlight were reaching into his so-called garden from either side. A bird flew by, what kind, who knew? The phone rang. Rang again. Then stopped — Mary must have picked it up.

On the one hand you had the lesson for the day, with its talk about wolves and lambs. On the other hand you had the Gospel, John 14, with its talk about spirit possession and last days. "And it shall come to pass, saith God, I will pour out of my Spirit upon all flesh; and your sons and daughters shall prophesy, and your young men shall see visions, and your old men shall dream dreams: the sun shall be turned into darkness, and the moon into blood. . . ."

But what about your middle-aged men, Richard thought. What were they supposed to be doing while the young men were having their visions and the old men their dreams? What about Carl Banner or James Trumbell? What about Piet Zeebrugge? What about the men who were actually running the world?

What Pentecost really was, he decided, with its optimistic talk and its pessimistic talk, was a story about what made a human life something more than meat. It was a story about what made a human life not just meat but something better, something capable of not just eating or being eaten. And it was also a story about what it took for a human being not to see other human beings as meat.

Suddenly the light changed; Mary was standing in the doorway, toweling dry her curly brown hair with one hand and holding the phone with the other.

"Darling, it's Warren," she said. "He says the organ isn't working."

"Not working? I don't even know what that means," Richard replied. "Don't you just press on the keys?"

"You're going to have to talk to him," Mary said, covering the receiver. "He's in a state."

She was already dressed for church in her navy linen sun dress — how he loved her tawny freckled shoulders, the way she walked toward him barefoot across the room, treading firmly and with her feet slightly turned out, like a peasant or a ballet dancer.

"He says the summer choir can't hold a tune *with* the organ, let alone without it," Mary reported.

Bells began ringing; the recorded bells of the Catholic church on Elm Street, very pretty, albeit a fraud.

Richard took the phone. "Warren," he said. "What seems to be the matter?" Then he pulled Mary close and kissed her at the base of her neck, in the little hollow place where the faint smell of sweat already pooled, together with the smell of lily-of-the-valley perfume and that mysterious toasty aroma that was Mary's and Mary's alone. "Okay," he said into the phone. "Okay, I'll be right over." He turned off the phone and ran his hand down Mary's spine.

It was always the same problem — trying to say two opposing things simultaneously. Language was never adequate to the task.

"What do *you* think happened in that upstairs room?" he asked his wife and, when she looked confused, added, "in Jerusalem. On Pentecost. Why do *you* think people want to tear one another limb from limb?"

"Oh, darling," she said, and for a moment a sad look passed across her face.

They were so happy, so well married. Granted, sometimes they had to sleep in separate beds, since Richard tended to snore and Mary to enact in her dreams the consummate backhand shot.

"I wish I knew what to tell you," Mary said.

Of course they both knew perfectly well that her view of the world tended to be more, well, *worldly* than Richard's. Mary had already spent an hour with the *New York Times* over coffee, which is to say, she had spent an hour confronting whatever form the devil had chosen to assume overnight, pleasantly smiling maybe, or waving his arms and screaming, or just dangling apparently pointlessly like a stuffed effigy of a living being in the sun.

Violets, the preferred food of the regal fritillary butterfly, were in bloom at the feet of the trees in the woods around Black Lake, but there weren't any regal fritillaries there to eat them, nor were they sitting on shrubs sunning themselves, slowly opening and closing their beautiful orange wings as they would usually do at this hour of the morning. This is because as a species they completely disappeared from the area sometime toward the end of the last century, along with many other butterflies, and birds, and animals, and plants.

Even given their tragic extinction, the morning smelled wonderful. The hot sun enhanced the fragrance of the milkweed and bedstraw growing in profusion on either side of Piet Zeebrugge as he ran up French Hill Road from the lake. The sky was pale blue, the way it is when the day is going to be hot. Because it was early Sunday, there was very little traffic, though even before he got past the alpine meadow Piet could see tiny Mr. Diamond steering his motorboat away from the public boat launch, with an even tinier Doozie in the bow.

Songbirds were singing: robins and warblers and phoebes and wrens. The white-throated sparrow. Maybe even a bobolink or meadowlark, though there were fewer of them than before. Theirs is a kind of music that lightens the human heart, and there is no telling what we'll do to one another when it finally stops.

Doozie sat curled in the bow of Mr. Diamond's motorboat on top of the orange life preserver. Doozie hadn't wanted to go in the boat, but Mr. Diamond had been feeling a little lonely today, for no obvious reason aside from the fact that sometimes even a beautiful day can seem to stretch endlessly ahead of a man with no obvious margin to it or point, and so he'd pressed Doozie into service as crew. His wife was still asleep. She loved to sleep late on Sunday and then don the long white peignoir from the Paris anniversary trip and make pancakes for herself and Mr. Diamond, who often as not would be returning to her from his early-morning expedition with a big appetite and a fish.

Water slapped the bottom of the boat. Dachshunds were bred in landlocked countries, and their special talent is for chasing badgers into their holes in the dirt and killing them.

The smell of fish and bilge — not good!

The boat motored toward Billie Carpenter's dock, where the beaver remained incarcerated in the Havahart trap. It was already awake and considering methods of escape when Doozie drifted past in Mr. Diamond's boat, cushioned on his orange life preserver like royalty in a gondola. Today Billie had to let the beaver loose, no matter what. She raised herself on her elbows and waved to Mr. Diamond, but he was too busy steering to notice. Doozie, on the other hand, who was high-strung by nature and already nervous from being so far from shore, began to bark at the beaver, sharp excited little barks that echoed around the surrounding hills, at which point the beaver also became agitated, making a low-pitched snorting noise and banging against the walls of its trap.

I'm going to have to open the door and let him go, she thought, and though she knew perfectly well that she was thinking about the beaver, she also had to admit that the thought might apply to Piet Zeebrugge as well. Now, she thought. Now, Billie. First thing, before we even dream of eating breakfast. She turned her head to the left and found herself looking right into the beaver's eyes and for a moment, it is true, Billie found herself unsure who or what exactly had had sex with her last night.

In any case, she was more than satisfied. The best sex was that way — like a heathen god had momentarily paid a visit. Baal, protector of livestock and crops and killer of infants. In some stories the creator took Beaver from his right side and divided it into twelve pieces, which were men.

Piet Zeebrugge ran along Adder Ridge and glanced at his watch, picking up speed. If he didn't make it back to Billie's house in exactly fifteen minutes, he would never manage to shower and change and get his mother to church in time for the ten o'clock service. She would see his lateness as a form of hostility; she'd read a lot of Freud in her day. Too much, if you asked Piet.

The sun was now shining brightly on the northern and southern extremities of Black Lake, turning the water there blue and gold and the air warm, though the middle of the lake, which remained in the shadow of Bliss Hill, was black, the air cool. The last of the traps Beau O'Brien had left near the beaver slide were empty; his plan was to sleep off his hangover and remove them sometime midafternoon, since the beaver population of Black Lake now appeared to be holding at exactly zero.

Mr. Diamond got a bite — a bullhead, dozing in the muck at the bottom of the lake and feeling around with its whiskers for something to eat. He was anchored directly opposite the point where the Murdocks' house sat, all of the bindery's many windows turned opaque like hammered brass by the rising sun. The house was empty, Danny having gone back north after settling Andrea in an extended-care facility outside of Boston; eventually a couple from Manhattan would buy the house and make a doomed attempt to turn it into a restaurant. Of course Dorothy Diamond would never dream of cooking such a thing as a bullhead. When she was in Paris, it had been all she could do to make herself swallow a single escargot.

Margaret, meanwhile — who'd managed to get away from Sophy Kipp the night before when somehow she'd slipped her head free from the red collar she'd been wearing most of her adult life and took off into Fair's Woods with Sophy trailing after her, leash and empty collar in hand, calling (firmly at first and then furiously and then piteously and finally in a complete panic), *Margaret! Margaret! Margaret!* all to no avail, while Margaret herself was having a ball chasing a porcupine to the top of Adder Ridge where she cornered it against a hornbeam tree and got a noseful of quills — Margaret was curled on the Crocketts' front lawn, utterly worn out and her nose like a pincushion, but also relieved to know that her girl was inside the exact house that she was lying outside of, keeping watch.

The day got warmer; Piet Zeebrugge was drenched with sweat by the time he made it back to Billie Carpenter's dock.

"Hey!" Billie said, rolling onto her side and smiling up at him.

"Hey," Piet replied, looking off across the lake. He felt spent; he felt heroic. He considered the fact that his father had been born on a day like this. "I need to get a move on if I'm going to pick up my mother," he said.

Billie arose, stark naked, and stretched, raising her arms high above her head and spreading her fingers like a stick person. "What time is it?" she asked. "I was just going to fix breakfast."

"Jesus, Billie. Do you want to give that old guy in the boat a heart attack?" Piet captured her hands and drew them down around his waist, pulling her close and kissing her on the lips. "No time for breakfast," he said. "How about a rain check."

Don't go, Billie thought, but she knew she had to get ready, too. It was her week to usher; James Trumbell literally had a fit when she was late. Sometimes he even foamed a little at the mouth. "You can't go," she said. "I'm your human shield."

"You wish." Piet kissed her again. He was reedy to look at, borderline scrawny, but had a heaviness about him that had nothing to do with the potbelly, being purely erotic. "After," he said, releasing her. "We'll eat after." Then he pointed at the beaver. "What about him?" he asked. "You can't just leave him here like this."

"I know." Billie got down on her haunches and returned the beaver's stare, its eyes all pupil, like looking down gun barrels. What was so bad about being in a trap? she thought, opening the door.

"It's okay, Billie," Piet said. He put his hand on her shoulder. "He's going to be okay."

"I know," she repeated, her voice catching as she watched the beaver slide out of the cage and off the dock, making a soft splash before disappearing under the water.

From the middle of Black Lake it was hard to tell the Crocketts' house from all of the other houses on the Knoll. You couldn't tell, for instance, that the Crocketts' house was the only one that had three full bathrooms and two powder rooms, one upstairs and one down, nor could you tell that Mees Kipp had locked herself in the downstairs powder room, where she was in the process of putting on her favorite pink dress.

The Day of Pentecost — Holy Eucharist, Rite Two

Entrance Hymn, "Glorious Things of Thee Are Spoken" . . 608
Opening Sentences
Hymn, "That Day of Wrath, That Dreadful Day" 432
The Collect of the Day
THE LESSONS:
A Reading from Isaiah 11:1–9
Hear What the Spirit Is Saying to the Church.
Psalm 118
A Reading from 1 Corinthians 12:4–13
Hear What the Spirit Is Saying to the Church.
Sequence Hymn, "Breathe on Me, Breath of God" 486
The Holy Gospel of Our Lord Jesus Christ According to John
14:21–29
Glory to You, Lord Christ
The Sermon: The Rev. Richard Jenkins
The Nicene Creed
THE PRAYERS OF THE PEOPLE, Form 3
Confession of Sin
Offertory Anthem . . . ."Lovely Appear"

EUCHARISTIC PRAYER A
Recessional Hymn, "God, My King, Thy Might
    Confessing" 414

PARISH ANNOUNCEMENTS:
The flowers today were given by Helen Zeebrugge to the
    glory of God and in memory of her husband, John Zee-
    brugge.
Flowers are needed for all Sundays in July.
On Sunday, July 13, Carl and Glenda Banner will be renew-
    ing their marriage vows. A reception follows.
Tuesdays at 12:15 and Thursdays at 5:45, the Holy Eucharist
    will be celebrated, with the Anointing of the Sick at the
    Tuesday service.

St. Luke's Episcopal Church was chartered in 1836. The first site of the church was on lower Main Street, across from the post office, but an angry mob of red-shirted granite workers burned that building to the ground during the Great Fire of 1849. The current church, a smallish neo-Gothic structure with a hundred-foot bell tower and spire, was built entirely from locally quarried granite and was dedicated in 1870 to the eternal worship and service of Almighty God by Bishop William Peck of the Diocese of Massachusetts.

Chief among St. Luke's attributes are its two rose windows (one above the entrance to the narthex and one above the altar), its ornately carved baptismal font (topped by a small sculpture of John the Baptist), its Jardine organ (not working at the moment), and its bell (weighing two tons and donated by the Ainsworth family).

On June 22, Pentecost Sunday, though it was twenty to ten and time for the second-service bell to be ringing, it wasn't, since Billie Carpenter was just pulling into the parking lot, and her partner, James Trumbell, was busy helping Warren Hommeyer track down the problem with the organ. The bell hung silent, its clapper dumbstruck, which was a lucky thing for the brown spider who'd spent the past week constructing her web inside it, while far below, the rope lay heaped in heavy coils on the dark bell-tower floor.

Meanwhile, bell or no bell, the church was starting to fill. Regular choir practice had been suspended a month earlier, just after Memorial Day, but the summer choir was expected to arrive half an hour early to warm up. Warren Hommeyer was leading them through the anthem a capella while James Trumbell checked the fuse box.

"Lovely appear over the mountains the feet of them that preach . . ."

You didn't have to audition for the summer choir, and you didn't get to wear a robe. Warren Hommeyer's already-limited patience was being put to the test by the sartorial decisions of several of his choristers, in particular, Mrs. Lendway's fishnet stockings and Mr. Ring's pink Bermuda shorts. The troubled soul without any hair of her own who'd pulled Billie's hair and whose name was Sally Edwards was also oddly dressed, in a white hooded sweatshirt and a pair of checkered pajama bottoms, but because it had turned out that she sang like an angel, Warren forgave her everything, even her occasional outbursts, including the time she bit him.

"Okay, okay, let's try it again," Warren said, "and tenors" — though it was a stretch to refer to Tim Lutz and Bill (Shooter) Carlson that way — "watch out for the high C in the tenth measure after the rest."

Dr. Christine Stokes and young Mr. Brackney were getting into their robes in the vestry, along with the little Hommeyer girl, Sheila, who was serving as acolyte. She was blind as a bat without her glasses but had decided not to wear them so as to make a favorable impression on Nate, the middle Crockett boy, on whom she had a major crush.

The side door next to the pulpit opened and in came Helen Zeebrugge on her son's arm. She liked to arrive early in order to get her regular pew, which because she no longer attended church regularly, was often apt to have someone else sitting in it, today a nice middle-aged couple from the Midwest, who it turned out were perfectly agreeable about scooting over and making room.

"Annalisa had heartburn for the whole last trimester," the nice middle-aged woman was saying to her husband. "Anyone could have told her the baby would be hairy."

Helen was barely able to see the altar flowers, a pair of blurs that were, in fact, a combination of mock orange, baptisia, lemon lilies, and loosestrife. She knew better than to ask Piet to describe them to her. He took after his father, who'd never paid attention to flowers. Men counted on women to bring beauty into their lives, except of course for gay men. Women trained men to have an eye for beauty, and then when the women stopped being beautiful, the well-trained men had to find their beauty elsewhere. You might even say it was an advantage to have a mate who didn't care. Helen fanned herself with her service leaflet and tried to catch her breath. The church was cool and dark, a relief after the forced march across the parking lot.

"Lovely appear over the mountains the feet of them that preach, and bring good news of peace. . . ."

Weird syntax but a nice tune.

As usual the summer choir sounded terrible. Except for the sopranos, that is, who were being led in a kind of unearthly descant by Sally Edwards, though you couldn't look at her face while she sang or it ruined everything.

Carl Banner strode down the aisle like a man destined for greatness. He felt great not only because Richard Jenkins had at last conceded that the church's security system left a lot to be desired, but also because he was alone today, Glenda having told him she had a summer cold. Of course the truth was that

Glenda couldn't get over Warren Hommeyer's betrayal two weeks earlier, when he gave away her rightful position as first soprano to that bald woman. Now all Glenda wanted was to stay in bed and nurse her hurt pride with the new Dean Koontz. The black fan that had originally belonged to her mother stood on the dresser, turning its head slowly and judgmentally from side to side just like her mother. Birds were singing, church bells pealing. But not at St. Luke's, Glenda thought, straining to hear.

White rose petals still littered the church floor and the kneelers and the pew cushions, as if there had been a light snow there the day before, not a wedding. *Mr. and Mrs. Nate Crockett,* mused little Sheila Hommeyer, squinting into the dark nave to see if her groom was there yet. *Sheila Hommeyer Crockett.* The bride a vision in her tea-length gown of cream peau de soie — though, really, Sheila knew her love for Nate was hopeless.

Sun broke through the rose window over the entrance and sent a beam of thick mote-filled light down the aisle all the way to the chancel. Richard Jenkins discovered, to his dismay, that the key to the ambry was missing, and that if there were going to be any wafers at Communion, he was going to have to pick the lock.

Florence Quill arrived, as usual, with her pockets full of money. Almost five thousand dollars in cash, to be exact, which she intended to heap like romaine lettuce in the collection plate.

"Everyone out!" said Mr. Crockett with false good humor as he double-parked in front of the church, and Lorna was pretty sure that though his idea was to make it seem like he was going to join them inside as soon as he found a parking space, he never would. Who was he trying to fool — he hadn't even shaved. Lorna used to envy adults their freedom, but after last night, she thought she knew better. Who was free? Babies? Yeah, right, Lorna — not to mention the whole diaper thing. Maybe old people, though by the time you got to be so old you didn't have to worry about other people, your body fell apart.

Kathy Crockett herded them down the aisle to the second pew on the left, where they always sat, behind that aging womanizer, Piet Zeebrugge, and his even older mother, Helen, who was dressed in a pale green pants suit. Today there was another couple sitting beside them, both of them smaller and better dressed.

"Sunny, keep an eye on the boys for me," Kathy said. "I have to find the rector."

"Rectum," said Nate.

"Grow up," said Sunny.

Mees was seated at the far end of the row, next to Lorna. Then came the three boys, and then Sunny, on the aisle.

The church felt empty to Mees. Empty but ready, like her chest. She looked at the stained-glass window nearest her, which showed Jesus carrying a lamb. You could tell it was Jesus because of the halo and the lamb, but His face was girlish and there was absolutely no expression in His eyes. It wasn't even as if He were *carrying* the lamb, since He didn't seem to feel the weight of it, and Mees knew Jesus felt the weight of everything.

"Throw up," said the youngest Crockett, doubling over with laughter.

"What?" said Kathy, returning to the pew with a pile of service leaflets that she began dealing out rapidly to everyone around her, including the midwestern couple and the Zeebrugges, all of whom already had leaflets of their own. "What do you mean? Do you need to go to the bathroom? Harry, listen to me. If you're going to be sick, do it now, before the service starts."

"It's okay, Mom," said Sunny. "He was just trying to be funny."

But Kathy was no longer paying attention, her sharp brown eye having been caught by the appearance in the entry door of Billie Carpenter, pink from the sun and slightly windblown and not only late for her ushering job but also for the service itself, which was just getting started.

"Announcements?" Richard Jenkins was asking, tall and splendid in his red Pentecostal vestments.

Tim Lutz's wife, Lily, said the Fourth of July rummage sale seemed to be shaping up nicely, though they could use more seasonal items like outdoor furniture or hibachis. Pam, the good Jenkins daughter, said Youth Group was canceled next week due to the holiday. Also, in case no one was aware of the fact, the homeless population in Varennes was growing. A vestry meeting July 7 would address the problem, said Chloe Brock, who had just arrived and seemed uncharacteristically flustered.

"That's the limit," Kathy Crockett remarked fiercely under her breath.

Lorna looked around to see what was making Mrs. Crockett so angry, but all she could see was the woman named Billie, who lived in the camp near the Knoll, holding on to a pile of service leaflets and waving them at the tall baldish man named Piet, who was Helen Zeebrugge's son, and who handled her father's investment portfolio.

The woman's name was Billie Carpenter, Lorna remembered. She was a writer, though she wrote for the newspaper, meaning she had to stick to the facts, whereas Lorna got to make things up, which Lorna was beginning to realize was a dubious advantage, since when you did that everyone could tell what was going on inside your brain.

Billie's still-damp hair was bunched on top of her head and tied with a red bandana. She'd put on a little lipstick and looked sort of pretty for a change.

It was the moment of incipience — things could go either way.

"Glorious things of Thee are spoken," sang the summer choir, and, gloriously, everyone joined in.

Outside in the parking lot, the air was hot and humid and as swarming with bugs as a brain is with ideas. Or so thought Malcolm Brock, leaning against the back of his ex-wife's small blue car, swatting at flies and mosquitoes. Malcolm's ideas swarmed around and around until one idea happened to bump into another idea, at which point there might be a battle of some sort, or else they'd engage in elaborate foreplay, followed by spectacular sex, which if Malcolm was lucky, might be followed by the birth of a brand-new idea. His latest was that we'd gotten the idea of evolution backward and that the further we crept from the primal ooze, the worse we became, the more monstrous and predatory, requiring a whole new set of environmental niches to accommodate us in our wickedness. As usual, though, Malcolm failed to make practical application of this idea. If he had, he might have noticed a connection between it and his most recent hero, whose arrival he was anxiously anticipating.

Des — where was he? The sun shone in Malcolm's eyes and he squinted. A group of young people walked past him toward the far side of the parking lot near the Dumpsters, one of whom appeared to be an extremely good-looking girl.

Des had promised to meet Malcolm behind the church at ten-thirty, and it was twenty after. "Are you ready?" Des had asked. "This is it. No fucking around."

By now the huge shade trees of Cummings Street, which formed the back wall of the parking lot, had all leafed in. They were no longer yellowish-green as they'd been only a month earlier, nor were they black-green as they'd be at summer's end.

Then it would be hard to ignore how *final* they looked, how immensely *complete,* and not to think it should have been obvious to anyone with half a brain the way things had been headed, were now, were always headed.

A young woman with a Trojan warrior–like brush of mahogany-colored hair and a brand-new tongue piercing bicycled past Malcolm, late for work at the Crockett Home and cursing loudly. The heathens were out buying Sunday papers; the Unitarians, whose church actually shut down for the summer, were still in bed. Beulah, the little black-and-white cat who had been missing for two weeks, suddenly emerged from behind the rectory and wove her way among the parked cars, slipping past the shade trees and onto the back porch of her mistress's house on Cummings Street, where she mewed pitifully to be let in, as if she'd been mewing there forever to no avail. In fact, Beulah had spent the past two weeks on Adder Ridge with Ellen Fair, and though she had grown plump from her diet of heavy cream and canned tuna, she had also become impatient with the old lady's fierce need to pick her up and hold her on her lap.

A small round cloud floated by above Malcolm's head and it looked so soft and so innocent and so oblivious to everything going on down below that for a moment it crossed his mind that he might possibly be on the verge of making the biggest mistake of his life, an idea that swam boldly across the sea of his brain and, meeting no opposing or mutually attractive idea, drifted right over the edge, the way boats used to do before Columbus.

Ten twenty-eight. David Crockett, who had momentarily parked his white SUV on the Cummings Street side of the lot in order to place a call on his cell phone to a sound-asleep (as it turned out) Liz Bamberger and who was now backing up, still talking, trying to convince her to let him drop in "for a cup of coffee," though the idea of the art teacher lying there in her bed with her eyes half open made his penis so hard he was finding it difficult to pay any attention at all to what he was doing, suddenly backed into a rust-colored Dodge Dart that appeared as if out of nowhere going a million miles an hour.

"Fuck," David thought. It didn't matter how fast the other car was going; he knew perfectly well he was at fault, though he also knew that whatever damage he'd inflicted — and it was in any case negligible — would be impossible to distinguish from among the Dart's many existing dents and scratches.

David had stepped out of his SUV and was reaching into his back pocket for his wallet and his insurance card when the driver of the Dart came at him with the knife.

"Asshole," said Des.

A tour bus full of French Canadian tourists drove into the lot.

"Hello?" said Liz Bamberger, having heard what sounded like a grunt or a moan and sitting up fully awake now. "Are you all right?"

From their vantage point high in the bus, the French Canadians had an excellent view of American teenagers exchanging money for drugs as well as of a pale young man in his early thirties, with a shaved head and the powdery and somewhat insubstantial look of a moth or a ghost, lounging against a small blue car, lighting a cigarette. What they couldn't see, because his white SUV blocked their view, was David Crockett falling back against his passenger door, bleeding profusely, nor could they see the driver of the Dart lean down and retrieve the dropped phone.

"David?" said Liz Bamberger. "David?"

"David's busy right now," said Des. "Why don't you try later?" Then he hurled the phone over the lilac hedge and into the churchyard next door, where James Trumbell would find it lodged in a clump of hostas a week later when he was mowing the grass.

"Hey man," said Malcolm Brock as Des came sauntering toward him from the back of the lot, the Dart resting at a forty-five degree angle between the Crocketts' SUV and a yellow rental van. "Nice parking job."

"Put out that cigarette," Des said, and then he burst into laughter, since in addition to the way he kept the flame of rage burning in his heart at every hour of the day and night, he also took pride in his offbeat sense of humor.

To get to the back door of the church even an able-bodied person had to use the handicap access ramp, and that, together with the way the Virginia creeper covering the rear wall seemed to be alive with a million chirping birds and the way humidity was making the door stick and the squeaking sound of their shoes, was getting on Malcolm's nerves. Once inside, he found himself in a dark little hallway. To the right, though the door was closed, was obviously a bathroom, since he could hear a toilet flushing. To the left, though the door was open, was a room whose function was less obvious to him, with a lot of clothes hanging on coat hooks and with piles of books. Dead ahead, just beyond a small wooden table containing a handful of service leaflets and a vase of yellow roses, was a door to the church itself.

Everyone was sitting down, except for Sally Edwards. It was a great relief to her that the organ wasn't working. "They hem me in," she sang, Psalm 118. "They hem me in on every side." Sally hated the organ. The sound of the organ was like the sound of all the fluids in her body coursing through her all at once like gamma rays.

"In the name of the Lord I will repel them," responded the congregation.

Not a one of them could sing, especially not the bossy woman with too many children on the left side of the church with the dark brown hair and the light brown dress whom Sally also hated, named Kathy.

A stranger was standing opposite the choir in the lee of the banner that had a picture of a dove on it, on the left side of the church over near the pulpit. Sally figured he must have come in through the perplexing door that was at the back of the church on the outside and at the front of the church on the inside. She could smell the stranger's anger, which had a different smell from her own, mixed as it was with semen and blood. *Go home,* she told him with her brain, but his brain had no openings. No stomata, she corrected herself, the word appearing out of nowhere. The man's brain was like a boxing glove.

"I was pressed so hard that I almost fell," Sally sang, and she had to resist the urge to point.

Having completed the head count, James Trumbell returned to the back of the church. Eighty-seven, not including James himself and Billie, who'd excused herself to use the bathroom, saying she wanted to comb her hair. He switched on the walkie-talkie, hesitated, and then switched it off again, since he realized that he didn't know Billie well enough to know whether she was the kind of woman who'd resort to a euphemism like that or if combing her hair was all she really wanted to do. Someone had propped open the big entrance doors to the church, letting in sunlight and heat and traffic noise, and at this precise moment, James couldn't help but notice, a bird. He had no idea what kind, since he never paid attention to birds, but he knew Billie would know, and it interested him to realize that even if he didn't know a lot about her, he knew that much. She loved all sorts of animals; she was very gentle. In case of emergencies she kept cookies in her pocketbook, the cheap kind shaped like windmills you bought out of bins in the supermarket.

James switched the walkie-talkie back on. "Billie," he whispered. "Can you see what's the deal with those two guys up there near the pulpit?"

From her aisle seat in the front pew, left, Helen Zeebrugge had an unobstructed if unfocused view of the two men in question. Trouble, she thought, though of course nowadays you couldn't tell a thing from the way a person dressed. Both men seemed to have very round heads, and the one whose two dark nostrils made his face look like a shirt button seemed to be scanning the congregation as if he were trying to find someone he knew. Helen cast a quick glance at the midwestern couple to see if it could be them, but they were too busy returning their prayer books to the rack to notice.

Helen considered sharing her anxiety with Piet, but he, too, appeared distracted, drumming his fingers on his hymnal. In fact Piet was watching Billie, who had just emerged from the bathroom and then got stuck in the narrow hallway behind the two strangers. She was staring straight ahead, straight at him really, with a look of deep concentration, the broad and lightly freckled brow that he'd come to feel great affection for, housing as it did Billie's supple and kindly mind, slightly furrowed, and her freckled cheeks pinker than usual.

Look at me! ordered Sheila Hommeyer, concentrating on Nate Crockett with all her might, as Nate meanwhile was concentrating on poking his stoic little brother, Harry, in the ribs, thinking, *Go ahead and cry crybaby.*

Come on Billie, answer the phone! thought James Trumbell.

Jesus, thought Mees Kipp.

The great nave of the church was alive with unspoken wishes; it is this way in all places of human habitation, some of the air thick, some of it thin, unspooling lightly or dark and clotted, a terrible mixture, so sweet and heartbroken that like all human wishing it could make you get down on the cold stone floor of a church (like Sally Edwards) and start crawling, as if we'd never actually got around to getting up on our hind legs in the first place, though getting up did no good, Sally thought, no good, no good at all.

Chloe Brock arose from her seat on the right side of the church near the stained-glass window in memory of the eight drowned children. It was her week to read the Epistle, and she wore a pale blue sundress from the overpriced shop in the hotel concourse that catered to the wives of the town fathers and had pulled her wild yellow hair back into a tight, conservative bun.

"Now there are diversities of gifts, but the same Spirit —" Chloe had just mounted the steps to the lectern and started reading when a man with a skinny little Chinese pigtail down his back snuck up on her as if from out of nowhere and grabbed her from behind.

"Oh my God," Billie said into her walkie-talkie. "He's got a knife."

Mees stiffened when Lorna grabbed her hand. "Don't," Mees said. "Don't touch me!"

"Stay where you are," Piet called out to Billie, but it was too late.

"I'm scared," said Sunny. "Mom?"

"What's happening?" Helen asked Piet. "I can't see."

"Shh," Lorna said. "Shh."

From Buddy's house Margaret began by trotting along the
road that was mostly empty and dry and hot and smelled like
dust or nothing interesting except where a skunk had just
walked past and also where a chipmunk got run over, but by
the time she came to the crossroads traffic had picked up,
including a truck carrying a block of granite the size of a tool-
shed that came at her suddenly, like a person with bad ideas,
and she took off into the forest.

Stinking great day.

First a squirrel, then a rabbit, then a squirrel. A mouse. Her
teeth could feel it. Not a pop like a frog but a bite.

As for the quills in her nose, she'd stopped thinking about
them ages ago, the minute she saw Mees getting into the
Crocketts' SUV and the SUV backing out of the garage with
Mees in it.

The forest between the crossroads and the elementary school
was old growth, its floor spongy and uneven and crisscrossed
with deadfall, decayed trunks of trees that had died long before
the town was incorporated, also trees that were dead and
hadn't fallen yet, also rotting trunks covered with moss and the
sun so far away you might as well be at the bottom of a well.
Just before the school came a clearing where the trees had
burned and now there was fireweed growing there, tall with
pink flowers, absolutely still in the absolute stillness of the day.

Then the forest was back again, hot and moist and dark and look! — another mouse!

In the forest there were fewer species of trees than before, and the ones that remained were home to tent caterpillars, long-horned beetles, and thrips. You couldn't tell unless you knew that this meant the forest was in bad shape, just as you couldn't tell from looking at a house who was in it or not in it, but you could smell their presence or absence like a good thing or a bad thing.

All animals can smell good or bad approaching.

Though usually what happens is not so much good or bad as routine, sacrifice having gotten built into the physical world along with everything else, like mountains and lakes.

Billie's beaver, for example, his attention captured by the tender young aspen shoot baiting the trap.

One being sacrificed to make way for another.

Meanwhile James Trumbell — once he'd left behind the heat and light at the back of the church and started walking toward the high shadowy altar where the sevenfold mystical drama of Pentecost was either continuing to unfold or had come completely unfolded, speaking into his walkie-talkie but receiving no answer from Billie Carpenter, who was standing in the front aisle between the pulpit and the first pew with her arms pinned behind her back by a bald young man who was also holding a gun to her head and talking to her a mile a minute, or from Richard Jenkins, who had just left the pulpit and headed out through the sacristy to get help when the man with the pigtail told him he was going to slit Chloe Brock's throat if anyone so much as thought of leaving the building and the bald young man said that went double for Billie — James Trumbell wasn't interested in seeing anyone get sacrificed.

He watched as the woman from the summer choir crept along the marble floor toward the steps leading to the chancel, at the foot of which Chloe Brock stood frozen in her blue sundress with a knife at her throat. The woman from the summer choir was like the serpent after the Lord had cursed it to crawl on its belly and eat nothing but dust for all the days of its life, a serpent in a white hooded sweatshirt being regarded with more than routine interest by the handsome bronze eagle mounted on the lectern.

Eagle, symbol of Saint John, the most mystical of the Evangelists, eagles being able to look directly into the sun.

The expression on Billie's face was one James had never seen before on any human face. It was like the expression he'd seen on a cat's face when it was sitting as still as it possibly could, watching a mouse frozen with fear trying to decide whether it was safe to make a run for its hole. Her hazel eyes grave and still as death.

Not death, though, James corrected himself, crossing himself. Wrong word. Still as a statue, rather. As if rooted to the spot. Stone.

By now James Trumbell had reached the central aisle, where he paused for a moment between the brightly dressed Jamaican apple pickers on the left and the lugubrious Ring family, minus Mr. Ring, on the right. So far the young man holding Billie hostage didn't seem to have noticed him, but it would only be a matter of time before he did; the one holding Chloe had, though, and was therefore unaware of the approach of Sally Edwards. James didn't know if this was good or bad — whether whatever Sally Edwards did would make things better or worse.

Things were about to change, he thought. Try and stop them.

He made a last attempt to rouse Richard Jenkins on the walkie-talkie and finally got through.

"I've called nine-one-one," Richard said. "But the one with the pigtail says if we let anyone in from outside, both women are dead. I've put Tommy at the door to the parking lot and Carl in the narthex."

"What do they want?" James whispered.

"The one with the pigtail seems angry. I think they want

the collection money, though it beats me how they knew about Florence. The money — I think that's what they want."

"Mrs. Quill's money?" said James, glancing up toward the lectern.

"Yes," Richard said.

Chloe's face, unlike Billie's, looked calm and placid and a little bored.

James walked closer, level with the organ. At some point Dr. Stokes had left the sacristy and was rummaging in her Mexican reticule as if maybe she actually kept something useful inside it. A grenade? George Mason was holding his mother Marjory's hand for dear life and had his eyes shut, praying. *Our Father who art in Heaven, hallowed be thy —*

Then there was a scream.

"Fuck, man. Fuck."

Another scream. A gunshot.

Sally Edwards had sunk her teeth into the tender flesh of the calf of the man who was holding Chloe Brock, and he was so startled he dropped the knife, whereupon Sally grabbed it and, rearing up all at once with the hooded and venomous grace of a cobra, stabbed the man in the heart. She knew where his heart was because years and years earlier, before the gates and doorways and hatches and flaps of her once-excellent mind had started shutting or opening and closing the wrong way, Sally had studied medicine. You had to aim just right, or you'd bang into the breastbone.

"Oh my God," Chloe said. But she wasn't talking about the man named Des who was now sprawled across the marble floor of the church at the foot of the rood screen, where the chipping sparrow James Trumbell saw fly into the church had come to rest, but about her ex-husband, Malcolm, who had just shot Billie Carpenter and was running toward the back door and into the arms of Piet Zeebrugge, as meanwhile his gun came clattering across the marble tiles, spinning around and around like cosmic debris, before coming to rest at Helen Zeebrugge's big ducklike feet.

*Tues June 17, 1872 — At home   raining   Papa very nice today
   no letter from V*
*Wed June 18, 1872 — At home   did not do much   sewed some
   read some   no line from V yet   what can be the reason   Mr
   Jones here   took Aunt Tinys picture*
*Thurs June 19, 1872 — another day has taken its weary hours into
   eternity and with no letter from V   this waiting is terrible for
   me to bear (O! Darling!)*
Rest of page blank . . .

There was a good place and a bad place.

The good place was off-limits, Mees could tell. She really didn't even stop there, pausing by the woman's side just long enough to make sure. In the good place, you could barely see past the entrance but what you saw was complete and very inviting, the edge of a grassy yard, a blue lawn chair, a large bowl-shaped glass with a pink umbrella and a bent yellow straw in it. You could hear birds chirping and ducks quacking and dripping sounds like someone pulling herself up out of the water and walking across the dock and a voice saying, *There's no room for you.* Like someone else's dream, maybe — sunlight filling the leaves the twigs the drops of water, and the woman's soul taking up all the room. *Let her go. Let her go. She doesn't need you.*

In the bad place, there was way too much room and the sky, if you could call it that, was the color of what came out of a thermometer when you broke it and was poisonous and beautiful and interesting to watch, rippling and thick and breaking apart into many silver balls, but you'd die if you ate it, her mother said. Mercury.

The bad place was like a desert, a little warm wind blowing, disturbing the yellow sand and lifting grains of it into a cloud shaped like two arms reaching into thin air. *Measle measle you are my own. Give me your answer true.*

The foxes have lairs, and the birds of the sky have places where they may lodge, but the Son of Man has nowhere where He may lay His head.

No animals in the bad place or any living thing.

Like those shaggy-dog stories Lorna's father thought were so hilarious, drawing you on with the promise of an ending when there wasn't one, as if a false promise was actually funny instead of being (as it really was) cruel. A kind of path, for instance, that you knew right away wasn't going to get you anywhere.

I'm lonely, Mees said. She felt the cold marble floor of the church breathing its cold breath up her dress. It smelled like nothing. She was wearing a pink dress that had a pleated skirt and a big white collar, with a pair of red cherries with green stems at each tip. No light shone on her, only to the left of her, where the man lay on his back in a pool of his dark gloppy blood.

Where are you? Mees said.

There was a pulsing sac at the root of the man's tongue, the skin so thin that if you got too close it would burst and the glop inside would get out. There was such a thing as evil, and it was right there at the tongue's root, and you could let it out and that would be the end for you, the end, the end, the end, and there wouldn't be any way out for you, even if you got a second chance like Mr. Banner or a third or an eighth or even a ninth like most cats.

Mees couldn't believe what she was seeing, but she was forgetting she wasn't the one seeing what she was seeing.

Come here, Jesus told her. *Come here. You're going too far away. Come closer.*

I love you that much.

You are the apple of my eye.

It hadn't been this way before, in Buddy for example, or Mr. Banner.

The thing about evil is that it can convince you that it can trump everything and also that you can triumph over it.

And when you are convinced of that, then there will be nothing more to see, and stone by stone and mica and glint and step by step and doorway you'll die and there will be just one less impediment, one less lump of earth and flesh and breath for all of that life to surge around and through.

The rule was: I am the light. If you trust in me.

Julian of Norwich said light is charity. Imagine the fen country, flat and gray and pierced with silver arrows of light. The arrows reached toward her as she lay dying, her body dead to all sensation from the waist down and also from the waist up.

The light reached through the three windows of her little stone cell attached to the church: one window to hear Mass through, one to call her servant through, one to give advice through. There were also three forms of light or charity, these being charity uncreated, which is God; charity created, which is our soul in God; and charity given, which is virtue.

The dead were waiting for Julian, their souls lengthening, reaching with enormous interest toward her approaching ghost. This is what the dying see when they talk about a bright light or tall figures like guardians or guides standing at the foot of their deathbed. The dead are completely fascinated by the dying, the way the living love gossip.

Outdoors the Black Death. The world, as always, hard on the flesh, and in the Lollards pit on the other side of the river, the bodies of Protestants burning.

Three windows, three kinds of charity.

"Mom," Sunny said. "Shouldn't we be doing something?"

If the scene at the altar hadn't been so terrifying, Lorna might have taken pleasure in the fact that for once Mrs. Crockett seemed unsure of herself, not even bothering to position her legs in such a way as to make her thighs look thinner but letting them blob out side by side on the red pew cushion.

"Let her go," Lorna had warned, when Mrs. Crockett tried to hold Mees back. "Measle," Lorna had said, starting to cry. "Mees."

"I can't believe no one's doing anything," Sunny said.

It was an indictment, Lorna knew, of Lorna herself, who was supposed to be Mees's best friend, whereas Sunny was merely linked to Mees through Lorna; Lorna was the conduit. But Lorna knew she had to leave Mees alone to do whatever it was she was doing, kneeling first beside Billie Carpenter, staring intently at Billie's extremely white freckle-dotted face, before moving on to the man.

The congregation was getting restless.

"Is she dead?" asked James Trumbell. "Is Billie dead?"

"Quiet," said Kathy Crockett. "I'm trying to hear." She punched in David's number on her cell phone and got his message immediately, meaning he was probably on the phone.

But this was Lorna's fear, exactly: Billie must either be unhurt, which she obviously wasn't, or dead. Why would Mees leave her and focus her attention on the man? "I don't choose!" Lorna remembered Mees yelling at her when she asked why out of all the people in the world she'd chosen to help Mr. Banner.

The sevenfold mystical drama of Pentecost was uncurling everywhere inside the church like scraps of paper in a pocket, shopping lists, credit-card receipts, ticket stubs. As they uncurled they made extra room, but room that was too small to see and infused with the light that shines in deep space and isn't like light but silvered glass, mirroring back the dark face of every created thing. Lorna could hardly believe that outside the church there was a sun and it was shining and there were people sitting across the street under red-and-white-striped umbrellas, laughing and talking and drinking iced coffee and ignoring the sound of sirens coming closer and closer.

Piet held his mother's hand and squeezed it, as if human touch on its own could correct the worst the universe had to offer. *Not here, not here in the darkness,* Piet thought, *in this twittering world.* It was astonishing where the human mind went in moments of terror. He could see Dr. Stokes bent over Billie, doing something to her neck with a length of altar cloth.

You could try making sense out of the universe, but you were too small and the parts you needed to see were too large or even smaller.

"What's happening now?" Helen asked, her voice moist and wavering like an old lady's, which she was.

"I'm going to see if I can find out," Piet told her. But when he started to leave the pew, she held on tighter.

"I don't like this," she said. "Please don't go. I smell blood."

The midwestern woman was sobbing, her husband speaking into a cell phone. "I can't hear you," he was hollering. "You're breaking up."

Mees Kipp sat crouched beside the man with the pigtail. He was lying there on his back, bleeding onto the cool marble floor, getting his blood all over her favorite pink dress.

"I don't understand," Sunny said. "Let me go!" she added, since Lorna had grabbed her wrist and was stopping her circulation like a tourniquet. Lorna's bones were long and elegant, Sunny's thick and strong, almost as if the image of that single gesture — Lorna's hand around Sunny's wrist — projected into the future, could seal their individual fates.

Of course we have free will, but not as much as we think we have. Otherwise we wouldn't also have dreams; we wouldn't need them.

Des cast a fishing line into the same lake on which Inez Fair's boat had capsized, releasing its screaming cargo of Sunday School picnickers into the mica-specked depths that got darker and darker the farther down they went. It's amazing but true: dreams share landscapes, especially the dreams of the wretched. He saw Inez's face just before she fainted, and it occurred to him that she was a good-looking woman. A good-looking woman consigned for eternity to feel the little limbs drift past her, always close enough to feel, always far enough away to be just out of reach.

A glint of mica here, a glint there. Churches are hospitable to spirits, though rarely haunted. Sunlight poured from the narthex, where the doors were still propped open. A car honked its horn; a breeze flew in, smelling like the river. The same paramedics who had stretchered Janet Peake from the floor behind the faulty treadmill three weeks earlier appeared and conferred with Piet Zeebrugge, as if he actually understood what should be done.

"This woman requires immediate attention," said Dr. Stokes.

"You need to get out of the way," the taller of the two para-medics said to Mees, who needless to say stayed put.

Afterward, no one could agree on what had happened.

It was Pentecost; the spirit came down and said, Listen to me!

When, for instance, had Margaret come into the church? Dogs weren't allowed inside except once a year for the Blessing of the Animals, which last year had included Dr. Stokes's ferret and a little capuchin monkey belonging to a tourist. Had the monkey traveled in the tourist's car, in a car seat, like a baby? The whole time Richard Jenkins was blessing it, it chattered with apparent ecstasy, its beady eyes bright as thought.

Margaret had followed her girl all the way from the Crock-etts' house to town, the *fact* of her drawing Margaret on — a smell without color but something she couldn't live without, like *water bowl, food bowl,* or the dream in the sun of the sun on her flanks, her breathing getting slower, deeper, her fur baking in the sun, golden.

"We need room," said the shorter paramedic, who'd been eating fast food and drinking beer when the alarm sounded, but when he tried to pull Margaret away from Mees, looping an arm around her collarless neck and tugging, gently, though he'd never owned a dog or any animal, being allergic and timid in their presence, Margaret snarled at him and he saw her long canines, curved and white and brown at the tops from a lifetime of kibble and her black eyes blacker than black, ready to kill.

Her girl. Her girl. Her face and her kisses and hands like a mole going into a hole in the snow. Quick.

There was a bee in the altar flowers, buzzing around a lemon lily. There was an ant crawling up the stem of the chal-ice, attracted by the sugar in the wine. If you're a bee or an ant, you love sweetness. Sweet sweet sweet, the world says to you, I am *sweet,* and then, often as not, a human hand comes down like the shadow of the world and that is that.

Not today, though. The human hands were all busy with other humans.

Lorna knew she should have guessed when that rusty car slowed ages ago: the cigarette pack twisted in the sleeve of the man's T-shirt, the long dark hair, the foreign license plate, the knife.

And then suddenly Sunny was there at the altar, grabbing Mees from behind. *Stop it!* Mees ordered, because this was the worst, the absolute worst. Sunny was trying to pull Mees away at the exact moment when Mees was trying to hook her own finger through the eel-like loops of the long coiling piece of stuff that connected the man's stabbed heart to his soul. *Go away!* Mees ordered, but the only way to shake Sunny loose was to move farther in, and then she ran the risk that it might not be in the right direction, not toward Jesus but away from Sunny. Then she made a mistake. She ran away from Sunny and into the black throbbing place at the root of the tongue.

I wish I wish O I wish in vain I wish I was a girl again. . . .

Kathy Crockett sat patting Helen Zeebrugge's shoulder, patting and patting, on and on, the way she'd pat Buddy when she really wanted someone to be patting her. Sunny was up there at the altar and had just jumped back from Mees Kipp as if she'd been slapped, a hurt expression on her face, though Mees didn't seem to have touched her. Mees was too busy bent over the man Sally Edwards had stabbed in the heart, her face right up against his.

Kathy again tried punching in David's cell phone number. The sparrow on the rood screen was starting to chirp.

Billie was lifted onto a stretcher, and Piet Zeebrugge was

helping the taller of the two paramedics carry her to the waiting ambulance.

The Brackney baby considered howling.

Margaret sat beside Mees, who sat beside the man with the pigtail. Margaret sat beside a lump of nothing she knew and beside the long green valley that was Mees. She too wanted to howl, but her jaw locked on the note. A moan in a box. Want to go out? Want to go, Margaret? The sevenfold mysteries of Pentecost unfolded and drew her in.

There was a man who was searching for the meaning of life. He went here, he went there. He went uphill and down. He went over land and sea. Etc. etc. You could drag this out to last for hours. In any case, he was very old when he finally came upon the even-older sage, who was said to know the answer. "Life is a fountain," the sage told him. "You're kidding," the man replied. "Life is a *fountain?*"

Margaret opened her mouth. "Beloved," she said.

Police Log — Monday, June 30

1:13 a.m. Sprinkler alarm activated at River Street restaurant.

1:59 a.m. Loose dogs reported on High School Drive.

4:00 a.m. Domestic complaint at French Hill residence.

6:15 a.m. Rear-ender on Route 10.

9:02 a.m. Woman sweeping in Summer Street rotary.

10:57 a.m. Young boys riding go-karts in roadway on Perry Street.

12:18 p.m. Theft of camera from Locust Inn lobby.

2:45 p.m. Possible animal abuse reported on Bank Street.

4:04 p.m. Two males involved in a 10-10 in post office parking lot.

7:20 p.m Security alarm tripped at Farwell Free Library.

9:47 p.m. Large dog "Margaret" missing.

11:30 p.m. Bear reported in Terrace Street yard.

It was Pentecost; the spirit came down and spoke.

No one died. Not then, anyway.

After the trial, Chloe Brock left Varennes. She moved to Colorado, where she coached girl's hockey at a small private school. Chloe had a series of lovers, none of them very interesting or important, and she died of congestive heart failure at an advanced age, unlike Malcolm Brock, who died of a drug overdose while in jail, or Byron Desilets, the thirty-nine-year-old Caucasian male who had been wanted in Three Rivers Quebec for armed robbery and manslaughter and was at last apprehended and brought to justice — meaning that once he'd recovered (miraculously, by all accounts) from his knife wound, he was remanded to Malpecque Prison, where he died of natural causes.

Mignonette hated Colorado. But she was put out of her misery by a bald eagle, who swooped down one day while she was sunning herself on Chloe's deck and carried her off to eat.

Many of the old people died within three years of one another: first Florence Quill, who changed her will in September, leaving the bulk of her fortune to the Republican Party before suffering a massive stroke; next Marjory Mason, who choked on a lima bean during Christmas dinner at the Crockett Home, closely followed by Janet Peake, who had never fully recovered from her fall off the treadmill, and finally Helen

Zeebrugge, who died peacefully in her sleep, dreaming of herself rising on the stalk of a green and pliant universe that opened like a water lily.

Carl Banner harbored the weak vessel in the brain that, unbeknownst to him, had felled him that morning in May and died years later a few doors down from Andrea Murdock, in the same level-three nursing home, miles and miles from Varennes and from the crack in the ice that Danny Murdock slipped through five years after Andrea finally expired, never to be seen again.

George Mason tried suing Kathy Crockett for the wrongful death of his mother, but the judge's sympathies lay with the defendant, whose life had never been the same since the day her husband's spinal cord was severed by a knife at the second cervical vertebra, paralyzing him from the neck down. In any case, quadriplegics never live very long, and Kathy never remarried, almost as if she'd actually loved David, though she confessed to Sunny on her deathbed that the only person she'd ever really loved was Richard Jenkins, who died himself, together with his wife, Mary, and Henry Fine, and Sophy Kipp, and a lot of other people all at once and in a terrible way that wasn't natural.

The young people all died too, but many years later. Even the Brackney baby.

Buddy got shot by a hunter from Connecticut who thought he was a deer. Doozie slipped a disk.

Margaret's heart was broken. As if Mees had died that day in the church or gone away forever, which in a manner of speaking she had, the gift that made her Mees having remained inside Des, whose cell mate came to think of him as a regular Saint Francis.

Mees became normal, meaning she repeated sixth grade without the help of the anticipated aide, and when the time came to put on the end-of-the-year operetta — *Pinafore,* this time — she sang along with the other sisters and cousins and aunts and allowed Miss Kowicki to make up her face without complaint. A tractable girl, a mediocre student, she went on to become a teaching aide herself, and she could no longer save the life of anything, human or otherwise.

The bullet sped through Billie Carpenter's neck, just barely missing the carotid artery, and she spent six hours laid out on a table as surgeons and scrub nurses hovered above her like mantises in their long green gowns in the insane light of the operating theater, hinged at the waist and wielding knives while machines monitored the coming into her and the going out of her of her breath. Billie dreamed; her life was in her dream. She walked into shallow water; the sand was red and gooey, the water warm, uniformly calf deep. Something was wrong with it, though. It was specked with tiny bits of green algae and it wasn't moving. She looked back toward the beach for one second, just one little second, and the water was suddenly all gone and there was a huge wave taking shape on the horizon.

Then she awoke in her hospital bed and saw Piet Zeebrugge looking down at her.

It was the first morning of the world. It was the first morning of the world, and later it was finished.

About the Author

Kathryn Davis has received a Kafka Prize for fiction by an American woman, the Morton Dauwen Zabel Award from the American Academy of Arts and Letters, and a Guggenheim Fellowship. She is the Fannie M. Hurst Senior Writer-in-Residence in the graduate writing program at Washington University in St. Louis. *The Thin Place* is her sixth novel.

BACK BAY · READERS' PICK

Reading Group Guide

The Thin Place

A NOVEL

Kathryn Davis

A conversation with
the author of *The Thin Place*

Kathryn Davis talks with Donna Seaman of
WLUW's *Open Books*

Beginning with *Labrador* (1988), a story of two young sisters that metamorphoses into a complex and otherworldly story, Kathryn Davis has cast a spell that has held readers transfixed over the course of six original and affecting novels. Each is a fresh embarkation for Davis in which she illuminates a radically different realm in a distinctive and piquant narrative style and a unique blending of genres. Yet within each brilliantly imagined, often fantastic fictional realm, she seeks understanding of the mysterious workings of fate, especially the unpredictable spiral of events set in motion by human creativity and its evil twin, obsession. Fables, music, cuisine, diabolical computer software, architecture, metaphysics, and the life force itself drive her complex, genre-altering plots, and her adventurous characters, most of them young women.

This conversation took place when Kathryn Davis came to Chicago in February 2006, a visit that included an appearance on *Open Books,* on WLUW.

I've been laughing over something Joy Press at the Village Voice *wrote about you. She described you as the love child of Virginia*

Woolf and Lewis Carroll. I imagine that you were influenced by these seminal writers.

Oh, absolutely. The very first book I was infatuated with was *Alice in Wonderland*. When I was in third grade we were supposed to bring our favorite book to school. The teacher was going to read from it, but when I brought in *Alice* she made me take it home. She said that it wasn't a book for children, which came as a surprise to me because my mother had been reading it to me from day one. This was a key moment for me because it made me realize that something I cherished had something a little bit edgy about it, something a little beyond the pale, and that made me love it all the more.

I encountered Virginia Woolf in high school when I saw *Who's Afraid of Virginia Woolf?* and asked my English teacher "So who's Virginia Woolf?" and he handed me *To the Lighthouse* and said, "Take a look." I bonded with that book in the same way I did with *Alice*. I don't think they're similar, but I did feel like they were written for me.

I think the fact that Carroll and Woolf are such different writers relates to part of what intrigues me about your fiction, which is the tension in your novels. There are at least two opposing forces at work, high literary writing like that of Virginia Woolf and Henry James, and elements of thrillers or speculative fiction. Can you explain how that happens?

Increasingly I feel that I want to make sure that what I write about is what interests me most. I love detective fiction. I've read murder mysteries for almost as long as I've read *Alice in Wonderland*. My mother doled them out to me, especially

Agatha Christie. And I've also had a real taste for speculative fiction of one sort or another, which is, I think, the legacy of *Alice in Wonderland*. The idea that you can enter another world is just one of the things that keeps me from feeling bored with life on this planet, that you could open a door and find something unexpected.

I'm fascinated with the way you contrast artifice with nature. They share a certain dynamic because human beings are part of nature, and what we do is inherently organic, yet our creativity results in inventions that are detrimental to the rest of life. That's a difficult thing to get at in fiction in a subtle and meaningful way.

As I get older, it becomes clear to me that that is one of my obsessions. The ways we mess around with the natural world — and the dire consequences of our interference — troubles me more than anything else, as should be obvious in *The Thin Place*. Yet there are good aspects of art and artifice as well. I mean, we make beautiful things that we then handle irresponsibly. In *The Walking Tour* the beautiful things become foul and demonic.

I don't want to give the impression that your books are in any way polemic or overtly message-oriented. They are not. And yet I can't help but ask you if following the news about the state of the natural world (I'm thinking about the mounting evidence of global warming) influences your work.

I'm alarmed and enraged that the world is being irretrievably changed in these ways, that there's no going back. It wasn't an accident that Katrina overwhelmed New Orleans. I think we're much closer than anyone wants to believe to the point where things like that are going to be happening regularly. And yet we're constantly reassured that there are good economic reasons for all of our crimes against the planet.

The fact that we've been hearing about global warming for decades is infuriating. If there is a future civilization able to look back at this, they will have fun writing about how foolish people were in the twentieth century.

I hope there's somebody around to say how foolish we were, because often it seems like that will not be the case. It makes me sad. The world is a beautiful thing. I mean, it's also horrible, but it will be sad to lose it.

That's so much of what The Thin Place *is about. I wonder if you could explain the title.*

The "thin place" is a term from Celtic mythology. I first heard about it when I was visiting a friend who was a lay member of a religious community, a bunch of sisters at a convent in Peekskill. They were talking about how they were going to have to sell the place where they lived because they couldn't afford to keep up these huge, gorgeous, drafty buildings for only a handful of nuns. They were sad to be leaving, they said, because it was a thin place. I'd never heard the phrase before, so I asked what it meant and one of the sisters explained that a thin place is a place where the membrane between this world and the other world — the world of spirit, the part of life we can't see — is very, very weak. So things leak back and forth between the two. I knew then that that was my title. I didn't know precisely where the book was going to be set. I thought maybe it was going to be the seashore, a place I've always wanted to visit in my fiction, but this wasn't the book to do that. I also knew that there were going to be lots of living things in it. That was kind of all I knew.

The Thin Place is full of creatures. I think of it as a symphony of consciousnesses. You tune in to the consciousnesses of dogs and cats, and even plants, corn and lichen. You capture the energy and sense of constant communication and communion in nature.

You know, it just occurred to me this very minute that all along I've been saying that what I wanted to do in *The Thin Place* was something like what Flaubert did in the novella *A Simple Heart,* where the narrative dips in and out of the sensibilities of different people living in a little village in Normandy. But what I'm now realizing is that giving voice to everything is exactly what both Lewis Carroll and Virginia Woolf do. It just dawned on me. In Lewis Carroll things are always talking that do not normally talk. And Virginia Woolf also spends a lot of time deep inside of the sensibilities of people and places; there's a feeling of place having a kind of presence, a voice.

Another striking aspect of The Thin Place *is the witty narrator. I think of it as a she, and find her omniscient in a very interesting way. How did you channel this voice?*

Well, it's not surprising that you hear the omniscient narrator as female, because she is me. What I wanted to do was give myself complete license to talk about the way the world presents itself to me as if I could hover above it. Not too far above, just enough to see everything and sort of swoop in and out. I wanted that feeling because I think that is what interests me about being a part of life, of the world — that there is all of this stuff going on all at the same time. I am, I think, 99 percent curiosity. I mean, I would not hesitate to put a glass to a door to try and listen to a conversation going on on the other side. I'm living in a duplex apartment right now, and I'm riveted by the noises overhead, trying to figure out what's happening up there. Curiosity — that's where the narrative point of view came from for *The Thin Place*.

You're eavesdropping on the cosmos.

And looking at it. Someone said it was like looking at a drop of water under a microscope and seeing everything teeming with life there. You focus on this, focus on that, get a better look at this person's face, what this person is saying to that person, what this cat is thinking as it scampers off.

The Thin Place *is full of prose poems, lush paragraphs in which you tell us all about a certain animal, or a plant. Did you read a lot of natural history or science textbooks?*

Some. But *The Thin Place* is much less researched than, say, *Versailles*. I would occasionally look something up when I wanted a piece of factual information. A friend had given me a really wonderful book, a field guide to the life in and around ponds and streams, and I just loved that book and used it for the names of the little microscopic creatures living in the water. I'm obsessed with murder mysteries and cookbooks and field guides. I love field guides. I love to look up something that I've found in the world and discover what it is. And I've also read them thinking, "Maybe one day I'll see one of those, if I'm lucky."

So in The Thin Place *we have all this life, all these organisms, all this activity, and we also have cosmology. We have a church, a school, an old persons' home . . .*

The key institutions.

And a trinity of girls on the brink of womanhood. I'm guessing one of them, Lorna, who is hoping to be a writer and who is reading Agatha Christie, is closest to you.

Partly. After I created those three girls and set them loose in the book, it was clear to me that I had used pieces of me and my friends. I've often found myself in trios, which is a difficult combination for girls, starting with the street I grew up on with Peggy and Ellen, where we used to fight with one another about who was going to be Nancy when we played Nancy Drew and who was going to be stuck being fat Bess. None of us really lines up precisely with Sunny, Mees, and Lorna in *The Thin Place*. I put a little bit of myself into each of them, and a little bit of other friends I've had over the years so that they're composites. In some ways I identify with Lorna, and in some ways Lorna is very much like my friend Elaine, an adult friend. There are unattractive qualities in Sunny that I feel I share, so it's a mixture.

The Thin Place runs on several time tracks, the present seen from various perspectives, and different layers of the past, some geologic, some illuminated in a diary kept during the 1800s. And you work on different scales, from the cosmic perspective, the bird's-eye view, and the microscopic. This simultaneity is the ultimate realism.*

I do think it's very realistic.

The Thin Place *is lavishly plotted, but there is also a metaphysical discussion going on. I'm intrigued with your interest in the soul.* Versailles *is narrated by your fictionalized version of Marie Antoinette, and the novel's opening sentence is: "My soul is going on a trip."*

I remember hearing that we have a soul when I was a very little child. I went to church with my parents and didn't understand what a soul was, but I thought about it a lot, and about the fact that I was alive. I was obsessed with the idea that there was something about me that might continue after I died, and it upset me. I became an insomniac, worried about the idea of forever and ever. That the soul would endure forever just seemed horrifying. It's something I have thought about my whole life long: what is it that gives us life, that makes us not just be a table. I guess I'm always going to write about that even if I'm trying very hard to stop myself from doing it.

That explains a lot of what goes on in The Thin Place. *I don't want to reveal too much, but Mees, who is named after a river, has a gift, a power that depends on the idea of a thin place, of being able to cross over between worlds of the living and the dead. You write about animal souls as well as human souls. Your cats and beavers embody intelligence and spirit, and you refer to Inuit stories, which are based on the belief that animals are wholly sentient beings. This was a nearly universal belief in pre-industrial cultures.*

I think I've always believed it, too. My parents did a lot of things wrong, frankly, but one thing they did right was to instill in us early on a love of animals. My father was also a gardener. Certainly we knew that when you look into an animal's eyes, you see the light of more than brute force. And the beavers, well, that is a very autobiographic part of the book.

I don't think I've talked about this, but I lived by a pond in Vermont that was fed by a larger lake. It's a very beautiful pond with a waterfall, one of the beauty spots of the village, and people come and take pictures of it. When beavers built a dam at the lip of the big lake, the water stopped flowing into the pond, and so the pond, just like in *The Thin Place,* turned into a kind of mud bog. Everybody was very upset, so the neighborhood banded together. First we dismantled the beavers' dam, and it was very hard to do. You had to put on work gloves because the beavers put in frighteningly sharp things as they became increasingly determined to prevent us from dismantling their dam. So we would take the dam down and the water would come in, and the pond would start to fill up, and then everybody would go to sleep, and while we were asleep the beavers would go out and build the dam back up again. And what happened was, I, the great animal lover, became filled with murderous hate for the beavers. Then we hired a beaver trapper, and he put some traps in the pond, and that didn't work. The beavers are quite devious, it turns out. I finally gave up, and just decided I wasn't going to worry about it anymore, but I hadn't changed my opinion of the beavers.

When I started to write about the beavers in the book, though, I was appalled that I'd ever wanted to murder them. I became really interested in their lives and the grace of their project even though it was so infuriating, and I felt horrible that I'd contributed any money to hire the beaver trapper.

Not only do you avoid preachiness, you also manage to be funny even while contemplating the dark side.

I think that one way you create humor is to combine the sense of the darkness of the world with an interest in or curiosity about life. This is what I inherited from my father, who took a very dim view of certain aspects of our existence, but also took delight in the way the dachshund looked running across the floor.

Adapted from an interview first published on Bookslut.com (May 2, 2006). Reprinted by permission.

Donna Seaman is an associate editor at Booklist *and host of the radio program* Open Books *on WLUW, where this interview originally aired. Her author interviews are collected in* Writers on the Air: Conversations about Books.

Questions and topics for discussion

1. Kathryn Davis once said that she "didn't want to write a polemic, but . . . I'm appalled by the disregard human beings have for the place where we live." In what ways does *The Thin Place* address the impact humans have on the environment?

2. A "thin place," according to Celtic legend, is a place where the membrane separating the physical world from the spiritual world is almost nonexistent. How does this idea play out in the novel? Do you believe that there are some places on the earth that are more connected to a spiritual plane than others?

3. At the beginning of *The Thin Place,* Mees Kipp discovers that she has the ability to bring the dead back to life. Although this may be the most startling example, the theme of resurrection also surfaces at several other points in Davis's novel. Identify some of these passages.

4. Davis uses sermons, horoscopes, almanacs, and police blotters, among other things, to give a vivid and complete picture of life in the New England town of Varennes. What

other novels have you read that provide all-encompassing portraits of specific places? How are they different from this novel?

5. Helen Zeebrugge celebrates her ninety-third birthday during the course of *The Thin Place*. In what ways is Helen as vital as the younger characters in the novel? What special wisdom comes with her age?

6. How do the narrator's references to geological time affect your thoughts about the significance of the people of Varennes? The value of life on earth? What does the line "Human time is much too thin to be discerned" (page 72) conjure up in your mind?

7. In what ways are Sunny, Mees, and Lorna similar as sixth-grade girls, and in what ways, apart from Mees's special powers, do they differ? How have their families affected their interests and personalities?

8. Does Kathryn Davis's flexible use of the colloquial, as well as her mastery of formal and lyrical language, help you to accept the fantastic aspects of *The Thin Place?* Does her sense of humor?

9. What clues about outsiders led you to suspect that the safety of Varennes would be threatened in the end? What is the larger threat to all living creatures that the novel considers?

10. In the precarious contemporary time of *The Thin Place,* how is Kathryn Davis able to convey joy?

Look for these other novels by
Kathryn Davis

Versailles
"A splendid novel. . . . It is rapturous, like an aria. Indeed, it is
a kind of aria, being the story of Marie Antoinette's life. . . .
She's very much alive here, and she's magnificent."
— Stacey D'Erasmo, *New York Times Book Review*

The Girl Who Trod on a Loaf
"Magnificent, a bravura performance of grand imagination
and fierce intelligence. . . . Kathryn Davis is a writer of original
gifts and haunting power."
— Ephraim Paul, *Philadelphia Inquirer*

Hell
"*Hell* weaves together three tales of domestic undoing in
exquisitely charged language that will make the hairs on the
back of your neck stand straight up." — *Elle*

"A gripping, hallucinatory novel. . . . The reader closes the
book as if waking from a dream." — *The New Yorker*

Back Bay Books • Available wherever paperbacks are sold